Dark Spy's Resolution

THE CHILDREN OF THE GODS
BOOK THIRTY-SEVEN

I. T. LUCAS

Dark Spy's Resolution is a work of fiction! Names, characters, places and incidents are products of the author's imagination or are used fictitiously and are not to be construed as real. Any similarity to actual persons, organizations and/or events is purely coincidental.

Copyright © 2020 by I. T. Lucas

All rights reserved.

No part of this book may be reproduced in any form or by any electronic or mechanical means, including information storage and retrieval systems, without written permission from the author, except for the use of brief quotations in a book review.

Published by Evening Star Press

Also by I. T. Lucas

THE CHILDREN OF THE GODS ORIGINS
1: Goddess's Choice
2: Goddess's Hope

THE CHILDREN OF THE GODS

Dark Stranger
1: Dark Stranger The Dream
2: Dark Stranger Revealed
3: Dark Stranger Immortal

Dark Enemy
4: Dark Enemy Taken
5: Dark Enemy Captive
6: Dark Enemy Redeemed

Kri & Michael's Story
6.5: My Dark Amazon

Dark Warrior
7: Dark Warrior Mine
8: Dark Warrior's Promise
9: Dark Warrior's Destiny
10: Dark Warrior's Legacy

Dark Guardian
11: Dark Guardian Found
12: Dark Guardian Craved
13: Dark Guardian's Mate

Dark Angel
14: Dark Angel's Obsession
15: Dark Angel's Seduction
16: Dark Angel's Surrender

Dark Operative

17: Dark Operative: A Shadow of Death
18: Dark Operative: A Glimmer of Hope
19: Dark Operative: The Dawn of Love

Dark Survivor
20: Dark Survivor Awakened
21: Dark Survivor Echoes of Love
22: Dark Survivor Reunited

Dark Widow
23: Dark Widow's Secret
24: Dark Widow's Curse
25: Dark Widow's Blessing

Dark Dream
26: Dark Dream's Temptation
27: Dark Dream's Unraveling
28: Dark Dream's Trap

Dark Prince
29: Dark Prince's Enigma
30: Dark Prince's Dilemma
31: Dark Prince's Agenda

Dark Queen
32: Dark Queen's Quest
33: Dark Queen's Knight
34: Dark Queen's Army

Dark Spy
35: Dark Spy Conscripted
36: Dark Spy's Mission
37: Dark Spy's Resolution

Dark Overlord
38: Dark Overlord New Horizon
39: Dark Overlord's Wife
40: Dark Overlord's Clan

Dark Choices
41: Dark Choices The Quandary
42: Dark Choices Paradigm Shift
43: Dark Choices The Accord

Dark Secrets
44: Dark Secrets Resurgence
45: Dark Secrets Unveiled
46: Dark Secrets Absolved

Dark Haven
47: Dark Haven Illusion
48: Dark Haven Unmasked
49: Dark Haven Found

Dark Power
50: Dark Power Untamed
51: Dark Power Unleashed
52: Dark Power Convergence

Dark Memories
53: Dark Memories Submerged
54: Dark Memories Emerge
55: Dark Memories Restored

Dark Hunter
56: Dark Hunter's Query
57: Dark Hunter's Prey
58: Dark Hunter's Boon

Dark God
59: Dark God's Avatar
60: Dark God's Reviviscence
61: Dark God Destinies Converge

Dark Whispers
62: Dark Whispers From The Past
63: Dark Whispers From Afar

64: Dark Whispers From Beyond

Dark Gambit
65: Dark Gambit The Pawn
66: Dark Gambit The Play
67: Dark Gambit Reliance

Dark Alliance
68: Dark Alliance Kindred Souls
69: Dark Alliance Turbulent Waters
70: Dark Alliance Perfect Storm

Dark Healing
71: Dark Healing Blind Justice
72: Dark Healing Blind Trust
73: Dark healing Blind Curve

Dark Encounters
74: Dark Encounters of the Close Kind
75: Dark Encounters of the Unexpected Kind
76: Dark Encounters of the Fated Kind

Dark Voyage
77: Dark Voyage Matters of the Heart

PERFECT MATCH
Vampire's Consort
King's Chosen
Captain's Conquest
The Thief Who Loved Me
My Merman Prince
The Dragon King
My Werewolf Romeo

The Channeler's Companion

The Children of the Gods Series Sets

Books 1-3: Dark Stranger trilogy—Includes a bonus short story: **The Fates take a Vacation**

<u>Books 4-6: Dark Enemy Trilogy</u> —Includes a bonus short story—**The Fates' Post-Wedding Celebration**

Books 7-10: Dark Warrior Tetralogy

Books 11-13: Dark Guardian Trilogy

Books 14-16: Dark Angel Trilogy

Books 17-19: Dark Operative Trilogy

Books 20-22: Dark Survivor Trilogy

Books 23-25: Dark Widow Trilogy

Books 26-28: Dark Dream Trilogy

Books 29-31: Dark Prince Trilogy

Books 32-34: Dark Queen Trilogy

Books 35-37: Dark Spy Trilogy

Books 38-40: Dark Overlord Trilogy

Books 41-43: Dark Choices Trilogy

Books 44-46: Dark Secrets Trilogy

Books 47-49: Dark Haven Trilogy

Books 50-52: Dark Power Trilogy

Books 53-55: Dark Memories Trilogy

Books 56-58: Dark Hunter Trilogy

Books 59-61: Dark God Trilogy

Books 62-64: Dark Whispers Trilogy

Books 65-67: Dark Gambit Trilogy

Books 68-70: Dark Alliance Trilogy

Books 71-73: Dark healing Trilogy

MEGA SETS
include character lists
The Children of the Gods: Books 1-6
The Children of the Gods: Books 6.5-10

PERFECT MATCH BUNDLE 1

CHECK OUT THE SPECIALS ON
ITLUCAS.COM
(https://itlucas.com/specials)

FOR EXCLUSIVE PEEKS AT UPCOMING RELEASES &
A FREE I. T. LUCAS COMPANION BOOK

JOIN MY *VIP CLUB* AND GAIN ACCESS TO THE VIP PORTAL AT ITLUCAS.COM

To Join, go to:
http://eepurl.com/blMTpD

Find out more details about what's included with your free membership on the book's last page.

TRY THE CHILDREN OF THE GODS SERIES ON
AUDIBLE

2 FREE audiobooks with your new Audible subscription!

Kalugal

Kalugal watched the monitor, following the steps as the program ran through the lockdown protocol. Once the bunker was secure, he pulled his immortal captive's earpiece out of his pocket, put it in his ear, and tapped it to activate.

"Everyone listening can move and talk now. Good night."

"Wait! What have you done with Arwel?"

Kalugal paused with his finger a fraction of an inch away from the device.

Should he disconnect? Or should he engage?

A dilemma.

On the one hand, he was eager to start questioning his captive, but on the other hand, this was an opportunity to talk with the team's commander and learn what he had in mind as far as escalating things.

Was the guy on the other side of the connection in charge of the operation?

His quick recovery from compulsion indicated that he had a good head on his shoulders and a strong personality, which were both prerequisites for a command position. Most people would have needed several moments to collect their wits.

This should be an interesting conversation.

Leaning back in his chair, Kalugal crossed his legs at the ankles. "So that's Flyboy's name. I haven't had the opportunity to chat with him and his girlfriend yet."

"Flyboy? And what girlfriend are you talking about?"

Kalugal sighed. He hated it when people played dumb.

"Your man sailed over the crowd to knock out the shooter, which was very impressive, but it also gave him away. Then Flyboy's immune girlfriend rushed to save him and fought like a hellcat. But don't worry, we handled them both with care. As you are aware, I don't need to use force to extract information from people."

"She is not his girlfriend, and we know where you've taken them. As we speak, your place is being surrounded."

Even if the guy wasn't bluffing about knowing the location of Kalugal's compound, there was no way Arwel's pals had made it there so fast. Except, he might have had additional warriors stationed nearby or some that hadn't been connected to Arwel's channel when Kalugal had compelled them to freeze.

His immediate safety was not an issue.

While locked down, the bunker was nearly impenetrable, and they had enough supplies stored to last them for months. The problem would be getting out of there while a large force was surrounding the place.

Two tunnels led in and out of the bunker, but one went into the house, which wasn't going to be helpful as an escape route, and the other led to a grate in the sidewalk on the other side of his property, which wasn't very useful either.

That was the trouble with building a bunker inside an established and affluent community. Digging under existing houses had not been possible.

If the force outside wasn't large, he could just walk out and compel the men surrounding his property to let him through, but there was a limit to how many immortals he could compel at once.

Kalugal wasn't as powerful as his father. Not yet. Twenty or so warriors were the most he could handle at the same time.

With a few quick taps on the keyboard, he flipped through the feeds from the perimeter's cameras and was relieved to find no one outside the compound or on its grounds. That meant that his initial assessment had been correct. The team that had been sent after him wasn't large, and they were all still in the vicinity of the club. Or so he hoped. Whoever had organized this operation might be sending reinforcements.

It was time to issue some threats of his own. "I can just command them to freeze again. Should I do it now?"

"They are no longer connected to this channel. It's just you and me."

Smart move, which Kalugal had anticipated.

"Who am I talking to? Are you the head of this operation?"

"I'm just the communications guy. The head of the operation is going to join us in a moment."

That wasn't good. A small unit didn't need a dedicated communications person, which implied that he was dealing with a large force after all.

The most logical conclusion was that it belonged to Annani's clan. Except, what did they want with him?

He had never bothered them or tried to find them, and they had left him alone as well. Kalugal was surprised that they even knew of his existence.

He was supposed to be dead.

Why the sudden interest? Perhaps they sought his cooperation against his father?

If that was why Annani had sent men to follow him around, she would be disappointed. Kalugal had no such intentions.

He lifted his legs and put his feet on the desk. "Wonderful. I can't wait."

"If you are planning to compel him as well, it's not going to help you. His second-in-command is an immune."

The possibility of compelling the commander hadn't even crossed Kalugal's mind. At this point, all he wanted was to find out why Annani's clan was after him, and then to get them off his back as soon as possible. Which probably meant releasing the warrior and his girlfriend.

He would gladly do that, but only after interrogating them. There was little chance that an opportunity to learn about Annani's clan and what they were up to would present itself again.

Regrettably, once this was over he would have to relocate, and that was a damn shame. Kalugal liked the neighborhood and its proximity to Stanford, and the bunker had cost him a fortune to build, not to mention the hassle it had been. But his location had been compromised, and he couldn't allow the clan to breathe down his neck and interfere with his plans.

"How fascinating. I can't wait to hear who your boss is, and to find out what he wants with me."

"Hello, cousin."

Cousin?

All immortals had common ancestry, but to call him cousin was a stretch.

"Who is this?"

"I am Kian, son of Annani, your mother's sister."

What?

"You heard me right. Areana, your mother, is my mother's sister, which makes us cousins."

Kalugal wasn't aware that he'd voiced his astonishment.

It took a brief moment for the shock to subside and for the gears in his mind to start spinning again. The guy couldn't be talking about Annani the goddess. Many of the clan's daughters were probably named after her.

Had Navuh stolen Annani's sister from the clan?

Was that why they had been stalking him? To get her back?

His mother hadn't said anything about the clan. But then Kalugal had been a young boy the last time he'd seen her, and the subject of the clan and how she'd come to be in Navuh's possession hadn't come up in their conversations.

"Are you still there?" Kian asked.

"I can't help you recover your clanswoman. If I could have, I would have freed my mother a long time ago. Regrettably, she loves my father, and even though I must assume that he kidnapped her and forced her to mate him, she wants to stay with him. I guess Areana is suffering from prolonged Stockholm syndrome."

Kian

Kian felt like scratching his head.

What the hell was Kalugal talking about? Could it be that he didn't know who Annani was?

Navuh had kept Annani's survival secret from her sister, but not from the Brotherhood. Since the very beginning of the conflict, he'd been using her and the supposed evils she and her clan were committing to unify his men behind his so-called cause.

Perhaps Kalugal was suffering from amnesia?

Could it be that he hadn't escaped during WWII but had been buried in stasis for decades, only to revive recently?

It had happened to Wonder, so it wasn't an implausible scenario.

"Do you know who Annani is?"

"I know who *the Annani* is, but naturally, I don't know any of her namesake descendants. If memory serves me correctly, and I'm quite sure that it does, my mother has never mentioned her sister, by name or otherwise."

That explained it.

Kalugal assumed that Kian's mother was an immortal named after Annani, not the goddess herself. And given that Areana hadn't revealed her true identity to her son, Kalugal's assumption made sense.

Unfortunately, the wind had already been knocked out from under the bombastic proclamation that Kian had hoped would have such a profound impact on Kalugal.

How disappointing.

On the other hand, lengthy explanations were precisely what Kian was after. The longer he kept Kalugal talking, the more time he would buy Kri and Jin to get out of the area, and the Guardians to surround the complex.

"No clan females are named after Annani. My mother is the goddess, and your mother is her half-sister."

There was a long moment of silence before Kalugal responded. "What you are saying is impossible. If my mother were a goddess, she would be more powerful than my father, and she obviously is not."

"Areana is a very weak goddess, and Navuh is a very powerful immortal. Still, Navuh doesn't want anyone to know that his mate is a goddess who outranks him in the gene hierarchy. That's the reason he's hiding her in the harem, and that's also the reason he didn't allow her sons to grow up with her."

"He doesn't allow any of his children to be raised in the harem. He thinks that by preventing his sons from being raised in the harem he is protecting them from killing each other over succession rights. If we don't know who our mothers are, we also don't know the hierarchy of who was born to a wife and who was born to a concubine, and Navuh does not play favorites. No one knows who he is going to choose."

Kian shook his head. He'd assumed that Kalugal knew so much more than he actually did, but he should have realized that Areana couldn't have told all that to a five-year-old boy. He'd been too young to understand harem politics and the web of lies and deceit that Navuh had created.

"Navuh has only two sons. You and Lokan. The others were fathered by human males who look like him. I loathe saying anything positive about your father, but he loves your mother and has been loyal to her throughout the years."

As Kalugal processed that nugget of information, there was another long moment of silence.

"Are you saying that the other women in my father's harem are having relations with the human male servants? That means that other than Lokan, my other so-called brothers are not related to me at all."

"That's right."

"I'll be damned. My father actually cares. That's an ingenious way to protect Lokan's and my identity. With numerous fake sons, no one suspects who Navuh's real successors are, or rather is. I have no intention of taking over. Lokan can have it all."

That hadn't been the take-home value Kian had hoped for, but it didn't matter. His main goal was to keep Kalugal talking and asking questions until Turner confirmed that Jin was safe and that the Guardians were in position.

"I'm not sure that you've got it right. Whatever Navuh does serves him and no one else. Technically, you and your brother outrank him as far as godly genes go. While Navuh is the son of a god with a mortal, and therefore only half a god, you and your brother are three-quarter gods. It's just as important for him to keep that information from you as it is to hide his mate's godly identity."

Kalugal chuckled. "Following that logic, unless Annani found a first-generation immortal to mate with, my brother and I outrank you as well."

That was regrettably true, but Kian wasn't going to provide Kalugal with any more information than he absolutely had to.

"You, Lokan, and I are not competing for positions."

"That's true. I'm not interested in your job any more than I'm interested in my father's. So, if that's why you sought me out and sent your warriors after me, rest assured that your clan is of no interest to me. You are not my enemy, and you are not my friend either. Can we leave it at that?"

Albeit mistaken, that was another logical conclusion on Kalugal's part.

The guy was level-headed, smart, and he wasn't easily shaken either. His cousin was a worthy opponent, of whom Kian would be wise to be wary.

"I have no reason to fear you, Kalugal. I sought you out because your mother asked mine to find you. She is worried about you, and she misses you."

Jin

Kri tapped her fingers on the steering wheel. "What if the Guardians surrounding Kalugal's place are given really good earplugs so they can't hear him?"

Jin's heart fluttered with renewed hope. "That's a very good question. His shrouds and his compulsion don't work the same way. It seems that he needs to be heard in order for the compulsion to work. Otherwise, he wouldn't have bothered with Arwel's earpiece. But he can shroud himself without being heard."

Kri nodded. "That's no less problematic than his compulsion. Even if he can't compel them because they have earplugs in, he can shroud himself and his men to be invisible and waltz out of there. The Guardians are not going to see them leave."

"True. But if there is a camera pointed at his gate, and the watchers are all the way back in the village, his shroud is not going to affect them. They will see him and can tell the Guardians."

Kri cast Jin a sidelong glance. "Very clever. I need to call Magnus and have him get everyone the best earplugs he can find. Roni, our hacker, can tell Magnus what to do about installing a surveillance camera." Kri pulled to the side and parked. "Damn. We forgot about Arwel's phone. He has everyone's numbers on it, and Kalugal can start calling people and compel them to do all kinds of shit."

"I can check if he has the phone." Jin closed her eyes and followed the tether to Kalugal. "He is still talking with Kian. I'll check on Jacki." She followed the tether to her friend. "She and Arwel are whispering in each other's ears. They are in a prison cell, but it's not nice like the ones in the keep. It has bars instead of a door, and I can see the toilet. Gross. It doesn't have a privacy wall or anything. It's just there, sitting against the back wall."

Kri grimaced. "It's just getting better and better, isn't it?" She turned to her phone and scrolled through her contacts until she found the right one and placed the call. "Roni. Can you erase Arwel's phone remotely?" A brief moment passed. "Good. I wasn't sure he would think of it."

Disconnecting, Kri huffed out a breath. "Onegus has already told Roni to do that. This is a nightmare. No one's come up with an SOP for dealing with a compeller. We are so unprepared."

The clan had known about Kalugal's ability for a while, and someone should have come up with a protocol before poking the bear. In hindsight, the entire operation appeared amateurish and gung-ho.

"You said that you are going to call Magnus about my idea."

"Right." This time Kri put the call on speaker. "Magnus, Jin and I have some ideas that we would like to run by you."

"Shoot."

"The Guardians surrounding Kalugal's place should have earplugs in, maybe the noise-canceling ones, so he can't compel them to do things. But since he can shroud himself and probably anyone else that he wants to, we need a camera installed somewhere to watch the gate, with the feed going to the village. That's too far for his shroud to reach."

"Good thinking," Magnus said. "I just need to figure out a way to communicate with my men while they are deaf."

"That's easy." Jin waved a hand. "Tell them to put their phones on vibrate and communicate via text messages."

"Excellent solution. Except, I'll have to find a store that sells quality earplugs and rob it, because I can't wait for it to open in the morning."

"You can leave money on the counter with a note," Jin said.

"I can do that. Thank you both for the excellent suggestions. You were thinking outside the box."

Kri lifted her hand for a high five, and Jin slapped it.

"That's why you need women on the force," Kri said.

"You won't hear me arguing against that. But there are no candidates for the position."

Kri nodded. "Wonder would have made a great Guardian, but her heart is not in it."

Jin had no wish to become a Guardian either, but that didn't mean that she couldn't help in other ways. "Please tell Kian that I'm fine with him trading me for Arwel."

"That's not going to happen."

"Please, just tell him that. Trading me for Arwel before Kalugal has a chance to get him to talk will solve the most urgent problem. Later, Kian can figure out a way to get me out, either by negotiating and bargaining or by threatening."

The more she talked, the more convinced Jin became that this was the only solution to the clusterfuck they found themselves in. "Kalugal is not a bad man. He made sure to get the gunman out of the club so he wouldn't shoot people when he woke up, and he told everyone who was listening to pull over before freezing them, so they wouldn't cause accidents. He's not heartless, and he's not going to hurt me. I'm sure of that. Please, Magnus. I appreciate the chivalry, but it would be really stupid on Kian's part not to use me to get Arwel and Jacki out. I beg you to convince him that this is the best option for everyone."

There was a long moment of silence before Magnus replied. "I'll convey your message to Onegus and have him explain the pros and cons to Kian. But just so you know, if we do that, Arwel is never going to forgive any of us."

"Once this is all over, I'll deal with Arwel. Right now, the future of everyone in the village is in jeopardy. That should be our first priority."

"I can't argue with that."

Jin let out a relieved breath. "Thank you."

When Magnus ended the call, she closed her eyes and followed the tether to Jacki. Everything was still the same as it had been the last time she'd checked. They were still alone in the cell, talking in hushed voices. She listened for a few moments, but it felt awkward to spy on them, so she moved to Kalugal.

Jin had no qualms about spying on him, not after he had taken her man and her friend and put them in a freaking prison cell with a damn toilet that was in full view of everyone passing by in the hallway outside.

Arwel

Jacki glanced at the toilet at the back of the cell. "If you need to use the loo, I will look away," she whispered.

"I'm good. You go first." Arwel closed his eyes and leaned against the wall.

"Can you also put your hands over your ears?"

"No problem."

Kalugal's underground bunker was no keep, and the cell they were in looked like what the name implied.

It was a prison.

The front wall was made of bars, two narrow bunk beds were the only furniture, and the toilet had no privacy wall. There was a sink, but no shower, and there were no towels.

Kalugal's men had dumped him and Jacki on the bottom bunk without bothering to untie her. She had to wait for him to unfreeze first so he could release her.

It had been cruel and unnecessary.

Jacki was human, and being tied up for an extended length of time messed up her circulation and caused muscle spasms.

Curiously, Jacki hadn't asked him any questions yet. Since he'd freed her from her bindings, she'd been quietly massaging the stiff muscles in her arms and legs, and other than thanking him, she hadn't spoken at all.

Not typical behavior for someone who had just discovered that she'd gone down the rabbit hole into a world she hadn't known existed.

Could it be that she'd forgotten Kalugal's comment about Arwel being an immortal?

Getting tied up and stuffed in the trunk of a car could mess with anyone's head. Still, even if Jacki didn't remember that, Kalugal almost certainly was going to repeat it at some point, which meant that he probably had no intention of ever letting Jacki go.

No matter on which side of the divide immortals were, they had one thing in common. Keeping their existence secret from humans was necessary for their survival, and since Kalugal couldn't thrall Jacki's memories away, he must either plan to kill her or to keep her imprisoned for life.

The only way things could have been worse was if Kalugal had also captured Jin.

Thank the merciful Fates that the guy hadn't made the connection between the girl bumping into him with what had happened shortly after that.

Jin's tether to Kalugal might help Kian with storming the place. If he had access to everything Kalugal said and did, he might even get from her the override code to unlock the bunker.

As the bed sank under Jacki's weight, Arwel opened his eyes and removed his hands from his ears. "You know that they can see you, right?" He motioned with his head toward the camera mounted near the ceiling.

"I can't do anything about it, so screw them." She flipped a finger at the camera.

"Antagonizing your captors is not a good strategy."

"It doesn't matter." Jacki kicked her shoes off, lifted her feet onto the bed, and wrapped her arms around her knees. "They are going to kill me anyway. Probably you too."

So, she'd figured it out.

Smart girl.

Except, it would have been better for her not to be so clever. As the saying went, ignorance was bliss.

He moved closer to her and whispered in her ear. "The boss is going to get us out."

She arched a brow. "How?"

"I don't know. But between him and his brilliant right-hand man, I'm sure they will figure out something."

Hopefully not by bombing the place, but Arwel couldn't discount the possibility. To keep the clan safe, Kian might decide to sacrifice them. It wouldn't be his first choice, but if everything else failed, this might be a last resort move.

Jacki leaned closer. "I still have Jin's thing, so if you want to say something to her, you can pretend that you are talking to me. Anyway, they assume that we are a couple."

The ability to talk to Jin was the one bright spot illuminating their bleak circumstances. He just wished that the communication went both ways.

Looking into Jacki's blue eyes, Arwel pretended that they were Jin's big brown ones. "I love you. Please don't do anything stupid. Stay safe."

Jacki put her head on his shoulder, probably to maintain the illusion of them being a couple. "What do you think she is going to do?"

He wrapped his arm around her shoulders. "Offer to trade for us."

"Yeah, she might do that. If I were in her shoes, that's what I would do."

That was bad. Jacki had known Jin longer than he had, and if she thought that Jin would offer to sacrifice herself, then she was probably right.

"The boss would never agree to that."

"He might have no choice." She lifted her head off his shoulder and looked at him. "Is Kalugal really his cousin?"

"It doesn't mean much to either of them."

"Are they also immortals like you?"

Damn, she hadn't forgotten.

Arwel nodded.

"Enemies?"

He nodded again, but then tilted his head. "Kalugal's father is our enemy. We don't know whether Kalugal counts himself as one too. I guess we will find out soon."

Jacki leaned against the wall. "You've come up with a good cover story. An organization of paranormally talented people made sense to me." She shook her head. "If you'd told me that you were immortal, I wouldn't have believed you. Is Jin also immortal?"

"No. But I'd rather not talk about it in here."

Even though they were whispering in each other's ears, with the proper equipment their whispers could be amplified.

"Do all immortals have paranormal talents?"

He could answer that. "To some extent. Some are stronger than others. But our mind tricks usually work only on humans. Kalugal and his father are the only immortals we know of who can affect other immortals. That's what makes them so powerful."

Annani could do that too, but that was because she was a goddess, and a powerful one.

Jacki closed her eyes. "We are so screwed. What chance does your boss have against that?"

"There are more of us than there are of them, and we have better weapons." Or so he hoped. "Kalugal can't hide inside this bunker forever, and if he thinks that this place is impenetrable, he is wrong. With the right equipment, any structure can be penetrated."

That had been meant for Kalugal's ears.

There was little chance of Kian launching a massive ordnance penetrator into a bunker located in a suburban neighborhood, but Kalugal wouldn't know that.

Turner

While Kian kept Kalugal busy talking, Turner went into hyper mode, the gears in his brain picking up speed as he evaluated the situation, projected outcomes, and set things in motion.

His first priority was to get Jin to a safe location.

She, or rather the tether she had attached to Kalugal, was the best leverage they had over him. The Guardians, who in a few moments would surround his property, were more a show of strength than a tactical tool.

Once Magnus delivered the new earplugs and had cameras installed across from the compound's gate, they might prevent Kalugal and his men from leaving. But Turner had no doubt that the bunker they were in was well-stocked and could sustain them through a long siege.

Except, the clan couldn't keep the blockade up for long. They were in one of the most expensive neighborhoods in the country, and even with every immortal trick in their proverbial bag, there was no way they could maintain it for more than twenty-four hours.

In the meantime, Kalugal would learn everything there was to know about the clan.

Jin was the key to preventing that from happening. More than Kalugal wanted to learn the clan's secrets, he wanted to keep his.

Jin's tether would paralyze him, preventing Kalugal from doing anything he didn't want the clan to know.

To get rid of that, the guy would do anything, which meant that the moment Kian pulled out that trump card, Kalugal was going to divert every resource at his disposal to locating Jin.

Except, he wasn't going to find her, because Turner was going to stash her in the safest and most secret location on the globe.

The goddess's sanctuary in Alaska.

Since no one knew how to get there other than Annani and her Odus, Kalugal couldn't compel anyone to reveal the sanctuary's location.

Turner had already arranged for a private jet to pick up Jin and Kri. The airfield was ten minutes away from their current location, and the flight to Alaska would take about four and a half hours. From there, he had no clue how long it would take them to get to Annani's place.

Alaska was a big state.

It would be preferable to hold back on issuing the threat until Jin was in the sanctuary, but Turner figured that as soon as she was in the air, she would be safe from Kalugal and whoever he might deploy after her.

Kian seemed to be doing fine, and Turner had no doubt that he could keep Kalugal talking for twenty more minutes or so before the guy lost his patience and demanded that the real negotiations start.

After giving Kri the location of the airfield, Turner still had to arrange for one of Annani's Odus to pick them up from the private airfield outside of Anchorage.

Thankfully, he had Alena's phone number, which Kian had given him when she'd left for her modeling stint in New York.

Not wanting Kian to know where he was sending Jin, Turner typed a text. He would have preferred to speak to Alena, which would have been the proper thing to do, but he didn't want to chance Kian overhearing the conversation, and he couldn't leave the room as long as Kalugal was on the line.

It's an emergency, and I don't have time to explain. I need you to send a jet to pick up Kri and Jin from Sky airfield in Anchorage and take them to the sanctuary. They are leaving San Francisco in about fifteen minutes and will get there in about four and a half or five hours. One more thing. Don't text or call Kian about it until I tell you it's okay to do so. I'll explain once I can spare a moment.

Her return text arrived a few seconds later. *Consider it done. Let us know what's going on as soon as possible.*

He erased the exchange from his phone and typed a new message for Kian.

Keep Kalugal talking for at least fifteen more minutes before telling him about Jin's tether.

After reading it, Kian nodded and gave him the thumbs up.

Next order of business was to evacuate the keep and send Yamanu to San Francisco.

To maintain the siege, they needed to shroud the Guardians' presence from the human neighbors, or better yet, have Yamanu thrall them into leaving their homes for the entire day.

He also needed to get offensive weapons for the Guardians that could penetrate an underground bunker. The delivery of a mobile command center for William and attack drones for the force had already been arranged.

Hopefully they would never get deployed, but when engaged in negotiations, it was advisable to have as much leverage as possible.

Onegus could handle the evacuation, but Turner needed to take care of supplying the force and finding places for the evacuees that Arwel and Kian didn't know about.

After several back-and-forth texts with his subcontractors and friends, he texted Onegus the address of a cabin in Big Bear along with the code for the lock pad.

He also added a note about sending Yamanu to the Bay Area.

The chief might have thought of that already, but Turner didn't leave anything to chance, and he wasn't concerned with stepping on anyone's toes either.

When lives were at stake, everything else became irrelevant.

Onegus texted back. *Charlie is in the hangar, and I notified Yamanu. How many bedrooms are in that cabin? Other than Mey, Wendy, and Richard, we need room for the two Guardians watching over them and for Vlad and Ingrid, who happened to be in the keep.*

Turner shook his head. Sleeping arrangements were the least of his concerns at the moment.

It has five bedrooms and three baths. I don't know how many beds. They will have to figure it out. How many Guardians do you have stuck outside the village?

As he waited for Onegus's response, Turner shot a text to William. *A mobile command van is on its way to the house. Get ready to transfer your equipment.*

In the meantime, the return text from Onegus had arrived. *Fifteen.*

I want you to send them with Yamanu to the Bay Area. I also arranged for a mobile command center and attack drones to be delivered to the Guardians.

Onegus texted back. *I can send them to the airfield, but I'm worried about leaving the village with a skeleton force. I counted on them as backup.*

Turner typed. *The village is securely locked. The more men we have around Kalugal's compound, the better chance we have of defusing the situation before he learns anything from Arwel. And the stronger show of force we manage, the more willing Kalugal will be to negotiate.*

Kalugal

K alugal rubbed the spot over his heart.

His mother was worried about him, and she missed him.

If only the fantastic tale Kian had been weaving was true, but he was most likely making the entire story up.

Kalugal had no way of proving or disproving the information, but it made no sense for Kian to know all that. Areana was locked up in the harem and could tell her story to no one on the outside. And since no one ever left the harem, she couldn't send a message out either.

There were only two ways Kian could have obtained that information, and both were highly unlikely.

One was that someone had managed to escape the harem and deliver Areana's story to her sister. The other was that the clan had an extraordinarily talented remote viewer who could see what went on in the harem, and a powerful telepath who could converse remotely with Areana.

"With all due respect, I find your story hard to believe. I admire your imagination, though. Are you in the film industry?"

Kian chuckled. "Even if I was the creative type, which I'm not, I would never have come up with an unbelievable story like that. I would have thought of something that made more sense."

As Rufsur entered the room, Kalugal motioned for him to keep quiet and turned his chair around. "I'm sure that you can understand why I'm skeptical of your claims. What do you really want from me, Kian?"

"I told you the truth. Your mother asked mine to locate you, but I didn't want to approach you before investigating what you were up to. I don't know whether you have contact with your father or not, and with him seeking my clan's extinction, I'm not taking any chances."

"I'm curious to hear what you have learned."

Rufsur got up and waved his hand in front of Kalugal's face to get his attention. "Several cars are parked on the street, and more are arriving," he mouthed.

So, the communications guy hadn't been bluffing about that. Obviously, Kian's intention was to keep Kalugal talking long enough for his warriors to surround the property, but it didn't matter.

Kalugal was ready for a prolonged siege.

"I know that you made a fortune on the stock market, and I also know that you faked your own death and that of your entire platoon during WWII. You are very careful, never leaving the house without first shrouding yourself, and you keep a low profile. Still, that doesn't tell me what you are up to."

It seemed that Kian had been observing him for a while now. The question was how.

The compound's sophisticated monitoring equipment hadn't picked up any new signals from surveillance cameras, and what was there before belonged to their neighbors. It had to be boots on the ground.

"How did you find me?"

"It was purely coincidental. I like to believe that fate had something to do with it."

"Fate? You don't strike me as the kind of guy who believes in a mystical higher power. Please don't insult my intelligence, Kian. What do you want? And I mean other than buying time for your men to surround my property."

Kian chuckled. "Every word I said was true. But it's also true that I was buying time for my men to get in position. I want you to release the warrior and the woman you've abducted."

"And why would I do that? Your men are of no consequence to me. I can compel them to do anything I want."

"You said that my clan is of no interest to you, and that you are neither my enemy nor my friend. I hold the same position. If you release my people, I'll take it as a sign of good faith and remove the blockade. After that, you and I can continue our conversation and come to an agreement of peaceful coexistence, or maybe even cooperation."

"That's what you want now. But what did you want before I took the warrior and his girlfriend?"

"Precisely what I have already told you. Your mother wanted to find you, and my mother promised her help."

Kalugal turned back toward the monitor and checked the feed from the perimeter cameras. He counted seven vehicles parked along the street, which didn't tell him much about the number of men surrounding his property. If there were three immortals in each car or less, he could compel them all. But if there were four in each, it would be a stretch for him.

Kian didn't know that, though.

If the story he'd told was true, and Areana was indeed a goddess, then Kian must have assumed that Kalugal was as powerful as Navuh or more.

Naturally, he was going to reinforce that misconception and keep on bluffing.

Kian's objective was to get the warrior out before Kalugal had a chance to interrogate him, but Kalugal had no intention of allowing that. He had to find out what

Kian's real agenda was, as well as every clan secret the captured warrior had ever been privy to.

Knowledge equaled power.

Jin

No more than an hour had passed since Kri had dragged Jin into the car and driven her away from the club, but it seemed like they had been in that freaking car forever.

At some point, Kri had left the surface streets and had gotten on the freeway. She was obeying the speed limit, but they were getting further and further away from the city. By the time Magnus let them know where they were supposed to go, they could be all the way to Oregon for all she knew.

Were they even heading north?

Since Kri had turned the GPS off, Jin had no clue. Navigating by the stars had never been her strong suit. Heck, she could get lost leaving the mall.

Besides, Jin had been busy listening to Kalugal talking to Kian. She could barely hear Kian because he was speaking into Kalugal's ear using Arwel's earpiece, but even if she missed parts of it, she could still figure out what he'd said by Kalugal's responses.

So far, the negotiations hadn't started yet, and it seemed like Kian's main objective was to keep Kalugal talking. As long as he was on the line, he couldn't interrogate Arwel.

She'd also checked on Arwel and Jacki several times, but only for a couple of seconds to make sure that they were still in the cell together and neither was being tortured.

As much as she would have liked to gaze at Arwel's amazing eyes through Jacki's, Jin decided that keeping tabs on the conversation between Kian and Kalugal was more important.

"Turner gave me instructions." Kri's voice pulled Jin away from the tether. "We are going to the sanctuary."

"What's that?"

Kri glanced at her and smiled. "Annani's place. You are about to meet the goddess. Are you excited?"

Under different circumstances, Jin would have been thrilled, but meeting the goddess was not at the top of her priority list.

"Where is it?"

"No one other than her and her trusted servants know how to get there, but I know that it's somewhere in Alaska."

Jin's gut twisted in a knot. "How is Kian going to trade me if I'm so far away?"

"I told you that he's not going to do it. The most important thing right now is to get you to safety, and there is no safer place than the sanctuary. Kalugal can't get information about its location from Arwel or anyone else because no one has it."

"Can I talk to Turner?"

"Sure. He's going to call you as soon as we are on the plane." Kri turned on the GPS. "We are five minutes away from the airfield."

Looking down at her dirty T-shirt, Jin shook her head. "Is that a country airstrip?"

"Yup."

"So, on top of everything else, I'm going to meet the goddess in a snot-covered T-shirt."

Kri glanced at Jin's middle and grimaced. "I'm sure that Annani is not going to wait for us in the hangar. I can ask Alena to have someone prepare a change of clothes for you."

As the tears started leaking out of her eyes again, Jin whispered, "It's such a silly thing to be concerned with at a time like this."

Reaching over the center console, Kri took her hand. "It's going to be alright. Kian and Turner are going to negotiate Arwel and Jacki's release."

"With what? They need something to bargain with, but they are sending their best chip to freaking Alaska." She looked down at her shirt again. "I'm going to freeze."

In all the commotion, she'd left her coat at the club. Luckily, she still had her purse, but that was only because Kri had noticed it and shoved it into her hands before dragging her out of there.

Jin had left her purse on top of the bar before ducking behind it to hide, but the coat must have slipped down to the floor and then got kicked somewhere by the panicked people who'd been trying to get away.

"I'll give you my jacket," Kri offered. "You can take off the T-shirt, put the jacket on, and zip it all the way up."

"But then you'll be cold."

"I'm an immortal and a Guardian. I'll survive. You, on the other hand, are still a human and might get sick." Kri cast Jin a crooked smile. "Arwel will kick my butt if I let that happen."

She shrugged the leather jacket off and handed it to Jin. "Do it now. I don't want you getting out of the car without it."

Since there were no vehicles on the rural road Kri had turned onto, Jin pulled the T-shirt over her head, tossed it on the floor at her feet, and pulled Kri's jacket on.

"It's so warm. Thank you." She zipped it all the way up.

"The airstrip is over there." Kri pointed. "And our ride is already waiting for us. Turner is a freaking miracle worker."

It took another minute for Jin to see the lone aircraft waiting on what looked like just another country road. "I really don't want to go. I want to stay here, close to Arwel."

Kri patted her arm. "You need to do what Turner tells you because he knows what he's doing. He has a lot of experience in crisis management, while you have none."

Turner

Turner missed his yellow pad.

Without it, he had to keep all the details in his head, which wasn't a huge issue, but he didn't have the satisfaction of marking items as done.

While Kalugal was on the line with Kian and could compel him to do anything he wanted, Turner couldn't risk writing anything down.

Regrettably, despite his new immortal physical strength, Kian could still overpower him with ease and take his notes. First of all, the guy was about half a foot taller. Also, he was Annani's son. That alone made him more powerful than immortals with blood that had been diluted over many generations of breeding with humans.

What Kian couldn't do, though, was take the information from Turner's head. He could try to beat it out of him, but Turner had been trained to withstand torture.

He'd never been captured, so his training hadn't been put to the test, but he was pretty sure that it would kick in when needed.

Being stuck in the village was a sort of captivity, but he wasn't helpless. Like a chess master, he was moving the pieces around while trying to anticipate his opponent's moves.

He shouldn't be enjoying this so much, but it was incredible how much he'd managed to achieve in under half an hour. It was impressive, even in light of his usual high standards.

There were two things that he still needed to do. One was to verify that Jin was in the air, and the other was to contact Lokan.

Since Kian had asked him to contact Lokan, Turner didn't need to be secretive about it and decided to call instead of texting. It was the middle of the night in Washington, and Lokan was probably asleep, so he might not hear the incoming text.

When Lokan answered, he sounded alarmed and fully alert. "What's going on?"

"Your brother has Arwel and Jacki, and we need you to get on the plane and fly to San Francisco as soon as you can."

In the background, Turner heard Carol gasp. "I'm getting dressed," she informed Lokan.

"Wait. What exactly are you expecting me to do? Kalugal is not going to listen to me. He doesn't even know me."

"He might, or he might not, but we need all the ammunition we can get. Besides, we are in this mess because your mother asked Kian to help you find your brother. You can't stay home snuggled in your bed with your mate while we are dealing with him."

Lokan uttered a long-suffering sigh. "You're right. I'll be there as soon as I can. Damn. I have two important meetings scheduled for tomorrow that I will need to move."

The guy's priorities were skewed.

"You can claim to have fallen ill. That would reinforce your human cover."

Lokan huffed out a breath. "Where do you want me to go once I get there?"

"I'll let you know. Call me when you are about to land."

"It's going to be early morning your time."

"I'm not going to sleep anytime soon." Turner ended the call.

A couple of moments later, he got the text he'd been waiting for from Kri. *We are in the air.*

He was about to give Kian the thumbs up when another text came from Kri.

Jin wants me to tell you that she is offering herself to be traded for Arwel and Jacki. She wants you to tell Kian.

The girl was in love and not thinking straight. *That's the worst thing we can do. As long as Kalugal knows that he's being watched, he is practically paralyzed. We will negotiate Arwel and Jacki's release in exchange for the tether's removal, not the tetherer herself.*

Kri texted back. *She says that he will want to see proof of the tether's removal.*

Turner frowned. *I was under the impression that the tethered can be told what to pay attention to, and that once released, he can feel the difference. Kian told me that Edna even managed to detach the tether on her end.*

A long moment passed before the return text came in. *Jin says that it's impossible to demonstrate without removing the tether and reattaching it. She can remove it remotely, but she needs to touch Kalugal again to reattach it to him.*

That was a complication he hadn't foreseen.

He texted back. *We will try to work around it and tell Kalugal that he will feel the difference. Can Jin describe it to me?*

Jin says that from her side, releasing the tether feels like a mental weight was lifted. She says that you should call Edna and ask her how it felt to her.

I'll do that. Don't fall asleep. After Kian tells Kalugal about the tether, he will want proof. I'll call Jin and ask her to report what she sees.

Arwel

"I'm cold." Jacki pulled the blanket from the top bunk. "Do you want some?" She sat back down. "We can share."

"I'm not as sensitive to the cold as you are."

She wrapped the blanket around her shoulders. "Is it because you are immortal?"

He nodded.

"Can you tell me more? I mean things that are not top secret."

"Our very existence is a secret, but the cat is out of the bag on that."

Jacki put her feet up and tucked her legs under the blanket. "If I ever get out of here, no one is going to believe me anyway. It's like those poor folks who report alien encounters. They are ridiculed and dismissed." She cast him a sidelong glance. "Do you guys have anything to do with that?"

He shook his head. "None of us have ever met an alien."

"Really? I thought that you and the others like you were aliens."

"Maybe our ancestors were. We are the descendants of the mythological gods. The result of them taking human partners."

"Like in the Bible? And the sons of the gods saw that the daughters of men were fair and took them as wives?"

"Not only the sons of gods. The daughters did that as well. Except, they didn't take them as wives or husbands because they were considered too lowly for that. They took them as lovers, or if they were really fond of them as concubines and paramours. The reason behind the practice was the gods' low fertility rate and limited gene pool. Without the infusion of human genes, they would have died out. Even the gods couldn't live forever."

Jacki lifted a brow. "Isn't that the definition of immortal?"

"The gods could live hundreds of thousands of years. That's as immortal as it gets."

"What about you? The descendants are hybrids, so their genes are diluted. Does it go down to tens of thousands? Single-digit thousands?"

He chuckled. "I don't know. The longest living immortal is only five thousand years old, give or take a few centuries, and he is still in his prime. He is also Kalugal's father and our clan's arch-nemesis."

"I don't understand. If Kalugal is the son of your enemy, what made you think he could be a friend? Or was that just the story you told me?"

"Kalugal escaped his father and has lived in hiding ever since. What we don't know is whether he considers his father an enemy. If he does, that could make him our ally by default. The enemy of my enemy is my friend sort of thing."

Jacki leaned her chin on her upturned knees. "What happened to the gods?"

"Kalugal's grandfather dropped a bomb on their assembly, killing them all. What he hadn't expected was getting caught in the blast and dying with them."

"Why did he do that?"

"Jealousy or greed or a combination of both prompted him to kill another god by beheading him. When the assembly of gods sentenced him to entombment for his crime, Mortdh's solution was to kill them all."

Jacki sighed. "I wonder how Kalugal deals with a heritage like that. It must be difficult."

Since in Arwel's mind all Doomers were predisposed to evil, it hadn't occurred to him that Lokan and Kalugal were less so than others. They were the grandsons of Mortdh and the sons of Navuh.

It didn't get any worse than that.

Except, they were also the grandsons of Ahn and the sons of Areana.

Arwel didn't know much about Annani's father, but from what the goddess had shared about her half-sister, Areana was a gentle and benevolent soul. Carol's impression of her had been the same.

The question was which side was dominant.

Arwel had a feeling it was the paternal side. "Kalugal seems like a conceited bastard. He probably wears his murderous godly heritage like a badge of honor."

Jacki chuckled. "He's like a very handsome version of Doctor Evil from *Austin Powers*." She waved a hand. "He's polite, soft-spoken, and extremely intelligent."

Arwel arched a brow. "Isn't it a bit early for Stockholm syndrome to set in? You've been a captive for less than an hour, and you had contact with your captor for less than a minute."

Jacki huffed. "I'm not crushing on him if that's what you're thinking. I'm just stating the facts."

Kian

"As fun as it was chatting with you, cousin, it is late. Perhaps we could continue our fascinating conversation tomorrow?"

Like hell.

Kalugal was eager to start questioning Arwel, and Kian was not about to allow it. To keep him on the line, he would tell Kalugal the entire history of the clan if necessary, or rather the version of it he saw fit to share.

He glanced in Turner's direction, but the guy was in the back of the room, still talking to Lokan. Evidently, he hadn't gotten confirmation from Kri and Jin that they were in the air.

It was imperative to keep Kalugal talking.

"Using the earpiece is not very convenient. We should exchange phone numbers. Would you like to write mine down?"

"Certainly. Go ahead."

After dictating the numbers, Kian asked Kalugal to repeat them. It was an obvious ploy to buy time, but he only needed a couple of minutes.

"Is that your direct line?" Kalugal asked.

"Yes. You can call me day or night. My phone is always with me."

"I feel so privileged." Kalugal's tone was mocking. "And now I feel obliged to do the same. Here is mine." He rattled out the numbers.

"Let me read it back to you."

As Kian enunciated each number, he glanced at Turner again and finally got the thumbs up he'd been waiting for.

"That's correct. Good night, Kian," Kalugal said.

Kian leaned back in his chair. "Before we call it a night, there is something you should know."

Kalugal chuckled. "I'm well aware of your men surrounding my property. They are of no consequence to me."

"I'm sure you are. But what you are not aware of is that one of ours has a direct mental connection to you, and she can see and hear everything you do. There is no hiding from her, and there is no way to circumvent her tether. Everything you say, hear, or see is no longer private. I'm informed of your every move."

There was a long moment of silence as Kalugal processed the information.

"You are contradicting yourself, Kian. You said that you wanted to find out what I was up to. If you had such a fantastic spy working for you, you would have no need to send men to follow me."

"To attach the tether, she had to touch you. And for that to happen, we needed to get her to you. The plan was to do it without you noticing a thing, but as often happens, the best of plans go awry. We couldn't have anticipated a human psychopath showing up at the club and pulling out a gun."

This time the moment of silence was longer.

As the door to the war room opened, Kian turned his swivel chair around and lifted his hand to motion for whoever entered to stay quiet.

Ella came in with her arm wrapped around Parker, who was wearing his pajamas with a coat draped over his shoulders.

Kian had forgotten about asking for Parker to be brought over, and seeing the anxious expression on the kid's face, he felt guilty.

It seemed that there would be no need for Parker's compulsion removal services, but it wasn't a sure thing. So, even though he hated to involve the kid in the drama, he needed him to hang around until it was over.

Okidu entered right behind the siblings, pushing a rolling cart with food and drinks, and the last arrival was Syssi, who sent him an air kiss and then joined Ella and Parker at the back of the war room.

"I assume that you can prove this?" Kalugal asked.

"Naturally." Kian motioned for Turner to get closer. "What proof would you like? I'll have my second-in-command ask her. And just in case you forgot, he is an immune."

"I didn't forget. I want to know how she did it."

Kian repeated the question out loud. "It will take him a couple of moments to communicate with her."

"I'll wait."

As Turner got busy texting, Kian pushed to his feet and walked to the back of the room. Taking Syssi's hand, he mouthed, "You shouldn't have come."

She kissed his cheek and handed him a bottle of water from Okidu's cart.

He nodded and then examined the cart's contents.

Syssi chuckled, and then whispered, "If you are looking for beer, it's in the cooler on the bottom." She pulled one out for him.

"You are the best," he mouthed.

He had time for two heavenly gulps before Turner lifted his phone and motioned for Kian to pull out his right as it buzzed with an incoming message.

It was a copy of the one Turner had received from Jin, detailing in length her encounter with Kalugal.

"Let me read you her answer."

Kalugal

As Kalugal listened to Kian read the story from the girl's perspective, he closed his eyes and replayed in his mind the events preceding the appearance of the shooter.

In the excitement that had followed Flyboy's amazing display of acrobatics, Kalugal had forgotten all about the girl who'd spilled her drink over him and his dance partner.

Apparently, he hadn't been as indifferent to Blondie's charms as he'd thought he was. Between her ample cleavage and his irritation over her response to the spilled drink incident, he hadn't paid much attention to the girl who'd clung on to his arm for a couple of seconds too long.

Or maybe it had been his arrogance at play, assuming that the girl didn't want to let go of him because of his magnetic masculinity, which even his shroud couldn't hide.

She was tall, he remembered that, and not because she had high-heeled shoes on. Assuming footwear was the cause of her stumble, he'd glanced at her feet. She'd also had a lot of badly-applied cheap makeup on, but for some reason, he'd found her attractive despite her below-average looks.

The immune was tall as well, and she too had similarly done heavy makeup on...

Two tall females with bad hair and bad makeup.

Damn. How had he missed that?

They were the same two he'd encountered the night before outside the cigar lounge.

The tall Asian had stared at him looking stunned, and her friend had done all the talking. In hindsight, their behavior made perfect sense. The Asian was the one with the tethering talent, and the immune was there as a precaution against his compulsion.

After failing to tether him outside the lounge, they'd changed their appearance and completed their mission in the club. If not for the shooter, he wouldn't have noticed that anything was amiss.

Even though recounting the events was no proof of the tether's existence, the effort the woman had invested into putting her hand on him was convincing enough.

Still, before starting negotiations, he needed indisputable proof.

"Everything you are telling me could have been witnessed by hidden cameras or your spies. I need something more conclusive."

"Hold on. I'll ask."

As Kalugal waited, he tried to imagine what proof the spy could provide. Maybe describe the room he was in?

First, he turned his chair around, so he wasn't facing the monitor. That really wasn't necessary since she couldn't figure out anything from what was on the screen, but if she'd been watching earlier, she could have seen his entire lockdown protocol.

Thankfully, no codes had been displayed, and he hadn't been the one who had entered them. Phinas had done that.

"She asks that you write something on a note," Kian said. "After that, look at the note long enough to read it, but don't show it to anyone. She will tell you what you've written."

"Does she have a name? Or are we just going to call her the spy?"

"Her name is Jin."

Kalugal opened a drawer, pulled out a sheet of computer paper, and clicked on his pen. "I'm writing the note."

Hello, Jin. I wonder what you look like under all that ugly makeup. You looked prettier last night outside the cigar lounge.

Holding the page in front of him for several seconds, Kalugal read the note twice and then put it down. "Well?"

"Let me read it to you." Kian recited word for word exactly what he had written. "Need more convincing?"

As the last of his doubts was quashed, Kalugal felt chilled. His mind working quickly, he tried to come up with ways of working around the tether, but there were none. Regrettably, his talents didn't include telepathy, and he had never bothered to learn Morse code, which was the only other method of communication he could think of. While his auditory and visuals were compromised, the only thing left was touch. Except, the spy's talents might include that as well, and Kian had just failed to mention it, intentionally or not.

"No, that will do. What do you want in exchange for removing the tether?"

"That's obvious. I want you to release my people."

Kalugal had expected that. "They must be very important for you to give up an asset like that."

Either that or they had information that Kian could not afford to fall into Kalugal's hands. The immune hadn't even known about her boyfriend's immortality, so she probably held no value other than her immunity. The warrior was the important one. Maybe he was related to Kian?

A brother, perhaps?

No one knew who Annani's children were, and how many she had, but given the gods' low fertility rate, she couldn't have more than two. Since she had most likely mated with humans, she must have had at least one daughter to continue her line, and Kian had proclaimed himself as her son.

"Every member of my clan is important. Unlike your father, who doesn't care about the individual cogs in his war machine, I value each and every one of my people. We are a family."

They were a tight-knit community because there weren't as many of them, but Kalugal saw no reason to point it out. At this stage of the game, Kian had the winning card, and antagonizing him was not going to work in Kalugal's favor.

"That's admirable. Unlike my father, I also value my men. You and I have that in common." Pointing out similarities was always a good strategy. People, humans and immortals alike, were more positively predisposed toward those who they thought were like them. "What about the immune, though? Is she a member of your clan?"

With the love the clan had been showing humanity from its very start, it was possible that they had some living among them.

"She is not a member of my clan, but after she has graciously agreed to help us, I'm not going to abandon her."

Kalugal had a feeling that Kian was not just spouting those things to flaunt his benevolence. The guy believed in what he was saying.

Nevertheless, the sanctimonious verbiage grated on Kalugal's nerves because its purpose was to demonstrate Kian's moral superiority.

"So, her immunity has no bearing on her value to you?"

"Of course it does. But I would do the same for any human who risked herself to save one of mine."

"I must admit that I was impressed by her heroics. She must truly love your clansman to do something as stupid as that. Then again, he must love her too. He exposed his inhuman abilities to protect her."

"My warrior protected his team members, which is his job. And I assume that the immune acted out of desperation because she was the only one who was able to move."

"Then I'm even more impressed. The woman fought like a wildcat."

"Did you hurt her?" Kian's voice turned into a growl.

"Relax. She is fine. We handled her with utmost care."

"I was told that you stuffed her into the trunk of your car, bound and gagged."

"Regrettably, I had no choice. She was screaming rape, scratching and kicking, and there was nowhere else I could put her in my Ferrari. Your warrior was too big to fit in the trunk."

Kian

Kian stifled a chuckle. As critical as the situation was, it lifted his mood to imagine Jacki raising hell and fighting two immortals who were doing their best to subdue her without hurting her.

Even though she wasn't a member of the clan, not yet, he was damn proud of the girl. If she transitioned, Jacki should join the Guardian training program. She sure had the right spirit.

"Do we have a deal then? You will release my people, and I'll tell Jin to release the tether."

"I'll sleep on it."

Right, as if Kian was going to buy that.

"If you're thinking about sending one of your guys to interrogate either of the two, you should know that Jin has them both tethered. If either is questioned, I will know, and the deal will be off. You'll be forever stuck with me as your shadow, and I'll do my damndest to thwart your every move."

"Let's assume for a moment that I believe you, but naturally, I would like proof of that as well. I wonder, though. What does your warrior know that you are so afraid of me discovering? Were you planning on capturing me and selling me to my father? Maybe in exchange for one of yours that he's holding prisoner?"

Kian could understand Kalugal's suspicions.

He was imagining the worst possible scenarios from his perspective, which was the prudent thing to do.

"You have one hell of an imagination. But my reason is simpler than that. My clan's survival depends on our ability to hide. Your father's army outnumbers ours, and we can't afford him discovering our location. That's the big secret that I'm trying to protect, not any plot against you. In fact, I'm okay with you asking my guy whether we had any plans to capture you, or sell you, or harm you in any way. But I'm not okay with you asking about anything of strategic importance to my clan."

"I believe you because I'm in the same situation. After we solve our little problem, I'll be forced to relocate." Kalugal sighed. "It will be a shame. I like it here."

"We don't mean you harm, Kalugal. As long as you don't engage in trafficking, we won't bother you."

"Trafficking? What on earth makes you think I would ever do something as despicable as that?"

"That's your father's latest business endeavor."

"I don't believe that. Navuh wouldn't stoop so low."

"You'd be surprised. There isn't much work left in the world for his mercenary army, and he's looking for other sources of revenue. It also gives his men something to do. Restless soldiers might start thinking, and he can't allow that."

For a long moment, Kalugal was silent. Out of all the fascinating new things he had learned from Kian, his father's involvement in trafficking seemed to rattle him the most.

Should Kian mention the drugs as well?

"That's regrettable," Kalugal said. "I don't have much love for my father, nor do I approve of his methods, but until now, I respected him. I can no longer do that."

That was somewhat hypocritical of Kalugal. Even before his escape, he must have been aware of the influx of females to the island who had been conscripted into prostitution. Navuh had been paying traffickers to deliver the women. The only difference was that now the middlemen had been cut out, and the warriors had taken their place.

Nevertheless, Kalugal had just provided him with an excellent opening, and Kian wasn't going to ruin the opportunity by pointing out the hypocrisy.

"I'm glad we see eye to eye on this issue. Perhaps it is time for you to take over. The island needs a new leader, and you are the only one who can do that. As long as Navuh compels everyone's loyalty, no change is possible."

"I have no intention of going after Navuh's position. I made a promise to my mother to never go against my father, and I won't break that promise. But I wouldn't have done it regardless. I'm not interested in the island."

"What are you interested in?"

"Making money. I like my peaceful anonymity, and I intend to keep it. My brother can take over if he has such aspirations. For now, he can only compel humans, but perhaps in time, his power will grow."

"Your mother had him make a similar promise. He vowed never to kill his father."

"How do you know all that? Is my father suddenly letting my mother out of the harem? Has she told someone who delivered the news to her sister?"

"Areana is still locked in the harem, but we managed to smuggle a communication device to her. She talks with my mother almost every day. This little piece of technology was a life-changer for her. With my mother filling her in on what's happening in the world, Areana is no longer as isolated. She didn't even know that Annani or any of her people had survived."

"How did you manage to get anything to her? I've thought about doing just that for many years, and I've never come up with anything that was doable."

It was tempting to tell Kalugal about Lokan, and that it had been his idea that had made contact with Areana possible, but it was too early for that. Kalugal was still an enigma, and although Kian was quite sure that the son had no contact with the father, he wasn't willing to bet Lokan's safety on that.

Kalugal might use the information to gain leverage.

Telling him about Areana communicating with the outside world and how she was doing it was risky enough.

"I can't tell you the details because we are not friends yet. Once we are, and you prove your trustworthiness to me, I'll let you talk with your mother. I'm sure you are eager for the chance to speak with her again after so many years."

Kalugal

Kalugal's heart skipped a beat. Contact with his mother was a dream he had almost given up on. He'd been tempted by many fantasies of clever ways to achieve it, but none of them had ever passed a reality check.

His life and that of his men depended on him staying as far from the island as possible and not attracting any attention to themselves.

It grated that Kian had figured a way to make contact with Areana while Kalugal had failed to do so, but he wasn't going to hold it against his cousin, especially given what Kian had just offered.

Kalugal had about a thousand questions he wanted to ask his mother, but the first and most important one was about her lineage, and through her, his. In the heat of the conversation and the bombs his cousin had been dropping one after the other, Kalugal had almost forgotten about that.

His mother was a goddess.

But even that was not as exciting as the possibility of actually talking to her. Would her voice be as lovely as he remembered it? Was she as angelically beautiful as he saw her in his mind's eye?

"I don't suppose the communication device you've smuggled into the harem has video as well as audio."

"Regrettably, no. But I can give you a copy of her portrait. We had a gifted forensic artist draw her from Annani's memory. It's a very accurate depiction."

Kalugal's heart missed another beat. "I would love to see it."

"As a gesture of goodwill, I'll send it to your phone, and I'll send you a full-sized replica at another time."

"What do you want for it?"

"Consider it a gift, a proof that what I've been telling you is true."

Kian didn't strike him as the sort of man who did something for nothing, but a moment later, Kalugal's phone pinged with an incoming text.

His hands shook only slightly as he opened the attachment, but when he saw the picture, he almost dropped the phone.

Sad, blue eyes looked at him from the most beautiful, pale face, framed by blond wavy hair that was almost white.

It was his mother. Exactly as he remembered her.

"Did you get it?" Kian asked.

Kalugal cleared his throat. "Yes."

"Is that how you remember your mother?"

"You were right about it being a very accurate depiction. Thank you. What do you want in exchange?"

"As I told you, it's a gesture of goodwill and proof of my claims. But since you are offering, you might consider moving my people to better accommodations as a gesture of your goodwill. My second-in-command has just shown me a text from Jin, and she is appalled by the prison cell you've thrown them in. She says it doesn't even have a modesty wall separating the toilet from the rest of the room, and the blankets on the bunk beds are so thin that her friend is shivering from cold."

If Kalugal wanted proof of the spy's tether to her friends, he'd just gotten it.

"I can do that."

"Also, Jin is requesting that you put them in a room with two good beds that have proper blankets, and a bathroom that has a shower. She also asks that you provide them both with a change of clothes."

"I'll see what I can do. This is a bunker, not a hotel."

"I'm sure you can manage something. I've seen the blueprints for your underground facility, and you have plenty of rooms with en-suite bathrooms. Jin also says that your men haven't fed her friends since their arrival or given them anything to drink."

To dig out the blueprints for the bunker, Kian must have been planning this for a long time. If not for the random interference from the shooter, he would have pulled it off without a hitch.

That deserved respect, but Kalugal didn't appreciate Kian's insinuation that he was mistreating his prisoners. "It hasn't been that long. It's not like they've been starving for days."

"Still, you might want to be a good host. Or, you can release them and save yourself the trouble. Once this is done, we can meet as friends, and I'll arrange for you to speak with your mother."

As much as Kalugal wanted to end this fiasco, he wasn't about to capitulate so quickly. Besides, he needed to figure out how to verify the tether's removal. He hadn't felt it being attached, and he still didn't feel anything different, but the proof Jin had provided had left no doubt as to its existence.

"Your spy is a demanding woman."

Kian chuckled. "Indeed. If I were you, I would play nice with the person who's privy to all my secrets."

"Noted." He lifted his phone and looked at his mother's picture. "Have your spy release the tether, and I'll let your people go."

"That's what I offered an hour ago, and I will sweeten the deal by letting you talk with Areana."

"I will need proof of the tether's removal."

A long moment passed until Kian answered. "I'll have to check with Jin whether she can describe the feeling of having it removed. I will also ask those who she tethered and then released what they felt."

"I'm sure you can understand why I can't agree to any deal without definite proof. And describing a feeling is too vague to prove anything."

Kian sighed. "We will work something out."

"I hope so. While you do that, I suggest that we take a break for the night. As a gesture of my goodwill, I will not question your people and will move them to a better room. I'll also send food and a change of clothing. You can have your spy verify that I'm good at keeping my promises."

Yamanu

As Yamanu walked into the bedroom, it wasn't to follow his original plan to make love to his mate.

It was to deliver bad news.

"Kalugal's captured Arwel and Jacki, and we need to leave the keep because its location might already be compromised."

Clutching the blanket to her breasts, Mey sat up. "What about Jin?"

"She is fine. She managed to tether him before everything went to shit. Kri has her, and she is driving out of the city. Turner is going to stash them somewhere safe."

"What happened?"

"Onegus didn't have time to give me the details, so I called Magnus. A gunman entered the club, and when Arwel felt his intention to kill, he ran in to stop him. His speed and strength gave him away, and when Kalugal realized that Arwel must be an immortal, he compelled everyone to freeze. When he took Arwel, Jacki ran after them, trying to save him, which resulted in her getting taken as well."

"That's so brave of her. But stupid. What did she hope to achieve?"

Yamanu rubbed the back of his neck. "That was my reaction as well, but Magnus pointed out that Jacki didn't know that she was going after immortals. If they had been a couple of human males, her bear-spray attack might have worked."

Mey ran a shaky hand over her mouth. "What's going to happen to Arwel and Jacki?"

"Kian is negotiating for their release." Yamanu pulled out his duffle bag from the closet and started shoving his clothes inside. "You should get dressed. We need to get going."

"Where?" As Mey flung the comforter off, her beautiful nude body momentarily distracted Yamanu from his task. She padded to the bathroom but left the door open. "Are we bringing Wendy and Richard to the village?"

He forced his eyes away and leaned to pick up his boots. "The village is locked down, which means that no one is getting in or out. Onegus gave me the address of a cabin in Big Bear. It belongs to a friend of Turner's, so Arwel doesn't know about it. You'll be safe there."

"You mean we, right?"

"I'm not coming with you." He walked into the bathroom and gathered her into his arms. "I'm needed in the Bay Area. The Guardians are surrounding Kalugal's compound, and I have to shroud them from the human neighbors. It's an upscale community, and with so many cars parked on the street at night, someone is bound to call the police."

He didn't want to worry her, but his shrouding might be needed to hide more than just parked cars. If they were forced to attack the compound, he would have to shroud the sounds, sights, and even smells of gunfire and explosions.

Mey clung to him. "I don't want to be separated from you."

"I know." He kissed the top of her head. "I don't want that either. But this is an emergency, and we have to play our respective parts."

"What's mine?"

"Taking care of Wendy and Richard. The Guardians will join you, of course, so you don't have to worry about security, but you'll be in charge of the household until the crisis is over."

"I think that Vlad is still here, and probably Ingrid as well. Since they can't go back to the village, do they come with us?"

Yamanu nodded. "They could rent rooms in a hotel, but it's probably better if they join you. They'll keep Wendy and Richard occupied."

"Don't you have another secret clan location? Like a safe house? A cabin in Big Bear is not secluded, and our guests will know where they are. I can demand that they wear blindfolds on the way up there, but once we are at the cabin, they will have to come off. What do I do then?"

"We have another location that could have been perfect, but Arwel knows about it."

"Damn." Mey rested her forehead on his chest. "What am I supposed to do if they decide to leave the cabin?

"We can no longer play this game with them. They will know where they are, and if they want to walk away, there isn't much you or the Guardians can do about it. The only way to prevent it is to make them terrified of getting discovered. I'll leave it up to you to get creative with all the possible scenarios. The more horrible, the better."

"I hope there is no landline in that cabin. It would be really difficult to explain why they can't use the phone."

"When you get there, Leon and Bowen will go in first and take care of the phones. Big Bear is about two hours away. Use that time to scare Richard and Wendy into compliance."

"I'll do what I can." Pulling out of his arms, Mey walked into the closet and took out a sweater and a pair of warm leggings. "What excuse am I going to give them for the rushed escape?"

"Tell them that Arwel and Jacki were captured by Kalugal, the head of a rival organization, and that he is planning to attack and capture all the talents he can find. That should scare them into cooperating. Make him sound really evil."

Mey paused with the leggings halfway up her thighs. "What if he really is? Kalugal's father is a heartless dictator who had no problem causing the deaths of millions of humans, and his grandfather was a god who had singlehandedly killed all the other gods except for Annani and Areana, ending their era."

"True. But Lokan shares the same genes as Kalugal, and he is a decent guy."

"Lokan might take after his mother, and we have no idea what kind of a man Kalugal is. Finding what he's about was the entire purpose of Jin's mission."

Yamanu zipped up his duffle bag. "So far, the only thing we know about him is that he is using his powers to make money. It's dishonest and immoral, but it's not in the same league as what his father is responsible for. I hope he's a reasonable man and that he'll agree to a deal. This whole thing might be over by tomorrow."

"From your lips to God's ears."

Yamanu smiled. "I'll beseech the merciful Fates to help us reach a peaceful agreement. But if that is not to be, we can overpower Kalugal despite his abilities. Right now, twenty-eight Guardians are positioned outside his estate, and I'm bringing fifteen more with me. That's more than half of the Guardian force. We can take him and his men."

"I hope it won't come to that. I don't want to even think about an all-out war between immortals in the middle of a human neighborhood. People could get caught in the crossfire."

Mey

Mey had kept up a brave face for Yamanu, but the truth was that she was scared and overwhelmed. She was only a baby immortal, and suddenly she was put in charge.

Saying goodbye to him had been hard, but there was no time to fall apart and cry. She had to ignore the heaviness in her chest, get herself into operational mode, and get everyone moving.

Thankfully, the two Guardians were there to help.

"Leon, can you get Ingrid and Vlad and explain what's going on? I will deal with Wendy and Richard."

The Guardian scratched his short stubble. "Vlad is in Wendy's room, and Ingrid is in Richard's. How am I going to excuse taking them aside?"

He had a point. "Can you text them?"

"That should work. I'll do it right now."

She lifted a hand to stop him. "Wait. I prepared a story to tell our guests, and I want to deliver it first. You can tell Vlad and Ingrid the truth later. Is Wendy's door open?"

Leon nodded. "They are playing William's video game."

"I'll start with her."

Mey rushed out, walking briskly toward Wendy's room.

She wanted to check on Jin, but first, she had to get everyone moving. Once they were on their way to Big Bear, she would text Jin and ask her how she was holding up.

Her sister was a strong woman, but with her mate taken by the enemy, she was probably freaking out. In fact, Mey was surprised that Jin hadn't called her yet. When they were younger and Jin got in trouble, she'd called Mey, not their parents.

But Jin was all grown up now, and apparently it hadn't crossed her mind to call her older sister.

Then again, Jin was probably following the tether to Kalugal and reporting to Kian what she was seeing. And if she had Jacki tethered as well, she was following that string too.

Poor Jin. She could use some handholding right now.

Slowing down right before she reached the door, Mey schooled her facial expression and affected a mask of calm. She rapped her fingers on the doorjamb. "Wendy, you need to pack up your things, sweetheart. We are moving to a different location."

The girl lifted a pair of frightened eyes to her. "What happened? Did they find us?"

"If by they you mean the government, then no. But Arwel was captured by a rival organization, and this location might be compromised. We need to get out of here fast."

"What are you talking about? What rival organization?"

"I don't have time to explain. I'll tell you more on the way." Mey looked at Vlad. "Are you coming with us?"

"I guess that going home is not an option, right?"

Smart kid. Mey nodded.

Wendy put her hand on his arm. "What's going on, Vlad? You are scared."

"Arwel's capture is bad. But Mey is right. We need to hurry up and get out of here. We can talk on the way." He got up and started shoving video games into his duffel bag. "I hope there is a games console where we are going."

"I don't know," Mey admitted. "All I have is an address. We will figure things out when we get there. I need to check on Richard and Ingrid."

"Wait." Wendy stopped her. "Do I take everything with me? And where am I going to put it? I don't have a suitcase."

"You can pull the sheet off the bed, pile everything on top of it, and then tie it up like a sack. Vlad can help you."

"Okay." Wendy's chin quivered.

Poor girl, she was frightened, and Mey didn't have time to handhold her through this. Heck, she needed some handholding herself.

When Mey walked out into the corridor, she saw that the door to Richard's room was open, and she could hear Ingrid cussing up a storm, with Richard trying to calm her down.

"What's going on?" Mey asked as she walked in.

"I can't go home! That's what's going on."

Apparently, Ingrid had learned about the village lockdown.

"You can't stay either. We need to get out of here."

"Where are we going?"

"To a safe location Turner has found for us. Think of it as a mini-vacation in the mountains."

"Are we going to the cabin?" Ingrid asked.

"Yes, but I don't think it's the same one you are referring to. Turner found a place for us to hide out in until this is over. But if you wish, you can stay in a hotel in the city. You don't have to come with us."

"Are Bowen and Leon going with you?"

Mey nodded.

"Then I'm coming too. There is safety in numbers."

Richard looked at Mey. "Are we under attack?"

"Not yet. But we might be. Arwel was captured by a rival organization, whose head can compel him to reveal everything he knows. They would like nothing more than to collect all the paranormal talents they can find, and that includes you and Wendy. Please hurry up and pack your things. You can use the bed sheet to create a carrying sack."

"You said that we are going to a cabin in the mountains. Does that imply snow?"

"I guess so. It's winter."

"We don't have warm clothing or proper shoes. I know it's not urgent right now, but I'm being practical."

Mey hadn't considered that. She still had her snow attire from the trip, but the others didn't have even warm coats. Richard and Wendy's coats had been burned, and Ingrid and Vlad didn't need them in Los Angeles's mild winter. Vlad had a hoodie on, and Ingrid probably had a sweater, but she wasn't wearing it now.

"We will get everything we need once we get there."

"Wendy and I don't have any money."

"Don't worry about it. I'll get you everything you need."

Lokan

"An hour is fine. Thank you." Lokan ended the call. "I need to pack."

Arranging for his private jet to be ready for takeoff this late at night had taken some maneuvering, but for the right sum of money, it wasn't hard to get people to cooperate.

"I'm going with you." Carol walked into the closet.

Stifling a groan, Lokan rubbed the back of his head. He didn't want Carol anywhere near Kalugal and his powers of compulsion, but convincing her to stay behind would start a major argument.

"We have proof now that I can't shield immortals from Kalugal. If he compels you, I would be powerless to do anything about it."

She walked out of the closet with a stack of clothes and dumped them on the bed. "Why would he do that?" She went back in and came out with a carry-on. "And how? I'm not going to be anywhere near him."

"Really? Are you going to stay behind in the hotel?"

He knew her better than that. Carol would want to take an active part in whatever was going on.

"Hopefully, I can stay with the others wherever they moved everyone to. I'm sure Turner's found them a safe house." She looked at him over her shoulder. "You need me there for moral support."

He stifled a snort. "So, if I have to negotiate with Kalugal face to face, you are going to keep away?"

Carol put the luggage on the bed. "I'm not stupid. If I come with you, he can use me as leverage against you. He can't compel you directly, but he could do it by compelling me." She chuckled. "If he told me to strip naked, you would freak out."

"Hmm." Lokan rubbed his hand over his chin. "If he does that, it will backfire. He'll be mesmerized by your beauty, and then you can compel him to do anything you want."

He was teasing, of course, but he'd done it with a straight face to see if she'd take the bait.

Given the spike in her excitement, she had. "You'd actually let me do that? You wouldn't mind your brother seeing me nude?"

Wrapping an arm around Carol's waist, Lokan pulled her close. "We are mated, love, and that means you are mine, and I trust you. I have no fear of my brother's charms winning you over, but I don't trust him. I don't want his eyes on you, neither nude nor fully dressed."

Carol shook her head. "This could be an opportunity for you and Kalugal to get closer, to become real brothers, a family. Don't go into it expecting the worst. He might surprise you."

"I'd rather expect the worst and get surprised for the better than the other way around." He dipped his head and kissed her lightly. "You are my family, Carol."

She smiled. "You are so sweet. But I'm not your only family. In a small way, you have your mother back, and you are getting to know her a little better with each phone call. Wouldn't it be nice to have the same connection with Kalugal?"

"That's different. I can trust Areana because she is my mother, and she has as much to lose as I do if my father discovers our clandestine communications. Kalugal is an unknown. I don't know what his agenda is."

"Whatever it is, it's not about the island." Carol put the stack of clothes in the carry-on. "Do you want me to pack for you?"

"I'll do it." Lokan walked into the closet. "Kalugal could've been building up his power base and waiting until he's strong enough to take our father on."

Carol followed him inside. "Isn't that what you want?" She pulled a pair of boots off the shoe rack. "Without Kalugal's help, your dreams and aspirations for the island will remain just that. With him, you have a chance of making them a reality."

"It all depends on what kind of man Kalugal is, and what he wants. He might want nothing to do with the island, or he might want to take over without me because he doesn't need me."

And that was what bothered Lokan the most. On the one hand he needed Kalugal, but on the other hand he feared him.

Lokan's plans to take over the island had never been concrete, so even if Kalugal was willing to cooperate, Lokan had nothing to show him yet. His brother would realize right away that he didn't need Lokan to take over from Navuh if he so wished. And if he had no such aspirations, he definitely didn't need Lokan for anything else.

Brotherly love was a foreign concept to both of them.

Other than their genes and the unique powers that they had inherited from Navuh, he and Kalugal had very little in common.

Some would argue that blood-ties were enough, and that their shared genetics manifested in more than similar body build and facial features.

Their personalities were determined by their genes as well.

Given who his father was, however, Lokan preferred to think that wasn't the case. Because if everything was determined by biology, free will was an illusion, and no one should be held responsible for their actions.

Except, this was not the time to ponder a philosophical conundrum.

Right now, there was a private jet waiting for him and Carol at the airport, and they had to hurry up. The six-hour flight to San Francisco would be better utilized by coming up with a strategy for dealing with his brother and organizing his thoughts regarding the island's future. Perhaps if he could get Kalugal excited about the possibilities, his brother would feel more inclined to join forces with him.

Magnus

"A motel?" Magnus checked the address Turner had sent him. "That can't be right."

Vivian opened the window and looked up. "The lights in the sign are off, and there are no cars parked in front. The place seems deserted."

"Before we go in, I want to double check." Magnus placed the call to Turner. "Did you send us to a motel?"

"I should have mentioned it, but as you can imagine, I was in a rush. The owner is the brother-in-law of a buddy of mine, and he closed escrow on it less than a week ago. That's why it's vacant. He knows it's a covert operation and he's not going to ask any questions."

"What about the staff?"

"There isn't any. You'll have to make your own beds. The linens and everything else is in the housekeeping supply room. The code I sent you will open that too."

"Not a problem. How are things going with the negotiations?"

"They ended for tonight and will resume tomorrow. Kalugal promised not to interrogate Arwel and Jacki and to move them to a better room. Jin is verifying that he is keeping his promise."

"At some point, she will need to go to sleep."

If she were an immortal, she could get away with a short nap, but as a human she needed more than that.

"I'm aware of that, but Kalugal doesn't know when she's watching him and when she is not. He wouldn't risk it. Kian told him that if he questions Arwel, he's going to be stuck with her tether forever. He wants to get rid of that more than he wants to know the clan's secrets."

"Have you told Kian about her offer?"

"No, and I'm not going to unless I think there is no other way. What about the blockade, did you get decent earplugs for everyone?"

"I got the best, but don't ask me how because you'd become an accomplice to a crime. William's equipment is all in the van, and he is right here behind me. I'm going to leave Vivian and him in the motel and go back to the blockade."

Magnus had never been in charge of such a large force, but he knew each of the men well, and they were all capable fighters.

In fact, he was glad of the opportunity to show Onegus and Kian that he and the other old-timers were just as good as the head Guardians, and that they could be entrusted with more than rescuing trafficking victims.

It didn't matter that some of the men were still better with a sword than a rifle. Being a warrior was not about the mastery of a particular weapon, it was about grit and attitude, and after centuries of service, they all still had it despite their temporary retirement.

"Who did you leave in charge?"

"Gregor. He is an experienced and capable Guardian who has proven himself many times over."

"You don't have to defend your choices. You are the field commander, and you call the shots. Good thinking with the earplugs."

"It was Kri's idea. Or maybe Jin's. Are they safely hidden?"

Magnus didn't expect Turner to tell him where he had stashed them. Even with the earplugs, it was better that those who could be compelled didn't know where Jin was. Finding her would be Kalugal's top priority, and the guy would stop at nothing to get her.

"Rest assured, they are out of his reach."

"Good. That's one less thing to worry about."

"Yamanu should be arriving with the reinforcements shortly. I told him to head straight to Kalugal's complex. He needs to shroud the vehicles and take care of the neighbors. Lokan is on his way as well, and I gave him the motel's address. I don't know if he will be needed, but just in case, I want him nearby."

"Is that a smart thing to do? He can't do anything about Kalugal's compulsion. His preventive measures didn't work."

"That's true, but since Lokan is immune to his father's compulsion, we can be pretty sure that Kalugal can't compel him either. If needed, he could do the negotiating for us."

"Or against us. Do you trust him?"

"We have no choice. I have to stay here to guard Kian. In case Kalugal takes control of him, I will have to take over command. Lokan is the only other immune we have, and you might need him on location. Besides, this is his chance to prove his loyalty, and if we want Lokan's help against his brother, we can't keep treating him as an outsider."

Magnus smoothed his hand over his goatee. "I understand your reasoning. But I'm not convinced that testing Lokan's loyalty during a crisis that involves his brother is a good idea."

"I'll use him only as a last resort. If possible, I don't want Kalugal to know that his brother is working with us. It's better not to expose the connection before we know what Kalugal's intentions are. But I want Lokan in the area in case all else fails."

"Got it. Are you calling it a night, or are you going to stay in the command center?"

"I'm not going anywhere until this is over. By the way, your son is here. Kian brought him to the war room."

Vivian grimaced. "I know. Ella called me. But Parker can't help remove Kalugal's compulsion. Lokan, who is more powerful than my son, failed to safeguard us against it."

"We don't know that for sure. But in any case, since the negotiations are done for tonight, Kian is sending Parker and Ella home."

"Can you tell Ella to call me once she is out of the war room?"

"No problem. Good night, Vivian."

After Turner ended the call, Magnus put the phone away and took Vivian's hand. "Parker is tough, and I'm sure that he feels two feet taller because Kian asked for his help."

Vivian shook her head. "The village is locked down, everyone is terrified of Kalugal and what he might do, and Parker is just a boy. He's probably scared and shaking in his pajama pants."

Magnus chuckled. "I know that you don't want to hear this, but at his age, I was already wielding a sword."

"Yeah, but this is now, and a thirteen-year-old is not equipped to deal with a situation like that. Kian shouldn't have asked him to come."

Kian

After ending the conversation with Kalugal, Kian leaned back in his chair, closed his eyes, and let out a long breath.

"That was intense." Turner walked over. "Ready for updates?"

"Let me grab another beer first." He pushed to his feet and walked to the back of the room where Syssi was waiting for him.

The beer was an excuse.

What he really wanted was to hold his wife in his arms and absorb the positive energy she emitted. Syssi was his rock, his foundation, his life.

"How are you doing?" she asked.

"I'm drained, but I'm relieved that Kalugal and I were able to reach an agreement."

She chuckled. "You didn't leave him much choice."

"Negotiation at its best is holding a big stick in one hand and offering a treat with the other. Some people respond better to the promise of a reward, while others are more afraid of sustaining a loss than they are eager for a profit. I like to cover both bases."

From the corner of his eye, Kian caught Parker nodding sagely.

The kid no longer looked shell-shocked. A good meal combined with Syssi's calming presence had done the trick.

He turned toward the boy and offered him his hand. "Thanks for coming, Parker. I really appreciate it."

Parker shook it. "I didn't do anything."

"But you were here in case I needed you. It must've been stressful."

Parker nodded. "I didn't know what was going on, and when Syssi explained that you were talking with someone who could compel immortals, I got really scared because I don't think I can override a compeller that powerful. But I listened to you negotiate with him, and you seemed to have things under control." The kid smiled. "It was interesting, and I'm glad I got to be here. I even learned something I can use. I liked your stick and treat negotiation method."

Kian clapped him on the back. "You are a smart fellow, Parker. And who knows? Maybe your powers have grown since the last time you used them. If we manage to bring Kalugal to our side, I might ask him to help us test you."

Parker's eyes widened. "Do you think he'd agree?"

"It all depends on what he will gain by it. I have a feeling that Kalugal is an opportunist, not an idealist. Which is good. It makes him much easier to negotiate with."

"Why is that?"

"People are seldom willing to compromise on ideology, and beliefs are almost impossible to bend, let alone change. But Kalugal is a smart fellow who thinks logically, which makes him a good partner for the negotiation table." Kian leaned closer to Parker's ear. "Here's another lesson you should internalize. Not everyone can be reasoned with, and bullies respond best to a show of force."

"Is Kalugal a bully?"

"He might be. But he proved that he can at least listen to reason. That's the mark of an intelligent man."

Kian lifted his eyes to Ella, who was sitting on Parker's other side. "Thank you for bringing your brother here. It must have been difficult for you as well."

She waved a dismissive hand. "It was much scarier on the outside. When the lockdown was announced, Parker and I freaked out. We thought that the village was under attack. Then when Onegus called and told me to bring Parker, it was a relief to know that the lockdown was only a precaution because the location might have been compromised. Being here and knowing what is going on was less stressful than staying home and wondering when the explosions would start."

"God forbid." Syssi put a hand over her heart. "We would have been forced to move everyone into the underground facility." She lifted her eyes to Kian. "After this is over, I'm going to enlist Ingrid, and we will figure out how to house everyone down here. I know that we have emergency rations, but we don't have beds and blankets and everything else that's needed for a prolonged stay."

Turning the underground into an emergency shelter was a good idea, but the place hadn't been designed for that.

"We don't have enough room down here. And besides, aerial shelling is the last thing I'm worried about. The Doomers wouldn't dare attract that much attention. What I'm worried about is a siege. Our emergency rations will not last indefinitely."

"You need an escape tunnel," Turner said. "Or several of them. If the Doomers discover one, we can collapse it and use another."

Syssi waved a hand. "We've all gotten carried away, imagining doomsday scenarios. Can Parker and Ella go home now?"

Kian nodded. "But please keep the phone nearby in case I need Parker again."

The kid saluted. "Yes, sir."

After the two left, Syssi shook her head. "We were scaring Parker with all that talk about escape tunnels."

"I think he was more fascinated than scared," Turner said. "I'm not in favor of coddling children. Ignorance is bliss, but it's also dangerous."

"I agree." Kian pulled a beer out of the cooler. "You said that you had updates for me."

"William and his equipment are safe in the van, the Guardians surrounding Kalugal's estate are all wearing earplugs and communicating by texting. They have their phones set on vibrate."

"That's brilliant since Kalugal's compulsion is obviously delivered by auditory means. But I worry that no earplugs are good enough to block it completely. We need to test it, and there is no way to do it."

"I had the same reservations." Turner tossed his empty water bottle into the trash bin. "I figured that it's worth a try. Lokan is on his way to San Francisco, so we can have him test the earplugs' effectiveness on a human. Not that it matters at this point. We need the men there whether the earplugs work or not."

Syssi sighed. "There must be something in the sound waves compellers produce that has a hypnotic effect. I wish we could test it."

Turner nodded. "If it can be measured, it can be reproduced. Imagine having a weapon like that. It would trump all other nonlethal measures."

"It reminds me of *Dune*." Syssi lifted the thermos and poured coffee into three paper cups. "I was fascinated by the Order of the Bene Gesserit, women who could control others by modulating their voices."

Turner cracked a smile. "And I was fascinated by Kwisatz Haderach. I fantasized that it was me, the super-being that the sisterhood produced after thousands of years of careful genetic breeding."

Kian chuckled. "That would explain your god complex. It seems to me that you still believe you are that super-being."

"We are all entitled to our fantasies." Turner took one of the cups Syssi poured and took a sip. "I later learned that Kwisatz Haderach meant a leap of distance in Hebrew, and that Bene Gesserit meant the daughters who bridge. Frank Herbert didn't invent those names, he borrowed them from another language."

Syssi handed Kian a cup. "When I call Mey to check how they are doing, I'll ask her if she read *Dune* and noticed that."

He lifted a hand to stop her. "Don't tell me where they are. I don't want to know. And don't tell me where Jin is either."

"I couldn't even if I wanted to. I don't know where Turner sent them."

"They are safe from Kalugal," Turner said. "That's all you need to know."

Kalugal

"What are you going to do?" Rufsur got up and started pacing. "Capturing the immortal was not worth all this trouble."

Kalugal crossed his arms over his chest. "Taking him was the best thing in this fucked-up situation. Otherwise, I would have nothing to bargain with to get rid of the spy and her tether. I wouldn't even know that I was being spied on."

Rufsur nodded. "Then we got lucky."

"Yes, we did." Kalugal pushed to his feet. "I promised to give them better accommodations. Do we have a vacant room that can be locked from the outside? I don't want them to wander around."

"We don't, but I'll station a guard outside their door. The thing is, we don't have cameras inside the rooms in the residential side of the bunker. Do you want me to put one in before we move them?"

"That's a good idea. I want to know what those two are talking about. Kian and his communications guy both claim that the immune is not the warrior's girlfriend, but I don't believe them. She wouldn't have done a stupid thing like chasing after us to save a teammate. That was a desperate act of a woman in love."

Rufsur nodded. "They are also sitting huddled under one blanket on the lower bunk. I haven't seen them kissing, but they've been whispering in each other's ears like a couple of lovebirds."

Kalugal walked over to his desk and brought up the camera feed from the prison cell. "They are probably plotting an escape."

"From what I managed to hear, he was telling her about immortals."

"That should be interesting." Kalugal sat back down. "I wonder what Annani's people know about our history. It's probably more than my father bothered to share with us."

"Why would you think that? For all we know, Annani is just as bad as Navuh. A female despot."

Kalugal glanced at Rufsur over his shoulder. "That's what my father wanted us to believe. Given that she is my mother's sister, Annani must have good in her."

Rufsur nodded, but he didn't say anything.

Kalugal knew what his lieutenant was thinking. A five-year-old boy's memory of his mother was not reliable, and Areana was probably not the benevolent angel Kalugal remembered.

He waved a hand in dismissal. "Put a bug somewhere they won't notice."

"Yes, sir." Rufsur turned around and walked out.

His friend could think whatever he wanted, but even as a young boy Kalugal hadn't been naive, and as an adult he was basing his opinion on facts and not just speculation.

If Annani was indeed Areana's half-sister, then she couldn't be an evil dictator. His mother was the gentlest soul that Kalugal had ever encountered, and if Annani was only half as good, she was leaps and bounds better than Navuh.

Besides, if Annani was behind humanity's technological advancements, which was what Navuh accused her of, then her intentions were at least good.

Misguided, but not evil.

Humans were too susceptible to brainwashing and too violent to be entrusted with the future of the planet and their own survival. If not monitored and controlled by a strong and capable hand, they would destroy each other and the planet, which they unknowingly shared with immortals.

Kalugal was not going to let it happen. The humans might not care whether their descendants survived, but since Kalugal was still going to be around thousands of years from now, he had to ensure that he had a habitable planet and enough humans on it to keep the machine working.

Apparently, Annani wasn't smart enough to see the trajectory humanity was on, or maybe she naively hoped that her influence would change their doomed future.

Without him taking over, they would eventually nuke each other and every living thing out of existence.

It would only take one crazed fanatic to start the chain reaction.

Putting the earphones on, he listened to the recording, but the sound amplification distorted whatever his prisoners had been whispering to each other. He managed to catch a few words here and there, enough to confirm what Rufsur had said about the topic of their conversation, but not enough to piece together the story Arwel had been sharing with the immune.

Getting the warrior to talk and tell him everything he wanted to know could have been extremely satisfying. But Kalugal had made a promise, which he wasn't going to break regardless of the spy's tether.

He wasn't an honest man or even a good one, but he held himself to certain standards.

Going back on a promise was the mark of a lesser man.

Besides, now that the channel of communication was open between him and his cousin, he could just ask Kian to tell him what he knew about their shared ancestry.

It wasn't as if the information would provide Kalugal with a strategic advantage, so there was no reason for Kian to keep it from him.

In fact, if Kalugal played his hand well and pretended to want an alliance with his cousin, he might even get to meet the mother goddess herself.

According to Kian, Areana had asked her sister to search for him, but he didn't believe Annani would have agreed to do it unless she sought to gain some benefit from it. At the very least, she was probably curious about her nephew.

He was definitely curious about his aunt, and specifically whether she was susceptible to his compulsion.

If she was, that would open up some interesting possibilities.

Wendy

Wendy knew where she was, which was a big improvement.

The guards hadn't bothered to blindfold her or Richard, and as they left their underground prison, she'd seen high rises. But since she'd never been to Los Angeles before, it had taken several road signs until she'd figured it out. Then they had gone up and up, through narrow, serpentine roads that had snow piled up on the shoulders. When Bowen finally parked the car in the driveway of a fancy cabin, Wendy let out a relieved breath. Some of the narrower spots had been scary.

"Everyone stay in the car. I'm going to open the garage and park inside, so you don't have to brave the elements."

She wasn't going to argue with that.

The clothes she had on were not warm enough for snow. The heating in the car was on, and she was in no hurry to get out into the cold night.

Mey turned to look at her and Vlad. "Tomorrow, I'm going to get you proper clothing. Tonight, we are just going to blast the heat in the cabin."

As Bowen opened the garage doors, Wendy's eyes widened at the two snowmobiles parked in the smallest of the three bays. "Can we ride those?" She pointed.

"I'll have to check," Mey said. "I don't know if they are part of the package."

"I've never ridden a snowmobile. I really want to try it."

"Do you have a driving license?" Vlad asked.

"Of course. I didn't grow up in the boonies, you know."

He lifted his hands in the peace sign. "Not everyone gets a license right away, and not everyone owns a car."

"I didn't have a car of my own, but I got my driver's license as soon as I was eligible."

Her father would have never gotten her a car, and not because he couldn't afford it. It was just another way for him to control her every move.

After Bowen parked his car inside, the other guard drove in, and Bowen closed the garage doors. "It's freezing in there. I turned on the heating, but it will take time for the place to warm up. Until it does, I suggest that you grab blankets from the beds."

Bowen was wearing a light jacket like the rest of them, but the guy didn't seem bothered by the cold. Neither did Leon, the other guard.

In a surprising gesture, Vlad wrapped his thin arm around her. "I'll try to keep you warm until we get a blanket."

"Thanks." She let him pull her against his body, and it didn't even gross her out.

Maybe she was just too cold to care.

As they rushed inside, Vlad immediately zeroed in on the throw blanket draped over the couch's arm. "This one is for you." He wrapped it around her.

"Don't be silly. We can share it." She lifted one end for him to get in.

He looked at it longingly, but then shook his head. "I'll get the fireplace going first."

The guy was too nice for his own good.

"I like it." Ingrid walked into the middle of the room and turned in a circle. "Not to my standards, but with a few tweaks, I could make this place spectacular."

Richard headed for the stairs. "I'll get us blankets."

He seemed chilled to the bone, while Ingrid appeared as impervious to the cold as the two guards.

"Aren't you freezing?" Wendy asked.

Ingrid smiled and waved a dismissive hand. "I was born in Scotland. This is a warm day for me."

Well, that explained it. Bowen and Leon had slight Scottish accents too, so it must have felt warm to them as well.

Once Vlad had the fire crackling, he joined her on the couch. Too shy to take her up on her offer to share the blanket, he sat several inches away from her and wrapped his arms around himself to keep warm.

"Come here." Wendy lifted the blanket. "I'll warm you up."

"Thanks." He slid over, trying to get under the blanket while keeping a couple of inches between them.

"Get closer. I'm cold."

It wasn't as if he had enough body mass to warm her, but she had enough for both of them. The padding that she normally resented would finally be good for something.

"Okay."

When his hip touched hers, it was trembling, and at first, she thought that it was because he was cold. But tuning into his emotions revealed the real reason. Vlad was excited, and he was trying to hide it.

Strangely, though, his arousal didn't repulse her.

Maybe the reason it didn't bother her was that she knew Vlad would never act upon it without massive encouragement from her, which he wasn't going to get. He was safe, and that was something that Wendy had never felt around a male older than twelve.

They were all predators, and they all wanted sex. Not all of them wanted it from her, some wanted it from other guys, but this was what they were all thinking about.

Her father was an abuser and a liar, but he was right about that.

Except, Vlad's need had a different flavor to it. Maybe because he didn't believe that he had any chance of ever fulfilling it, his longing felt more sad than aggressive, and it touched on the dormant nurturer in her.

She wanted to take care of Vlad, to bring a smile to his sad, handsome face, to show him that he was wonderful and worthy, and that he was selling himself short.

But that wasn't going to happen. Instead, she was going to use him, and he was going to end up even less confident and more hurt.

Maybe it would teach him not to be so nice.

Good people were losers. Like sheep, they were just waiting for the big bad wolves to devour them.

For better or worse, Wendy had vowed a long time ago never to be a sheep.

She was a short, chubby wolf cub, but her bite was just as vicious as that of her big, bad compatriots.

Vlad

It took almost an hour for the cabin to get warm enough for Wendy to put down the blanket, and it was the best and also the most torturous hour Vlad had ever suffered through.

He'd never been so physically close to a girl. Huddling under one blanket, their thighs and their arms touching, he couldn't help but get excited. And since Wendy was an empath, she must have known what he was going through.

Talk about embarrassing.

Still, if given the opportunity again, he would seize it without hesitation.

Wendy was so soft, so feminine, and being close to her made him feel like a man. He could protect her, shield her from all threats.

Provided she'd let him.

Did he make her feel safe?

She was hard to read, and he wasn't an empath, but he was quite certain that she wasn't repulsed by him or afraid of him. That was already better than what most girls projected at him.

He should be grateful for that.

Mey leaned back in her armchair, cradling a hot mug of cocoa in her palms. "I didn't expect to find a 7-Eleven that was open twenty-four hours in such a small town. It would have been pretty miserable to have to wait until morning to get something to eat and drink."

Wendy lifted her own mug and saluted Mey with it. "This was a life saver. It warmed me from the inside."

Ingrid grimaced. "The sandwiches were terrible, but I was so hungry that I didn't care. I forgot that cold weather makes people hungrier."

Vlad wondered whether that was why he had wolfed down more than half a bag of Oreo cookies and had chugged down three full mugs of hot cocoa.

Not really. It had been warm under the blanket with Wendy, but it had made him nervous, and that was why he had eaten so much. It had given him something to do other than think about Wendy's soft thigh that was pressed against his.

Not that it had helped.

He was still acutely aware of it and savoring every moment.

"I love hot cocoa in the winter. Jin and I used to drink it while watching *Doctor Who*." Mey crossed her legs. "We need to figure out the sleeping arrangements. There are five bedrooms and three bathrooms in the cabin. The master bedroom has its own bathroom, and I think it should go to Richard and Ingrid." She glanced at the two, who were squeezed together in one armchair. "Is that okay with you?"

"We'll take it," Richard said.

Mey nodded. "That leaves four bedrooms and two bathrooms. We can divide them in two ways. Wendy and I can share the bedroom that has two beds, while Vlad, Bowen, and Leon each get their own room. Or, Bowen and Leon can share the bedroom, and the rest of us each get a room."

"Bowen and I will share," Leon said. "Since we are going to take turns guarding the place, we won't be sleeping at the same time anyway."

"Then it's settled." Mey pushed to her feet. "I don't know about you, but I want to take a hot shower and crawl into bed."

"Yeah, me too." Wendy put her mug down. "I hope there are televisions in the bedrooms." She folded the blanket and put it over the back of the couch. "Can I choose my room?"

"Of course."

As Mey walked over to the front door and lifted her suitcase, Wendy got up as well, depriving Vlad of her warmth.

"I'll get your stuff." He followed her.

Taking Wendy's bundle in one hand, he slung the strap of his guitar case over his arm and lifted the duffle bag full of video games and books with the other.

Regrettably, he didn't have a change of clothes in there, and anything he could borrow from Bowen or Leon would be six sizes too big.

"I can take that." Wendy reached for her bundle.

Vlad shook his head. "It's okay. I've got it."

Following Mey upstairs, they walked into the first bedroom.

Wendy eyed the television. "Can this one be mine?"

"Yes." Mey opened the door to a bathroom. "I'll take the room on the other side, so we can share the bathroom. The boys can use the bigger one that has a door to the hallway."

Vlad put Wendy's bundle on the bed and then stood there unsure of what to do next. "Do you want to maybe watch something together before going to sleep?"

He didn't expect her to say yes, but he loathed parting with her so soon.

"Yeah, that would be nice. But I want to shower first. Can you come back in half an hour?"

His heart started beating so fast that he was afraid she could hear it. "Of course. If Bowen and Leon don't hog the shower, I'll grab one myself." He was proud of managing a casual tone.

Wendy sat on the bed and started working on untying the knot on her bundle. "Do you have anything to change into?"

"I don't, but maybe one of the guys can lend me a pair of sweatpants. If not, I'll just sleep with nothing on." The moment the words left his mouth, Vlad felt his ears catch fire. "I have a room to myself, so it won't bother anyone." He pushed the strap of his duffle bag higher on his shoulder. "Have fun showering."

Damn. That was another wrong thing to say.

Imagining Wendy's curvy nude body as she stood under the spray, her long brown hair cascading down her back, Vlad felt the flame from his ears spread to the rest of his face, and not all of it was covered by his long bangs.

"I'll be back in half an hour." He turned around and rushed out the door.

Kian

Syssi glanced at her watch. "It's one o'clock in the morning. Is it too late to call Mey?"

Turner shook his head. "They arrived at their destination not too long ago. She is probably still awake."

"I'll send her a text first."

Kian doubted that anyone involved in the crisis was going to sleep anytime soon, and that included Kalugal. His cousin's claim that it was late and he was tired had been an excuse to get off the line and do some thinking.

He wondered what clever scheme the son of a despot would come up with.

There was no way out of his predicament, so no matter how much the guy strained his noggin, he wasn't going to come up with anything other than doing exactly what Kian wanted him to do.

The problem was arranging the exchange.

Kalugal would not give up Arwel and Jacki unless he was convinced that the tether was removed, and that was going to be a problem. And the same went for Kian. He wasn't going to let Jin remove the tether until Arwel and Jacki were released.

Hopefully, Turner could come up with a solution that would be acceptable to both sides because Kian had nothing.

Well, that wasn't entirely true. The easiest way to do it was to trade Jin for Arwel and Jacki, but Kian wasn't going to do that no matter what.

Kalugal might decide that the best way to get rid of the tether was to kill the one holding it. Or he might decide to keep Jin and never let her go. In either of those scenarios, not only would the clan lose a valuable asset and an almost certain Dormant, but they also might lose Arwel, who would never forgive Kian for allowing that to happen.

"Yamanu just texted me," Turner said. "He is on his way to the blockade, and he plans on thralling the neighbors to have a strong urge to leave early in the morning and not come back until nightfall. Do you want to talk to him?"

"Tell him that I like his plan. I need to call my mother and give her an update."

Turner nodded. "Do you want me to leave?"

"There is no need. You know everything that I'm going to tell her."

"I thought that you would like privacy."

Normally he would, but not tonight. Turner was indispensable, and having him near made the entire situation more tolerable.

Things would have been a lot scarier without an immune who Kian trusted to take over and run things as well, if not better than he could.

"This is still a crisis situation. I need you here." He pulled out his phone and checked the time in Alaska.

It was after midnight there, but he doubted his mother and sister were sleeping. In fact, they might not be there at all. Annani liked to travel, and she might be in Paris or London for all he knew.

Placing the call, he didn't expect her to answer before it even rang once.

"Kian. I was waiting for your call."

He'd forgotten about the grapevine. His mother always knew what was going on mere moments after it happened.

"I guess you heard about the village's lockdown."

"I did. What happened?"

"Do you remember the saying I'm so fond of?"

She chuckled. "There are many of them. Which one are you referring to?"

"The one about no good deed going unpunished. We found Kalugal, but things have gotten out of hand, and he captured Arwel and a human woman who is an immune and a possible Dormant. With his power of compulsion, Kalugal can get Arwel to tell him where the village is as well as everything else Arwel knows, which as head Guardian is basically everything."

"That is very troubling. What are you going to do?"

"I'm negotiating for their release. We were lucky that Jin managed to tether Kalugal before things went south, so I at least have a big stick to threaten him with. The carrot is Areana. If he releases our people, I'll let him talk to his mother."

"Did you tell him about her?"

"I did. Apparently, she never told him that she is a goddess. He thought that she was an immortal who Navuh stole from the clan."

"Why would he think that?"

Kian smiled. "That's actually a funny story. When I introduced myself as his cousin and Annani's son, he thought I was talking about a clan female who was named after you. He even apologized for not being able to help me retrieve my clanswoman. As you can imagine, I was very disappointed to have my thunder turned into a hiccup."

Annani laughed. "How uncooperative of Kalugal. He should have at least pretended to be stunned."

"He was. But it was too much for him to swallow, so he tried to rationalize it."

"Given that he did not know that his mother is a goddess, that is understandable. Can I tell Areana that she is about to hear her son's voice for the first time since he was a small boy? Or should I wait until the negotiations are done and the conflict is resolved?"

"You can tell her. After all, I'm using Areana as a bargaining chip. I need all the ammunition I have to dissuade Kalugal from trying to compel me. I have Turner with me, so if Kalugal tries anything, Turner will take over, but I'd rather stay in control."

In the moment of silence that followed, Kian braced for his mother's response.

"I should be there with you to protect you. Kalugal cannot compel me."

It was precisely what he'd expected her to say. "That would be the worst move we could make. Did you forget that the village is locked down because I fear the location might get compromised? You have no idea how glad I am that no one knows where you are, including me, so there is no one who can be compelled to reveal that information. Your safety is my number one priority."

Glancing at Syssi and her slightly rounded belly, Kian was no longer sure that his mother still held that position. At least not exclusively. Her safety was the number one priority as far as the world was concerned, but Syssi and their daughter were his top priority.

"I understand. Tell me, what is your impression of Kalugal?"

"He is full of himself, smart, eloquent, and not easily shaken."

"What about his morality? Is he good or bad?"

Kian raked his fingers through his hair. "I don't know. It's not the kind of thing that can be determined after one conversation, or even a thousand. People are complicated, and they might be good on one front and bad on another."

"What does your gut tell you?"

His mother was big on letting her subconscious answer difficult questions, which was what gut feelings were.

Not that she was wrong, sometimes the gut made a quicker and better assessment than the brain, but oftentimes it also got it all wrong. Emotions, prejudices, beliefs —they all contributed to the smorgasbord from which the subconscious gathered its data and processed it to produce gut feelings.

"My gut tells me to tread carefully. It would be a mistake to underestimate Kalugal and allow his amicable attitude and soft tone to lull me into a false sense of security."

Arwel

When Rufsur showed up with two more ex-Doomers, Arwel braced for the worst. And when the cell's bars started sliding aside, he was sure that it was interrogation time.

His only hope was that they wouldn't harm Jacki.

Rufsur grinned and motioned for them both to get up. "You are being moved to better accommodations. Please, follow me."

Arwel let out a soft breath.

"That's nice," Jacki said. "Do we get a toilet with a door?"

"Better. You are getting a nice room with an en-suite bathroom, a meal, and a change of clothes." He gave Jacki a once-over. "I apologize for not having any female clothing for you. The smallest I found are still going to be too big, but they are clean."

Jacki narrowed her eyes at him. "Why are you being so nice to us all of a sudden?"

One of the guards walking behind them coughed to cover up a chuckle.

"A gesture of goodwill. My boss is negotiating with yours, and certain concessions have been made."

Arwel hoped that those concessions didn't include giving up Jin, but he didn't want to ask questions that might reveal things Kalugal didn't know.

Jacki cast Rufsur a sidelong glance. "I hope that includes no cameras in the bathroom. I've given you perverts enough of a show already."

If he could, Arwel would have kicked her to shut her up. Antagonizing their captors wasn't smart, especially since she was the only female in the bunker. They might get ideas, and there was nothing he could do to prevent them from doing whatever they wanted to her.

Rufsur dipped his head. "My apologies, little lady. The cell was designed with males in mind. We never expected to have a female guest in there."

"I'm not little. And why do you have a prison cell to start with? Who do you bring down here?"

The Doomer gave her a lopsided smile. "Do you really expect me to answer that, or do you just like to hear yourself talk?"

"You are being rude."

Arwel lifted his eyes heavenward. *Fates, help us.*

Rufsur shrugged. "You called us perverts. That wasn't nice either." He stopped in front of a door marked number 31 and opened it. "Your new room."

It was a big improvement on the prison cell, but it was a far cry from the luxury of the keep. Apparently, none of Kalugal's men had a degree in interior design.

The room was utilitarian, but the bed looked comfortable, the blanket was thick, and there was even a couch he could sleep on.

Apparently, their captors had realized that he and Jacki were not a couple. Next to the stack of clothing on the couch, there was also a pillow and a folded blanket.

"This is so much better." Jacki opened the door to the en-suite. "Awesome. Tell your boss that he's forgiven for stuffing me in the trunk of his tiny car."

"I will." Rufsur turned to Arwel. "The door is not locked, but there will be a guard posted outside, so don't get ideas about snooping around. If you need anything, you can poke your head out the door and ask him, but don't step outside. Understood?"

Arwel nodded.

"And the same goes for you, little lady. I don't want any trouble from you."

Jacki rolled her eyes. "Stop calling me little, give us something to eat and drink, and I promise to behave."

"Your offer is accepted." He opened the door and motioned for a guy with a rolling cart to enter. "Enjoy your dinner."

"Thank you." Arwel spoke for the first time.

"You are welcome." Rufsur and the guy who'd delivered the food stepped out. "Good night."

Jacki lifted the covers off the two plates. "Not bad." She brought them over to the coffee table and then went back for two bottles of water.

"Are you just going to stand there? Come eat. With what their boss can do, they have no reason to drug us."

It hadn't even crossed his mind, but it was a legitimate concern. "They might."

She twisted the cap off the water bottle. "I'm willing to risk it."

When he sat next to her, Jacki leaned to whisper in his ear. "Kalugal knows about the tether. He moved us to a better room because Jin demanded it."

That had occurred to him as well, but he wasn't a hundred percent certain. "I'd rather not mention it in case we are wrong."

She leaned toward him again. "I'm certain of it, but you are right that it's better to keep quiet about it."

Arwel took the other bottle of water and opened it. "What makes you so sure?"

"Rufsur was trying to be polite despite the way I talked to him. He wouldn't have been so reserved if no one was watching." Jacki cut a piece of chicken and stuffed it in her mouth.

So that was why she'd acted so foolishly. Or rather smartly.

"My impression of Rufsur is that he's an amiable fellow. He wasn't rude or unnecessarily cruel when he apprehended you. I couldn't see much from where I was stuck frozen on the back seat, but from what I heard, you were fighting him with everything you had, and yet he was careful not to hurt you."

Jacki nodded. "True. Still, I insulted him and his comrades, calling them perverts. With no one watching, he would have done worse than the one slightly snide remark."

Jin

"Wake up, Jin." Kri nudged her shoulder. "You don't want to miss this."

"Miss what?" Jin cracked one eye open.

The shades on the jet's window were locked in the down position, so there was nothing to see outside, but the pressure in her ears told Jin that they were landing.

"The sanctuary, the goddess. You are the first human to ever set foot inside of it."

"Have you ever been there?"

"As a baby, and I don't remember anything, but I've heard stories, and the place sounds magical."

"I bet. Where else would a goddess reside?"

Kri smirked. "Wherever the goddess wished to."

"Is that supposed to be a joke? Because I don't get it."

After less than an hour of sleep, Jin's brain was sluggish.

Kri shrugged. "It's like the joke about where does the 800-pound gorilla sit? Anywhere it wants."

"Oh."

"You don't seem excited."

"I'm too tired and worried for that, and I want to check on Jacki and Arwel. Give me a moment."

When she found Jacki asleep, Jin followed the tether to Kalugal. He was awake, but he was alone and staring at the wall, so there wasn't much to see there either. Regrettably, her tether didn't give her access to his thoughts.

Since Arwel and Jacki had been taken, Jin had been wondering about that. Her hook was mental, so it was strange that she only had access to the visual and auditory parts of her targets' brains and not their thoughts.

"Anything interesting?" Kri asked.

"Jacki is asleep, and Kalugal is staring at a wall."

"No news is good news."

"True. How do I address the goddess? Do I bow? Curtsy? What's the protocol?"

"You can bow if you want to, but it's not required. You should address her as Clan Mother, but if she asks you to call her by her given name, don't argue and do as she says. Just be polite and don't use cuss words. Annani does not tolerate crude language."

Jin snorted. "Kian must have a real hard time with that. He likes his expletives."

"He has a hard time with her in general. He can't boss her around, and Annani is not as careful with her safety as he would like her to be. There are also some other issues that they disagree on, and it's difficult for him when she puts her foot down, and he has no choice but to obey."

Jin yawned and stretched her arms. "Does it happen a lot? Is she bossy?"

"She is definitely bossy, but she lets Kian and Sari run things as they see fit and only intervenes on rare occasions. Sari is Kian's counterpart in Europe."

"I know. Mey told me. She talked a lot about Alena and how nice she is. I'm glad of the opportunity to meet her, but I wish it was under different circumstances."

As the jet's wheels touched down, Jin released her seatbelt. "I'm going to brush my teeth."

"Hurry up. It's not a long runway."

In the jet's tiny bathroom, Jin used the toilet, brushed her teeth and her hair, and then adjusted the sweater that Alena had kindly sent for her with the pilot. It was warm and cozy, but most importantly, it made her look more presentable. She would have hated meeting the goddess wearing Kri's leather jacket with only a bra underneath.

Taking a deep breath, she opened the door and stepped out just as the plane came to a full stop.

"Ready?" Kri asked.

"Is anyone ever ready to meet a goddess?"

"I don't know if Annani will be there to greet us. We will probably be taken to our suite first."

"I hope that they put us together. I don't want to be alone."

In the short time that she had spent with Kri, Jin had come to depend on her. The Guardian was so strong, so confident, that it felt natural to do so.

Kri wrapped her arm around Jin's shoulders. "If they don't, I'll ask that they do."

"Thanks."

When the pilot opened the door, Jin expected a blast of cold air, but instead of snowy vistas, she saw the interior of a large hangar, and a tall blonde woman smiling and waving at her and Kri.

"Welcome to the sanctuary." She waited for Jin to come down and offered her hand. "I'm Alena."

Jin shook it. "Mey told me a lot about you. I just wish we'd met under more pleasant circumstances."

"Oh, sweetheart." Alena pulled her into her arms and hugged her fiercely. "Everything is going to be fine. The Fates work in mysterious ways, but so far, they have been kind to us. I'm sure they had a good reason for allowing this to happen."

"Like what?"

Alena let go of her. "I guess we will find out soon enough. Let me take you to your room." She looked at

Kri. "I figured that you would want to be near your charge, so I put you in a two-bedroom suite."

"That's perfect. Thank you."

Apparently Jin wasn't going to meet the goddess tonight. On the one hand it was a little disappointing, but on the other hand, it would be better to meet Annani when she wasn't as tired, and her brain was functioning properly.

There was just one more thing Jin needed to do, and that was to let Mey know that she'd landed in the sanctuary. Since it was four in the morning in Los Angeles, a text would be better than a phone call. After all, they had talked only a few hours ago, covering everything that had happened, and she had nothing new to report other than her safe arrival.

I'm in the sanctuary, and I met Alena. I'll get to meet the goddess tomorrow.

Mey replied almost immediately, which meant that she couldn't sleep. *Give Alena and Annani my best regards.*

Any pointers on how to talk to a freaking goddess?

Just be yourself. Annani is friendly, and once you get over the glowing skin, it will be like talking to a girlfriend, but one who happens to be a queen.

Kalugal

Kalugal had spent the night sitting in his armchair and thinking.

He might have dozed off a couple of times, but for no longer than several minutes at a time. His mind was too troubled for a peaceful sleep.

It had been ages since he'd been so perturbed by anything. Since escaping his father's control, his life had been uneventful.

Even boring.

He'd been busy amassing his fortune, which had been exciting at the beginning, but had quickly become just another routine. There was no challenge to it, and the money was just a means to an end. However, for the longest time, he couldn't decide what that elusive end was.

Freeing his mother could have been a worthy goal, but she didn't want to be freed. For better or worse, she loved Navuh.

It was one of the few things that grated on Kalugal's psyche and soured his mood whenever he thought about it. There was no solution that would make him and his mother happy at the same time.

Unless his father miraculously changed his entire outlook on the world, Kalugal was never going to see Areana, because to do so he would have to conquer the island and take Navuh down, which he'd promised his mother never to do.

During the negotiations with Kian, Kalugal had kept his cool, not letting his cousin know how tantalizing the prospect of talking to Areana was to him, but the truth was that it was on an almost equal footing with wanting the damn tether gone.

Perhaps since he'd last seen her, his mother had grown disillusioned with her mate and was willing to leave him?

That would be a game-changer for Kalugal.

He would divert his efforts from gaining global control to first taking over the island and getting his mother out.

His world domination plans could wait a few years longer.

Or maybe not.

If the Chinese beat him to it, which they were actively pursuing, wresting control from them would be a much tougher mission than gaining it before they managed to spread their tentacles over the entire world.

Kalugal might not be the most benevolent ruler imaginable, but he would be better than them. He at least would give humans the illusion of democracy and personal freedom. Under his control, most of humanity wouldn't even know about the puppet master who was running the show, and their elected officials would want to keep it that way.

The Chinese wouldn't bother with such niceties.

As a knock on the door interrupted his thoughts, Kalugal glanced at his watch. At five in the morning, only one person could be standing behind the door to his private suite.

"Come in, Rufsur."

His second-in-command walked in and closed the door behind him. "Did you spend all night sitting in this armchair?"

"Most of it. What brings you here so early in the morning?"

"I couldn't sleep, and I figured that you'd be awake too. We need a strategy."

Kalugal shook his head. "Have you forgotten that none of what is said in front of me is private?"

"I thought you would figure a way around it."

"If you and I could have learned Braille overnight, we could have done it that way. But neither of us is that talented."

"True. But it could be a long-term solution."

"It could. Right now, I'm more concerned with finding a way to confirm the tether's removal without demanding the spy be delivered to me."

Rufsur sat in the other armchair and crossed his legs at the ankles. "There is no other way. Besides, if she is here, it doesn't matter that she has you tethered. She can't tell anyone what she sees and hears."

"That's what Kian wants me to believe. What if she can? They might have staged the entire thing to create the perfect setup for a Trojan horse maneuver."

Rufsur arched a brow. "Do you really believe that?"

"No, but it's possible."

It all depended on the kind of man his cousin was. If he was indeed such a caring ruler who would do anything to free his people, he wouldn't sacrifice the spy. He must realize that the easiest way to get rid of her tether and the risk she represented would be to kill her.

But if his posturing was just for show, Kian might have orchestrated the entire thing to get the spy into the bunker. And if she was also very beautiful, he might have hoped that Kalugal would want to keep her at least for a little while.

Except, she wasn't even close.

All he could remember from their first encounter was that she was Asian, or maybe of mixed heritage, had a nice figure, and was pleasant-looking but not strikingly beautiful. Then again, her heavy makeup had been designed to obscure her features and not to make her look pretty. Perhaps she was beautiful under all that gunk.

He wondered if that was true of the immune as well. She was a feisty one, and he liked that in a woman.

"How are our guests doing?"

"The immune is snoring in the bed, and the warrior is lying on the couch, awake and looking worried."

"So, they really aren't a couple."

"They are not, but they seem to be either close friends or just at the beginning of their relationship. Until she fell asleep, they were whispering in each other's ears and it looked pretty damn intimate."

"Do you have it on tape?"

"Naturally. Do you want to listen to the recording?"

Kalugal shook his head. "Kian might view it as a breach of our agreement." He pushed to his feet. "I need a good cup of coffee before I call him."

"What are you going to offer him?"

"The better question is what is he going to offer me."

Kian

Syssi opened the sliding door and walked out, huddling inside her thick night robe. "Did you get any sleep at all?"

Kian extinguished his cigarillo and pushed to his feet. "You shouldn't be outside. It's too cold." He wrapped his arm around her and led her back inside. "And to answer your question, I slept for about two hours. That's enough to keep me going."

Leaning her head against his arm, she sighed. "Any news from the front, so to speak?"

He walked over to the couch, sat down, and pulled her onto his lap. "The Guardians are still surrounding the complex. Magnus had them take turns sleeping for a couple of hours each, so they are good to go. Yamanu thralled the neighbors to have an irresistible urge for a day trip, and some are leaving already. That's about it. I know that Jin has arrived safely at her destination, but I don't know where it is, and I'm not asking."

He had a feeling that Turner had sent her to the sanctuary. That would have been Kian's first choice because even he didn't know how to get there. But on the flip side, he could call his mother and ask her to send one of her Odus to pick him up, which he might do if Kalugal compelled him to do that.

It was better that he didn't know for sure that Jin was there. If Kalugal compelled him to reveal her location, he could truthfully answer that he didn't know where she was.

"What about Turner? Did he go to sleep?"

Sweet Syssi. Always thinking about everyone else.

"He stayed in the war room, so I don't know. He might have caught a catnap on the couch in my office." Kian leaned and kissed her soft lips. "Now that you have all the updates, how about you go back to bed? You need your rest." He put his hand on her rounded belly.

Syssi smiled. "I've heard of eating for two, but not sleeping for two. Since I turned, four hours is enough for me."

He arched a brow. "Could've fooled me. You never want to get out of bed before seven in the morning."

"That's because I like to cuddle and make love to you when I wake up, and after that, I'm too languid to get up."

"I love our mornings." He kissed her again. "And our evenings." Another kiss. "And our nights. But I don't like everything in between because you are not there with me."

Syssi rested her head against his chest. "Absence makes the heart grow fonder."

"My heart is fond of you twenty-four-seven."

"Mine too." She pushed up from his lap. "Would you like some coffee? I can make us cappuccinos."

"I can do that. I want you to go back to bed. All this stress is not good for the baby."

Syssi snorted. "She'd better get used to it. If she wants to hang around her daddy, stress is going to be an integral part of her life."

"That doesn't make me happy."

"I know, my love. I'm sure you didn't have it easy growing up as Annani's son. You told me that she'd never coddled you and expected you to shoulder many responsibilities from a young age."

"That is true. But I want my daughter to have a normal, carefree childhood."

Syssi lifted a brow. "Did you suffer so greatly growing up?"

"I can't say that I did. I was quite proud to be entrusted with important tasks as a boy. But it wasn't a normal childhood."

"What is normal?" She walked over to the cappuccino machine and turned it on. "Normalcy is subjective.

What's normal for a child in urban suburbia is not normal for a child growing up in the jungle. The parents' job is to teach their children survival skills that are appropriate for their environment. Our Allegra will have to learn to function in stressful situations and make hard decisions."

"That doesn't make me happy either. I don't want her to take over my job."

Syssi chuckled. "You are immortal, my love. You can keep your job indefinitely. But maybe she could assist you and ease your burden. Wouldn't it be nice to work together with your daughter?"

"How about we let her decide what she wants to do with her life?"

"Of course. But first, we need to give her all the tools we are able to and let her try things out, so she can choose wisely." Syssi handed him a cappuccino. "Besides, we have time to figure it all out."

He was about to answer that they needed to have a plan when his phone rang. Pulling it out of his pocket, he looked at the display.

"It's Kalugal." He hadn't expected the guy to call him this early, and talking to him without Turner right there next to him was dangerous.

He let the call go to voicemail.

"I have to leave."

Syssi nodded. "Call Turner and make sure that he is still in the war room. I'll bring you both breakfast."

"You are the best." He pulled her in for a quick kiss.

Kalugal

"Voicemail." Kalugal disconnected and put his phone down. "Kian is either sleeping or decided not to answer."

"It's early." Rufsur rose to his feet and walked over to the wet bar. "Do you want coffee?" He dropped a fresh packet in the coffeemaker.

"Yes."

"Did you eat anything?" Rufsur poured water into the machine and turned it on.

Kalugal shook his head. "I was too preoccupied to think of food, but now that you mention it, I'm hungry."

"Do you want breakfast brought over here, or do you want to go to the dining room?"

"I'd rather eat here. Kian is going to call me back soon."

"You didn't leave a message. He might not."

"He will. I'm sure he wasn't sleeping. He might have been in the bathroom, but what's more likely is that he didn't have his immune lieutenant next to him. Kian wouldn't risk talking to me without safeguards."

"I'll get you a tray."

"Thank you."

Rufsur could have called for one of the other men to bring the food in, but it wasn't in his nature. He liked doing things himself, mostly because he didn't trust anyone to do it as well as he could or as quickly.

If Kalugal's force ever grew substantially, Rufsur would no longer be the right man for the position of second-in-command. He was loyal to a fault, and Kalugal enjoyed his company, but leadership required the ability to delegate, and Rufsur had a problem with that.

Not that his friend had anything to worry about. Kalugal didn't plan on recruiting more men. The only way to get more immortal warriors was to steal them from his father, but that was too complicated and the quality of the men would be questionable. Kalugal didn't need a bunch of brainless yes-men. When he'd planned his escape during WWII, he'd carefully selected the warriors, handpicking them one at a time.

Regrettably he and his men didn't have access to Dormants or immortal females, so increasing their ranks the natural way was not going to happen either.

When the coffeemaker finished brewing, Kalugal poured himself a cup and went back to his armchair. The phone call he was waiting for came in a few minutes later.

Leaning back, he answered. "Good morning, cousin. Did you have a good night's sleep?"

"It was probably as good as yours."

Kalugal smiled. Talking with Kian was like playing a game of chess. "Did you decide on how you would like to proceed?"

"I believe that when we decided to break for the night, the ball was in your court."

"You are mistaken. You were supposed to check with your spy about her ability to provide conclusive proof of the tether's removal."

"It's not even six in the morning, and I haven't had a chance to talk to Jin yet. You called, so I assumed that you had come up with something."

He was right of course, and Kalugal had come up with the only viable solution, but he hadn't wanted to open with that.

"My solution is simple. You hand over the spy, and I hand over the warrior and the immune. We can do a middle of the road exchange."

Kian chuckled. "Nice try. I'm not handing her over."

"Then we are stuck. I doubt she can prove the removal of something I didn't feel her attaching. I still don't feel anything different. For all I know, the reading of the note I wrote could have been done by telepathy, and she might have access to me and my men anytime she wants."

"If that was the case, she wouldn't have to touch you. Why would we go to all the effort of getting her to you if that wasn't necessary?"

"She might need to touch a person to create the telepathic connection with him or her, but there is no tether and nothing to remove. Once it's done, it's there forever."

Kian sighed. "I understand your concern but think about it logically. If the connection was permanent, do you think I would have allowed her to do that to my Guardian? Or to the immune?"

"If you trust the spy, then why not?"

"They wouldn't have agreed to that. No one wants to be an open book to someone else, not even a loved one. It's crippling."

"That had occurred to me. If not for the spy's accurate description of the cell your people were originally in, I would have doubted her connection to them. In fact, I'm going to have my men check the two for hidden recording devices. Since it doesn't involve questioning, you can't view it as a breach of our agreement."

"It depends on how your men conduct the search. If you subject my people to anything humiliating or painful, I will consider it a breach. Do you have a female in your bunker who can search the immune?"

Unless Kian was one hell of an actor, his concern sounded genuine.

"I don't. But the woman doesn't need to be fully nude for the search. I can allow her to keep her underwear on."

"No patting down," Kian growled.

"There is no need. She can't record any visuals with clothes covering the camera. But her hair is a different story. My man will have to comb through it."

"That's acceptable."

"When will you talk to your spy?"

"Soon."

"Make it so. The neighbors are probably starting to wake up, and when they see all the cars parked along the street, they will call the police."

"Your neighbors are leaving their homes as we speak. I have a powerful thraller who is urging every human in your neighborhood to go on a day trip."

Kalugal doubted that was true. Even the most powerful thrallers couldn't cover an entire neighborhood. Kian's guy was probably going from house to house and convincing the closest neighbors to leave. Still, that might be enough for what Kian and his Guardians needed.

"That's an impressive skill."

"It's one of a kind. No one on your side of the fence has it."

Kalugal chuckled. "I'm not on either side of the fence or even anywhere near it. I'm an unaffiliated party, and I wish to stay that way."

Jin

"Are you awake?" Kri walked into Jin's bedroom.

"Yeah, I can't sleep." She scooted aside, making room for Kri to sit on the bed. "What are you doing awake?"

"I slept enough." The Guardian sat on the edge of the bed. "Immortal, remember?"

It was more than that. Kri was a tough cookie. Jin could imagine her sleeping in the trenches, bombs exploding all around her, and then waking up two hours later refreshed and ready to fight. She doubted other immortals were as resilient.

"It wouldn't have helped me even if I was post-transition. I kept waking up and immediately panicking that I might have missed something. I kept checking on Jacki and Arwel and on Kalugal."

"Anything interesting?"

"Jacki was still asleep, so no news from that front, and Kalugal just finished talking with Kian." Jin pushed up on the pillows. "Kian is under the impression that I have a tether to Arwel as well, or he might be bluffing so Kalugal doesn't separate them. The guy is seriously paranoid. He thinks that I'm a powerful telepath and that's how I knew what he wrote. He's going to have Jacki and Arwel checked for hidden cameras. But that's the small stuff. Just as I thought, he wants Kian to trade me for them."

"Did Kian agree?"

"No, but he will have no choice."

Kri shook her head. "He can't do that. Kalugal will kill you. That's the surest way to get rid of your tether or any other form of reporting he imagines you have."

Jin shivered. "No, he won't. Kalugal wants to be left alone. He doesn't want to start a war with the clan, and if he kills me, that's exactly what he'll get."

"I'm sorry for being so blunt." Kri gathered the blanket and pulled it all the way up to Jin's chin, tucking it around her shoulders. "Are you cold, or did I scare you that badly?"

"I'm cold, and scared, and tired. I don't feel so good." As another shiver rocked her body, Jin turned on her side and brought her knees up against her chest. "Do you think we can get some hot tea in here?"

"I'll get it. I'll also turn the heating up a notch."

"Thank you. For everything." A tear slid down Jin's cheek, but thankfully Kri didn't notice it.

Jin had done her best not to fall apart, but for some reason Kri's kindness had undone her. Maybe because she didn't think she deserved it?

"You're welcome. But I'm just doing my job." The Guardian got up and walked out of the bedroom.

Kri was so nice, and she was taking such good care of her, but that was no reason for tearing up.

Everything else was.

Talking with Mey would help, but it was too early to call her. Thinking about her sister alone in the mountains with a bunch of strangers added to Jin's stockpile of guilt. If not for her botching the assignment, Yamanu would be right there with Mey, sleeping or cuddling with her in bed.

Another salty tear made its way to Jin's lips.

She missed Arwel, she was worried sick about him and Jacki, and she felt responsible for the entire freaking mess. If she'd only left the club when Jacki had told her to, none of this would be happening.

But she hadn't been thinking straight. She had worried that Kalugal would see her leaving the club, and she'd wanted to listen to his conversation with his dance partner, but both reasons had been stupid. She could have used the back exit, and even if Kalugal had noticed, he would have assumed that she went to the ladies' room. And as for the conversation, she could have followed the tether from anywhere.

God. Why had she been so dumb?

When her phone rang, Jin reached for it with a shaky hand, hoping it was Mey.

But it was Kian.

Jin wasn't surprised that he was calling her after the talk he had with Kalugal, but she hadn't expected him to do it so soon.

"Hi, Kian."

"I hope I didn't wake you up."

"You didn't. I followed the tether to Kalugal before, so I know what you are calling about. You want to know how I can prove the tether's removal."

"Correct. Is there a way of doing it without you having to be there?"

"I can't do it remotely. When I tethered Edna, she didn't feel it at first. But after I removed it and then reattached it, she noticed the difference and was able to cut it from her end. Except, none of the others I've tethered were able to do that. Most didn't feel it being attached or removed, but then they weren't trying. I think that if I release and reattach it several times, Kalugal will be able to feel the difference. The problem is that I can remove the tether remotely, but I can't reattach it without touching him, which means that it will have to be done in person. You have to trade me, Kian."

"I can't do that. He will have no reason to let you go."

Kian wasn't as blunt as Kri, but he was probably thinking the same thing.

"You can keep something of his in exchange for me. He seems to really like his assistant, a guy named Rufsur. You could hold him hostage until I convince Kalugal that the tether is off."

"I'm afraid that he might sacrifice his right-hand man to free himself from your tether. I'll talk it over with Turner and let you know."

Jin bunched the comforter in her fist. "I just want you to know that I'm more than willing to be traded. This whole mess is my fault, and it's on me to get it resolved."

"How did you arrive at that conclusion? No one could have foreseen a crazy human gunman entering the club right when you were there. It was a freak coincidence."

"If I'd left five minutes earlier, which I could have done because I already had Kalugal tethered, none of this would be happening."

"Not necessarily. If Arwel wasn't there to stop the shooter, people would have died. Because you stayed five minutes longer than was necessary, those lives have been saved. I think that the Fates had something to do with that."

That was another way to look at it, and it eased her conscience a little, but not entirely.

Now she felt guilty for not thinking about the people whose lives Arwel had saved, and for still preferring to save Arwel and Jacki over strangers.

Annani

Alena walked into Annani's suite, a steaming mug in each hand. "I thought you could use some calming tea before calling Areana."

Annani smiled. "I am not nervous."

"It's a precaution."

"I don't know whether I should mention that Jin is here. I do not think it is risky to confide in Areana, but Kian might not second that opinion."

"He probably won't. Just in case, don't say anything about Jin's whereabouts, only that she is in hiding. I doubt Areana would ask where. And if she does, tell her that you don't know."

"But I do know."

"No, you don't. I didn't tell you which suite I put her and Kri in. Focus on that, and you won't be lying."

Annani took a sip of the tea and then put it down on the side table. "You have developed interesting skills during your New York adventure."

Alena chuckled. "It was the exposure to Eva. Jin should have trained with her before going after Kalugal."

"Indeed." Annani pulled her phone out of the hidden pocket in her gown. "I feel guilty for pushing Kian. Because of me, he rushed things and did not prepare Jin well enough."

Sitting down, Alena sighed. "It's everyone's and no one's fault. It is what it is." She glanced at her watch. "It's time."

At seven o'clock sharp, Annani's phone rang, but instead of William handling the call, it was Roni.

"Hello, Clan Mother. I have your sister on the line."

"Please connect her, Roni."

"Right away."

"Good morning." Areana opened with her regular greeting.

It had taken her a while to switch from saying good evening. Theoretically, she had been aware of the different time zones around the earth, but as someone who had never traveled, it was a foreign concept to her.

"Hello, Areana. I have good and bad news for you. The good news is that we have made contact with Kalugal.

The bad news is that he took two of our people and is holding them hostage."

Areana gasped. "Why did he do that?"

After Annani finished telling her an abbreviated version of what had happened, Areana released a long, suffering breath. "I need to talk to Kalugal and explain the situation. He would believe me when I tell him that the clan means him no harm."

"I am afraid that is out of the question at the moment. Kian is dangling communication with you as a reward for releasing our people. If he lets you talk to Kalugal without him making any concessions first, we will lose an important negotiating chip."

"I do not know how important that chip is. Kalugal is a grown man, and re-establishing contact with his mother might not be a top priority for him. He might not even remember me."

"I am sure he remembers, and I am also sure that he longs for contact with you, but he will most likely pretend that he does not care about you. It is all part of the negotiations. Besides, given how suspicious he is, Kalugal might not believe that it is you on the phone. I do not think you can persuade him to do or believe anything."

"He will know it is me. I remember every word we spoke to each other in those brief encounters when he snuck into the harem. He was only a little boy, so he might have forgotten, but I will remind him."

"That gladdens my heart. I was worried that you would have no proof other than your voice, which he might have forgotten as well."

Alena chuckled. "If Areana's laugh is anything like yours, that would be proof enough. No human or immortal female can make a sound like that."

"Your daughter is correct, which is why I never laugh out loud around anyone other than my mate and Tula."

Annani grimaced. She would never get used to hearing Areana talk lovingly about Navuh. How could her sister be so blind to what a monster her mate was?

Even if Navuh treated her like a queen in closed quarters, the fact remained that he kept her isolated from her children and the rest of the world.

Areana was willingly living in a gilded cage.

Even if she lacked the means to get free, she could at least feel resentful about the way he was treating her.

Annani was a big believer in love and its power to heal and unite. She also believed that the Fates required great sacrifices to grant the boon of great love, but this was taking it too far.

"I did not perceive Navuh as the humorous type," she said sarcastically and immediately regretted her tone. Making Areana feel bad had not been her intention. "Does he tell you funny stories to make you laugh?"

Annani did not imagine that Navuh did anything of the kind, but she tried to sound genuinely curious.

"On occasion. I am the only person he can let go around. With me, Navuh is not the iron-fisted ruler of the Brotherhood. He is only my mate."

Annani shook her head but bit her tongue to prevent herself from saying another thing she would regret. Instead, she changed the topic. "If Kian and Kalugal reach an agreement later today, your next scheduled call could be with your son."

"I cannot wait. Being able to talk to Lokan has given me so much. When I can do the same with Kalugal, my life will be complete."

This time, Annani could no longer hold her tongue. "What about holding your sons in your arms? And later your sons' children? How can your life be complete without that?"

Areana sighed. "None of us gets everything she or he wants. Life is about compromise and sacrifice. I accepted that truth a long time ago."

Arwel

As Jacki came out of the bathroom, dressed in the simple sweats Rufsur had given her, Arwel was startled by how beautiful she was. He'd seen her like that many times before, but he'd gotten used to her looking much less attractive, with the heavy makeup dulling her complexion and the mousy-brown wig covering her lustrous blonde hair.

She'd showered and changed last night, but since he'd given her as much privacy as he could by closing his eyes and pretending to be asleep, he hadn't seen the transformation.

Right now, she looked like her old self, with her long blonde hair cascading down her back and her peach-toned skin glowing with health.

The ex-Doomers might get ideas.

"You should put the wig back on. You look too good."

"Thank you." She sat next to him on the couch. "Without the makeup, the wig is not going to make much difference, and it would look very obvious that it's not my natural hair."

Regrettably, she was right. Besides, the Doomers had already seen her through the surveillance camera that he was sure was somewhere in the room. He'd tried to locate it without it being obvious, but the device must be very small and well hidden.

In his imagination, Arwel could see the guy in security calling his friends to take a look at the bombshell they had in their bunker.

This was bad.

"Prepare to stave off unwanted advances."

She shrugged. "What else is new. I've been doing that since I was twelve."

He arched a brow. "That young?"

"I was tall for my age, and my boobs started growing when I was eleven. I hated it. Old men were always giving me leering looks, and I felt disgusted." She chuckled. "At twelve, I thought that any guy over twenty was an old man."

At the sounds of footsteps out in the corridor, Arwel turned to look at the door. "Our first visitor of the day is approaching."

"Rufsur?"

"I think so."

Following a quick knock, Rufsur pushed the door open and walked in with a large tray in his arms. "Good morning. I brought your breakfast."

His lack of surprise at Jacki's new look confirmed Arwel's suspicion that there was a hidden camera somewhere in the room.

Rufsur put the tray on the coffee table. "Enjoy."

"Thank you." Jacki poured herself a cup of coffee from the thermos and added cream and sugar. "Do you want me to fix yours, Arwel?"

"Sure." He looked at their host, who didn't seem to be in a rush to leave. "Any news that you can share with us?"

Rufsur pushed the ottoman to the other side of the coffee table and sat down. "I'm afraid so. I was instructed to search you for hidden communication devices." He cast an apologetic glance at Jacki. "We don't have any ladies down here to search you, but I promise to be as gentlemanly as I can about it."

She put her cup down and crossed her arms over her chest. "I knew you guys were perverts. This is just an excuse to get me naked."

Rufsur shook his head. "I wouldn't ask that of you. If you can hand me the old clothes you arrived in, I will hand them to the men outside to search. After you are done with breakfast, I will kindly ask you to remove your outer clothing and leave only your undergarments on. I will have my men search the clothing you have on now, and promptly return them." He looked at her hair. "I won't put my hands on any part of you other than your hair. It's so thick that you could hide several devices in it."

"Why the sudden suspicion?" Arwel asked. "You didn't bother searching us last night."

Rufsur spread his arms. "We weren't prepared, and we didn't think things through. When your spy described your cell to your boss, and he repeated the description to mine, we didn't stop to think that there might be another, more mundane explanation for her being able to see where you were. This morning we realized that it might have been a clever hoax."

Arwel leaned back and crossed his legs. "Your boss must have demanded more than one proof."

"Correct. The spy also had my boss write a note and then repeated it word for word, but that can be achieved by strong telepathy. None of us have ever heard about a talent like hers, so naturally, we are skeptical."

"Makes sense for you to doubt it," Jacki said. "But the tether is real. You are not going to find any hidden cameras on us."

"I believe you. But I have my orders. If your spy has indeed tethered my boss, that's good news for you two. He is willing to trade you for her."

Arwel stifled the growl that threatened to escape his throat.

If Kian agreed to the trade and anything happened to Jin, Arwel was going to quit the force and dedicate his life to revenge. He would kill Kalugal and make Kian regret his decision for the rest of his immortal life. He wasn't sure how he was going to do that, but he would make Kian suffer. And after that was done, he was going to find a way to end his own life because living without her would be too painful.

The powerful response and the conviction behind it took Arwel by surprise.

Evidently, the bond between Jin and him had solidified after all, just without the fireworks that had accompanied Carol and Lokan's. Arwel had been waiting to experience exactly what they had, but apparently every couple was different, and for some the bonding happened quietly in the background, thickening and sprouting more and more roots until separation became impossible.

He couldn't wait to tell Jin. He could do that through her tether to Jacki, but it didn't feel right. This realization was as significant as realizing that he loved Jin, and telling her about it had to be done face to face.

Arwel had to believe that they would both come out in one piece on the other side of this crisis, and that he could take Jin in his arms and whisper in her ear that they were going to spend eternity together.

"Let's get it over with." Jacki pushed to her feet and glared at Rufsur. "Do you want me to undress here, or can I do it in the bathroom?"

Avoiding her eyes, Rufsur rubbed his jaw. "Here, if you don't mind. That will save me the trouble of searching the bathroom as well."

"I'll go first," Arwel offered. "Do I get to keep my underwear on? I'd rather not give Jacki a show."

She chuckled. "I'll turn around to give you privacy."

Rufsur nodded.

After he was done with Arwel and handed his clothes to the guy waiting outside the room, he turned to Jacki. "Arwel and I can turn our backs to you while you undress."

She huffed. "Yeah, as if that is going to do me any good. I know that there is a camera hidden somewhere in here and that the rest of your pervert friends are going to watch me strip." She waved a hand. "You might as well enjoy the show."

And a show she gave them. Removing the sweatshirt, she swung it around and tossed it on the bed, and then repeated the performance with the sweatpants.

The whole thing took less than a minute, but by the end of it Rufsur was breathing hard.

Nevertheless, he conducted the search just as he had promised, treating Jacki as if she were made from highly breakable glass and apologizing every couple of moments for having to comb his fingers through her hair.

In return, Arwel hadn't said anything about the guy's acute arousal. If Jacki didn't notice the boner he was sporting, Arwel wasn't going to mention it.

When Rufsur left, Jacki let out a breath. "That could have been so much worse."

"It will get much worse if Kian trades Jin for us."

She looked at him with a pair of sad eyes. "What choice does he have?"

"He can bomb the damn place. Invade it. Kalugal is outnumbered and outclassed. We have a much larger force, and the weapons at our disposal are the kind he can only dream about."

His words weren't meant for Jacki.

Arwel was talking to the hidden recording device, and also to Jin in case she was tuning in.

"Yeah, I know that." Jacki played along. "But that might kill us as well. Or just me, the accidental human."

Kian

His mood somber, Kian poked his fork at the blueberry pancakes Okidu had put on his plate.

It seemed like he had two choices. One was to trade Jin for Arwel and Jacki, and the other was to attack the bunker. Both were bad, but as much as he strained to come up with a third option, every idea he'd come up with had big holes in it.

"These are excellent." Turner put two more pancakes on his plate. "Can I get the recipe?"

Syssi smiled. "Okidu's waffles and pancakes are the best. I'll ask him to write the recipes down for you."

"Much appreciated."

Kian pushed the plate away. "What do you think of Jin's idea?"

"What idea?" Syssi asked.

Addressing the question to Turner, he'd forgotten that Syssi hadn't been there when he'd talked with Jin.

"She suggested that we trade her for Arwel and Jacki but also demand Kalugal's second-in-command as hostage. Once she convinces Kalugal that the tether is gone and he lets her go, we will release his guy."

"That's good." Syssi put her fork down and reached for her coffee cup. "But I think you should also hold off contact with Areana until he releases Jin. Give him double the incentive."

Turner shook his head. "Both might not be enough. If Jin can't prove the tether's removal, or if Kalugal doesn't believe that she can remove it, he could sacrifice his lieutenant as well as access to his mother to get rid of it, either by keeping Jin locked up or killing her."

Syssi put her cup down in the middle of her plate. "But we have his place surrounded." Using her finger, she drew an imaginary line around the cup. "If he does either of those things, we can attack, right? I'm sure he would rather avoid an all-out war with the clan."

"He might have an escape tunnel." Kian got up and started pacing. "We didn't find any, but that doesn't mean that there are none. He could have a tunnel leading into one of the neighbors' houses. Even one that's a couple of streets over. We can't post guards to cover the entire area. He could grab Jin and run or kill her and run. I can't risk that."

"I can bring in more drones and monitor the neighboring houses," Turner suggested. "But it's a temporary measure that can work only while Yamanu's thrall is keeping them out of their homes."

"Yamanu can thrall the neighbors to pay no attention to the drones," Syssi said. "The other option is to have Kalugal come to Jin instead of sending her to him. That way we control the situation." She looked at Turner. "You will need to be there."

Kian and Turner exchanged glances.

That would mean lifting the lockdown to allow Turner out of the village, and possibly Kian as well. Right now, it didn't seem like the village was in any danger, but things could quickly change if Kalugal decided to break his promise and interrogate Arwel.

He might figure out that by doing so he would gain even greater leverage over the clan. Like threatening to bomb the village in retaliation for them attacking his bunker.

Pulling out a chair, Kian sat back down. "Kalugal would agree to come to us only if I am held by his men at the same time. And that's too risky."

"Right. We can't have that." Syssi leaned back and crossed her arms over her chest. "What about Lokan? Can we use him in any capacity? We can threaten to do him harm if Kalugal harms Jin. Naturally we won't, but Kalugal doesn't know that."

Turner sighed. "He might not care about his brother either."

"Then let's wait," Syssi said. "Let him stew and chafe knowing that he can't make a move without us knowing about it. After a day or two, I bet he'll be willing to leave the safety of his bunker and come to us if it means getting rid of the tether."

As a contemplative silence stretched across the conference table, Kian ran through the various options. So far, taking Kalugal's second-in-command seemed like the best one, but it wasn't good enough.

"How long did it take Jin to demonstrate to Edna how it feels with and without the tether?" Turner asked.

"Not long." Kian remembered Jin walking out into the corridor a couple of times. "The entire experiment lasted about twenty minutes."

"Then we have another option. Kalugal will not take Jin into the bunker. Instead, they will meet outside in the yard, where we will have snipers ready to take him out if he tries to harm her or compel her to come with him. Naturally, he would have snipers aiming at her at the same time, but they wouldn't do anything as long as we have him in the crosshairs."

"A Mexican standoff," Syssi muttered. "That could work."

Kian took a deep breath. "Only if Kalugal is as attuned to his psyche as Edna is. If he is not, Jin won't be able to convince him that the tether is gone."

Jin

Jin finished her tea and put it on the nightstand. "I think I'm getting sick." She sneezed. "Damn. Do they have any tissues in this place?"

"I doubt it." Kri got up. "I'll get you toilet paper."

"Thanks."

A moment later, the Guardian came back and tossed the roll at Jin. "What exactly are you feeling?"

Jin put her hand on her forehead. "I think I have a fever, but it's not very high. My throat hurts, and I have a runny nose."

"Are those normal symptoms for a human?"

Jin chuckled. "It's like any other flu or cold. Why?"

Kri shrugged. "Transition usually starts with a fever. We should have the sanctuary's doctor check you out."

It had crossed Jin's mind, but unfortunately her symptoms were typical of a simple cold.

Except, as much as she wanted to transition, now was the worst time for it to start. How was Kian going to trade her if she was unconscious?

And even if he didn't trade her, she needed to be conscious to follow the tethers to Jacki and Kalugal.

"I'm not transitioning. Arwel told me what to expect, and it didn't include sneezing and coughing."

"When Michael's started, he thought that it was just a toothache. Everyone experiences it differently. I'm going to find the doctor."

That reminded Jin that Mey's symptoms had also started with a toothache, and that her gums had been swollen.

Was she growing fangs like Mey's?

The first thing Jin did after Kri left was to pat her gums with her fingers. It was a huge relief to find that everything was normal. No swollen gums and no wiggly canines.

With a sigh, she let her head drop back on the pillows.

Getting sick at a time like this was inconvenient, but it was better than entering transition. What if the loss of consciousness caused her to drop the tethers?

That didn't happen during sleep, so maybe it wouldn't happen then either, but she couldn't be sure of that, and losing the connection would have catastrophic consequences.

Ever since Jin had woken up, she'd been checking the connection every half an hour or so, and the last time was mere minutes ago, but she felt the urge to check again.

Closing her eyes, she followed the tether to Jacki, catching a fragment of a sentence. "...kill us as well. Or just me, the accidental human."

The sound of the bedroom door opening broke her concentration and Jin opened her eyes.

"The doctor is coming." Kri rushed into the room. "But so are Annani and Alena. Do you want to get dressed?"

"Oh my God." Jin flung the blanket off. "I can't meet the goddess in a sheer nightgown."

"You can put the robe on." Kri held the equally sheer garment out to her.

Both items were Alena's, but thankfully those weren't the only ones Kri and Jin had found waiting in the closet for them. Kian's sister had prepared outfits to last them several days.

Jin shook her head. "I'll get dressed."

As she pushed to her feet, her head spun, but she ignored the dizziness and padded to the closet.

A long, loose skirt wouldn't have been her first choice for a meeting with the goddess, but it looked comfy and elegant and it was hanging together with a matching loose sweater.

At least she would be color coordinated.

"They are here!" Kri called out just as Jin pulled the sweater over her head.

Damn. There was no time to duck into the bathroom to brush her hair. Combing it with her fingers, she pushed her feet into her boots and walked out of the closet as steadily as she could.

Kri opened the suite's door and bowed. "Good morning, Clan Mother."

As Kri stepped aside, Jin held her breath in anticipation of her first glimpse of the goddess.

Everything Mey had told her about Annani was true, and at the same time it wasn't.

She'd expected the glow, and she'd expected the beauty, she'd even expected the goddess's petite frame, but she hadn't expected to feel as overwhelmed by her otherworldliness.

There was no mistaking Annani for a stunningly beautiful human. She was clearly an alien, and an extremely powerful one.

For the first time, Jin understood what Spencer saw when he described people's auras. She didn't see Annani's Aura, but she felt it. It was like a force field of power, except it wasn't oppressive or terrifying. It was warm and welcoming.

Remembering her manners, Jin bowed. "Thank you for inviting me to your sanctuary, Clan Mother."

The goddess glided toward her. "You are most welcome, child." She reached for Jin's hand. "Let us sit down. I heard that you were not feeling well."

It was the oddest thing to have the goddess lead her by the hand to the couch.

When they were both seated, Annani smiled. "That is much better. You are so tall that I had to crane my neck to look into your beautiful eyes."

"They are just like Mey's." Alena walked in.

Jin had been so absorbed in Annani's awesome presence that she hadn't noticed the goddess's daughter enter behind her.

She took Alena's hand. "Mey sends her regards." She glanced at Annani. "To both of you."

Damn, it was hard to look at the goddess, but it was just as hard not to. Her beauty and power were mesmerizing, but they were too much to handle.

"Your sister is a lovely woman." Alena sat in an armchair facing the couch. "My mother and I are very fond of her."

"Such unique talents you both have." Annani patted Jin's knee. "When you feel better, I would like to see a demonstration of your tethering."

Jin swallowed. Hopefully, the goddess didn't mean for Jin to tether her. It would be like trying to tether the sun.

Alena laughed. "Don't look so terrified. My mother is not suggesting that you tether her. You can use me for your demonstration." She spread her arms wide. "I am an open book with nothing to hide."

"Your secrets are safe because I don't read thoughts. I will only hear what you hear and see what you see." Jin glanced at Annani. "I'm just afraid of creating a mental link with a goddess. I imagine it would be like connecting a battery-operated device to a high-voltage power line."

As Annani let out a melodic string of laughs, the sound was so beautiful that it sent shivers running down Jin's spine. The laughter was just as otherworldly as the female producing it. If she had to describe it, the best analogy Jin could come up with was crystal music, but that wasn't even close.

"We would not want that. What ails you, Jin? What do you feel?"

Jin waved a dismissive hand. "It's a simple cold. In the rush to get out of the club, I left my sweater and my coat behind and went out into the cold night with just a thin T-shirt on. My mother would have had a conniption."

Annani tilted her head. "This is a word I am not familiar with. What does it mean?"

"It means a fit," Alena said. "It's in Yiddish, but like many words from other languages, it was incorporated into English."

The goddess nodded sagely. "That is the fate of all tongues. My native one no longer exists in its original form, but many words have survived by being adopted into others. It gladdens my heart to hear them on occasion."

"The doctor is here." Kri got up and walked over to the door.

Jin hadn't heard anyone knock. Apparently the sanctuary's doors were soundproof just like the ones in the keep.

"Hello." A pretty brunette with a friendly smile walked in. "I apologize for the delay, Clan Mother." She dipped her head. "I misplaced my thermometer." She smiled apologetically at Jin. "No one ever gets fevers here."

Jin wondered if the doctor even knew how to examine a human. Except, if she had a real medical degree, she must have at least interned in a human hospital.

"I'm Doctor Rebecca." She offered Jin her hand. "Let's start with taking your temperature."

It was super weird to get examined while the goddess and her daughter were watching, but thankfully the doctor didn't ask her to remove her sweater but only to lift it a little so she could listen to her lungs and her heart.

After that, she checked Jin's throat and measured her blood pressure.

"It's just a cold." The doctor folded the pressure cuff and put it back in her bag. "I'd be very surprised if it's anything else. Your throat is a little red, but that's all." She pulled an unlabeled container of pills from her bag. "This is for the fever and should make you more comfortable." She chuckled. "I was lucky to find some that were not expired. As I mentioned before, no one gets fevers in here, but some suffer from the occasional headache."

"Thank you." Jin took the small bottle. "Should I take them only if I feel feverish?"

"And if you feel achy. Also drink lots of liquids and try to rest."

Kian

"So, this is how we are going to do it." Kian got up and started pacing.

"First, we will demand Arwel and Jacki's release and Kalugal's second-in-command as a hostage. Kalugal will come out, deliver the three to his driveway, and open the gate. The exchange will happen outside with sharpshooters aiming at Kalugal, and he will no doubt have sharpshooters aiming at Arwel, Jacki, and Jin. Ours will have earplugs in, so he won't be able to compel them. The removal of the tether will happen outside, while our sharpshooters are aiming at Kalugal's head. Once he is convinced the tether is removed, he will exchange Jin for his guy."

Kian looked at Turner. "Feel free to poke holes in my plan. I need your brain to flag the pitfalls."

Releasing a long breath, Turner leaned back in his chair. "The biggest possible pitfall is Jin's inability to prove the tether's removal. We need a contingency for that."

"If she weren't Arwel's mate," Onegus said, "a possible solution could have been for Kalugal to marry her. Maybe that's what the Fates had in mind all along."

Kian glared at the chief. "How can you even suggest that? After all that Arwel has sacrificed for the clan, the Fates wouldn't be so cruel to him. Jin is his mate."

Onegus shrugged. "Maybe there is a better one for him out there."

"Remember Robert and Carol?" Syssi asked. "He sacrificed everything for her, and yet she wasn't his fated mate. Sharon was his, and Lokan was Carol's."

Could that be possible?

As a headache started pulsating behind his eye sockets, Kian pushed his hair back and rubbed his temples. "We can't base our strategy on a hypothetical like that. I need a concrete contingency. If Kalugal refuses to release Jin, do we take him out? Do we attack the bunker? What do we do?"

"You threaten to expose his mother," Turner said. "And if that's not enough, threaten to kill her. We have the means to do that. We know when she is outside, and we can launch a missile from a boat at her." He looked at Kian. "All he needs to know is that we can, and you will have to convince him that you are heartless enough to do that. Make him believe that it's a matter of pride for you."

"He knows I would never do that because Annani wouldn't allow it."

"He doesn't know who runs the show. Kalugal is the product of a patriarchal society. It should be easy for you to convince him that you are in charge and that your mother is just the figurehead."

"I'm not sure that I'm that good of an actor."

"I can do that for you if you wish."

"Won't work. Up until now, Kalugal has been dealing exclusively with me, so if you suddenly take over the negotiations, he would immediately suspect that something is up."

Turner nodded. "I can coach you."

"How? By practicing on you?"

"You can do that if you wish. But what I have in mind is teaching you how to lie convincingly, or rather how to become a better actor. It starts with imagining the kind of asshole who wouldn't hesitate to kill his aunt to prove a point, and then becoming that person until Jin is safely back."

"It's called method acting," Syssi said. "But actors train for years to be able to immerse themselves fully into a role. Kian has hours."

"It will have to do," Turner said. "After all, you are not a novice. You have two thousand years of experience pretending to be human. That should be worth something."

"I'm not very good at it."

"And yet you pulled it off. Who will be your role model, so to speak?"

"Navuh," Onegus suggested. "I'm sure he would kill his own mother if it benefited him in any way."

"I don't know him well enough to emulate his act."

"How about Alex?" Syssi suggested. "Anyone who deals in trafficking is exactly that kind of monster."

"Not him. I could never immerse myself in a role like that."

"What about the Russian?" Turner offered. "Gorchenco is a cruel, emotionless son of a bitch, but he takes care of his people."

Kian grimaced. "He is also a rapist."

Turner shook his head. "I'm out of ideas. Immersing yourself in Mother Teresa's character is not going to help you achieve your objective."

"I'll create a fictional character. Or better yet, I'll pretend that Jin is my sister. If one of my sisters was captured by Kalugal, and killing Areana was the only way to save her, I might give it serious consideration."

"So, it's settled." Turner tapped the table. "When you talk with Kalugal, take into account that it will take Jin about six hours to get back to San Francisco. Perhaps I should tell her to get going already. If it's a no, she can always turn around and head back."

Now Kian was convinced that Jin was at Annani's sanctuary, but as long as Turner didn't verify it, he could claim ignorance. "There is no need to rush her back. I want the exchange to take place at night, and I prefer for her to stay out of reach until it's time."

"The neighbors will be back by then," Syssi pointed out.

"Yamanu will have to shroud the area. Those types of things are better handled in the dark."

Kalugal

"Did you look at the feed from the guest room this morning?" Given Rufsur's smirk, he was referring to the immune having to strip for him.

"What did I miss?"

"Miss Jacqueline the immune is a knockout. The makeup and the wig were designed to make her look plain, and the clothes made her look chunky, but she is perfectly shaped and beautiful. No wonder the warrior risked exposure to save her."

"You said that they are not a couple. They didn't share the bed."

Rufsur shrugged. "Not yet. But he's probably hopeful."

"How did he react to you searching her?"

"He watched me closely, making sure that I was professional about it."

"Were you?"

"Of course. The spy might have been watching. I'm also not into putting my hands on a woman who doesn't want them on her. There are more than enough willing females for me to choose from, and even if there weren't any, I would not debase myself like that. I'm an honorable male."

Kalugal nodded. The men under his command knew his position on proper seduction etiquette. Getting consent without the help of thralling was not negotiable.

"I assume that no recording devices have been found on our guests?"

"None."

"That's actually good news. It means that the tether is removable. Otherwise, those two would have never agreed to it."

Rufsur rubbed his hand over his jaw. "That's true only if the spy bothered to ask their permission. She might be forming a connection with everyone she touches, and it might not even be intentional. It just happens whether she wants it or not."

"That would make her life very difficult. She would be treated as a pariah by her own people."

Kalugal hadn't asked Kian whether Jin the spy was a clan member or just another talented human like the immune. When she'd touched him in the club, he hadn't felt anything different about her, but then immortal females didn't trigger an alarm like the males did, so there was no way to differentiate them from humans. Not unless they demonstrated unusual strength or enhanced senses.

But he wasn't sure about that either.

What if immortal females didn't have the same advantages as the males?

When he'd visited his mother all those years ago, Kalugal had been too young to ponder such questions, and his father was not forthcoming with information on the subject.

If the spy was an immortal, it would open up some interesting possibilities, though. If he married her, Kalugal would gain several advantages for himself, while Kian could not view that as a move against the clan. In fact, if Jin was an outcast because of her ability, he would be doing her and the clan a favor by taking her for himself.

Having an immortal mate could provide him with immortal children, or dormant children that could be later induced into immortality. And he would also have her special ability at his disposal.

As for her looks, just like the immune, she was probably much prettier without the makeup and the wig. But it wasn't a deal-breaker if she wasn't. Jin the spy was a great asset even if she was no beauty queen.

The more Kalugal thought about it, the more he liked the idea. By mating a clan member, he could not only defuse the situation, but also form an alliance with Kian.

That would be the best solution for everyone.

Kalugal wasn't interested in cooperation with the clan, but he wasn't interested in a conflict either. A non-interference agreement would suffice.

Rufsur frowned. "You're smirking, which means that you're plotting something. What devious plan have you concocted in that brilliant mind of yours?"

"A change in strategy. When Kian brings Jin the spy to me, I'm going to be the most gracious of hosts and lay on the charm. This troublesome situation could provide me with the most unexpected boon."

"You want to keep the spy?"

"Indeed."

"That would start a war."

"Not if I marry her."

Rufsur gaped, and then dropped onto the nearest chair. "Why didn't we think of that before? The clan has immortal females. If we play nice with Kian, we could get some for ourselves."

Kalugal lifted a hand. "Don't get carried away. I'll dangle the possibility of an alliance in front of Kian and see how he reacts to that. He might view us as not worthy of his clanswomen."

Rufsur grimaced. "If he judges us based on the Brotherhood's conduct toward females, that might be the case."

"He has no reason to think differently. He knows nothing about us."

Which was exactly what Kian used as an excuse for sending the spy after Kalugal in the first place.

Before initiating contact, Kian had wanted to know who he was dealing with. Or at least that was what he claimed.

What else could he have wanted, though?

The clan was not looking for a confrontation any more than Kalugal was, and both wished to fly under the Brotherhood's radar and remain hidden from Navuh.

Perhaps showing Kian that he and his men were nothing like his father and his organization was precisely what Kalugal needed to do.

Except, how could he prove that?

In Kian's eyes, he was guilty until proven innocent, and innocence was always harder to prove than guilt.

Wendy

"Can Vlad and I take out a snowmobile for a ride?" Wendy looked hopefully at Mey. "I have to get everyone warm clothing first. And then I need to ask if that's okay. I don't think the snowmobiles are included in the rental."

That wasn't a no. Mey not shooting down the idea right away was an encouraging sign.

"I hope they are. I've never ridden one." Wendy looked at Vlad. "Have you?"

He shook his head. "My mom took me skiing a few times, and I've ridden a jet ski but not a snowmobile."

That was more than Wendy had ever gotten to do. But then Vlad's parents were normal people who loved their son. Except, he'd only mentioned his mom.

"What about your dad? Did he go skiing with you?"

"I don't have a dad. I mean, I don't know who he is." Vlad looked into his cereal bowl and fished out the one remaining cornflake.

"Would you like more?" Mey asked.

"Yes, please."

It was his third serving, and that was in addition to two pieces of toast smothered with peanut butter and jam.

Wendy shook her head. "You are so lucky. If I ate as much as you do, I would turn into a ball. Where is all of that going?"

"I wish I knew. I try to gain weight, but no matter how much I eat, nothing sticks to my bones." He smiled shyly. "That's what my mother says."

"Your mom sounds nice."

"She is."

"I'm done." Bowen pushed away from the table. "Are you ready to go, Mey?"

"I need to write down everyone's sizes first." She pulled out her phone. "Ingrid, what's your shoe size?"

"Eight and a half. I wish I could go with you. I'm choosy about my footwear and my clothing."

"I'll send you pictures. You can't go out wearing a thin sweater and yoga pants. Besides, I'm only going to get basic stuff. Snowshoes, puffer coats, gloves, scarfs, hats, and warm socks. You and Vlad also need underwear and pajamas."

"Get me a swimsuit," Ingrid said. "I want to get into that hot tub out on the back patio."

"I must have some clairvoyant talent because I packed my swim shorts." Richard waggled his brows. "Although if the others promise not to peek, we can enjoy the hot tub in the nude."

"Ooh, you naughty boy. I like how you think."

Things seemed to be heating up between those two, and Wendy was happy for them. She was even happier about Richard's idea to share the hot tub with Ingrid in the nude. If they were busy with each other while Mey and Bowen went shopping, that would leave only Vlad and Leon to pay attention to her.

Perhaps that was her opportunity to sneak out?

Except, without a coat and proper shoes, she would probably freeze to death before reaching the town on foot.

Damn.

"I also brought mine," Mey said. "How about you, Wendy?"

"I have it. I was in a rush, so I just dumped everything I had on the bedsheet and brought it with me. I left nothing in the underground."

Mey glanced at Vlad. "Should I get you swimming trunks?"

He shook his head. "I'm not a fan of hot tubs."

185

Poor guy. He was probably embarrassed about being seen without clothes on.

As guilt assailed her once again, Wendy's gut twisted. It would have been so much easier to use Vlad if he were a jerk. Well, not easier because he would have been less trusting, but her conscience wouldn't have bothered her as much.

Every time he showed vulnerability, Wendy's resolve to betray him and the others faltered. But what choice did she have?

They couldn't offer her the safe future her uncle had arranged for her, and without his help, she wouldn't make it a week on the outside.

Maybe if she were a fighter like Jacki, she could've managed, but she wasn't. She had no skills, and no family to support her. All Wendy had was a paranormal talent that was mostly useless.

On her own, she would probably end up homeless. Or dead. A young girl alone on the streets had no chance of survival. She'd get raped on the first night.

The sad truth was that she couldn't afford to take the moral high ground. As sweet as Vlad was, and as nice as the others were, her life was more important than their hurt feelings.

Except, more than their feelings would get hurt.

If she managed to contact her uncle, all these nice people would end up in the paranormal program whether they wanted to or not. But even that wasn't worth giving her life up for. There were much worse fates than getting conscripted into a government program that paid extremely well and using their special talents to serve their country.

A small voice in the back of her head reminded Wendy of her uncle's super-babies breeding program, but she stifled it.

So what if the director and Marisol were compelling people to sleep with each other? There were much worse things than that too. And when she delivered a bunch of new paranormal talents to him, Wendy was going to demand to be excluded from that as her reward.

"Wendy, what's your shoe size?"

"Seven. And I wear a medium in some clothes and a large in others. It depends on the cut."

"Okay." Mey closed her phone. "I've got everything I need. Any special requests?"

"Meat," Leon said. "And lots of it." He glanced at Vlad. "And also potatoes. We are going to fatten this boy up."

"You can try," Vlad said. "But it's not going to work."

Leon cocked a brow. "Do you object to eating steak, ribs, and potatoes?"

"Not at all."

"That's what I thought."

Vlad

"I want to see the jacuzzi." As Wendy opened the sliding door to the back yard, a cold gust of wind swept through the cabin's living room.

Vlad grabbed the throw blanket from the back of the couch and rushed to wrap it around her. "You should have waited for Mey to come back with the coats."

She smiled up at him. "Thank you, but I only want to take a peek."

"I turned it on before breakfast," Richard said. "Check if it's warmed up yet."

"Okay." Vlad followed Wendy outside and closed the sliding door behind them.

Lifting her face toward the sunshine, she closed her eyes and took a deep breath. "It's so peaceful up here. And the air is so crisp. I wish I could live in a place like this."

Vlad commanded his heart to stop pounding like a locomotive. It was beating so hard that even a human could hear it, and if not that, then his labored breathing for sure.

The friendlier Wendy was toward him, the more he wanted her. His arousal had become almost constant, and he was thankful that his dark clothing and the long hoodie hid the erection that wouldn't let up. So far, his fangs hadn't elongated yet, but Vlad was afraid that the smallest touch would trigger that as well.

He'd never had that problem before.

Knowing what most girls thought of him stifled any attraction he might have felt. Perhaps it was the smidgen of hope that allowed him to feel things he'd been suppressing since puberty.

Wendy turned to look at him and smiled, her ruddy cheeks making her look even more beautiful than usual. "I love being surrounded by nature. Do you want to go for a hike later?"

"Sure. After Mey gets here with the clothes, though. I don't want you to get sick."

Vlad was cold, but he could tolerate it better than Wendy and he was not going to get sick.

"Of course." She lifted her foot to show him her sneakers. "These would get wet right away, and my toes would freeze." She walked to the side of the deck where the hot tub was. "But until Mey returns, we can sit here and keep our feet warm in the jacuzzi, or I can get into my swimsuit."

He would love to see Wendy in it, but he didn't want her to see him. If she felt even a little attraction toward him, that would be gone the moment she saw his scarecrow-like body.

"I'll check if the water is warm enough."

The hot tub was built into the deck, and Richard had left the cover on, but it wasn't tight, and steam was escaping through the sides. Crouching next to it, Vlad lifted the cover and dipped his fingers in the water. "I think it's good to go."

"For now, I'm just going to dip my feet in." Wendy sat on the deck and started taking her shoes off, but then stopped. "I can let Ingrid borrow my swimsuit." She pushed up. "Wait here. I'm just going to give it to her and come back. And put your feet in the water, that will warm you up."

He nodded.

His feet were okay looking, so there was no harm in Wendy seeing those. His calves, however, were just as skinny as the rest of him.

With a sigh, Vlad sat on the deck, removed his boots and socks, folded his black jeans up all the way above his knobby knees, and put his feet in the tub.

Wendy was right. The heat from the water spread from his toes all the way up, and the warm vapor heated the air. It would have been pleasant if he weren't so self-conscious about his knees.

When Wendy opened the sliding door, he quickly covered them with his hands. "Are Richard and Ingrid coming out?"

"Ingrid is trying on the swimsuit." Wendy kicked her shoes off and sat on the deck. "She is taller than me, so it might not fit. It's a one-piece."

Wendy took her socks off, pulled her leggings above her perfectly shaped knees, and swung her legs into the water. "Hot!" She pulled them back up. "Why didn't you warn me?" She cast him an accusing look.

"It wasn't hot for me, and it only feels hot to you because your feet were probably cold before. You'll get used to it."

She eyed the water suspiciously. "Yeah, and they are getting even colder now."

In a surprise move, she scooted closer to him, lifted the blanket that served as her coat, and wrapped it around his shoulders, cocooning them inside the same way they had done last night. "You don't have to act all macho and pretend the cold is not bothering you."

"Thank you," he managed to say through his rapidly elongating fangs.

Wendy

Vlad was aroused.

Wendy felt it every time she got close to him. Outwardly he acted like they were just friends, not making advances, not casting her suggestive looks or saying suggestive things, but that was only because he totally lacked confidence.

Which was probably the only reason she had the courage to continue with the charade. If he made a move, she would most likely run away as fast as her short legs could carry her.

Liar.

The truth was that the more time she was spending with Vlad, the more he appealed to her. She no longer saw the skinny, hunched-over guy who hid his face behind a mop of black, glossy hair. Instead, she saw a very tall young man, who was handsome in his own unique way, and who was also kind, intelligent, and oddly protective of her.

In daylight, he appeared even more vampiric than in the underground's artificial lighting, but Wendy found that kind of sexy too. She liked that he was different in just about every possible way.

The question was whether she was attracted to him enough to kiss him.

Maybe.

The turning point had been when Vlad had sung for her. His voice was deep, soothing, and beautiful. There was a softness to it, but also strength, and for the first time in her life, Wendy had felt a stirring. Listening to his voice had transported her to a different place, and in those moments, she could have imagined herself kissing him.

"Can you sing for me?" she blurted.

He arched a brow. "Here?"

"Why not? Do you need your guitar to sing?"

"No, but we are outside."

"So what? There is no one around to hear you."

"Richard and Ingrid are about to come out."

"So they'll get a treat too. You are very good."

Vlad shook his head. "I can't. Maybe later."

Oddly, the emotion she picked up from him was fear, not embarrassment.

What was he afraid of? Wild animals coming closer to hear him sing? She was about to tease him with that, when the sliding door opened and Richard rushed out, wearing only swim shorts and a towel draped around his shivering shoulders.

Anticipating his next move, Wendy scooted back. "He's going to jump!" she warned Vlad.

Since the hot tub wasn't big, it ended up being more of a hop than a jump, but they still got sprayed with hot water.

"Richard!" Wendy admonished. "You've got us wet."

"I'm sorry." He didn't even affect an apologetic expression. "It's so damn cold out here, and we don't have robes."

He crouched, submerging his body all the way up to his nose.

A moment later, Ingrid came out wearing similar attire, but instead of running, she sauntered casually, displaying her hot body in Wendy's swimsuit. The thing looked enviably better on the interior designer.

Richard lifted a couple of inches out of the water. "Aren't you freezing?"

"It's nothing." She waved a dismissive hand. "This is like summertime in the Highlands."

After dropping the towel on the deck, Ingrid gracefully sat on the hot tub's edge, swung her legs over, and slid inside.

Wendy had expected Vlad to steal glances at Ingrid, but even though the woman was hot and moved like a ballet dancer, he paid her no attention. His sole focus was on Wendy, and that felt nice.

Leaning closer to him, she whispered in his ear, "We should go inside. They probably want to be alone out here."

Ingrid smirked as if she'd heard that, which was not likely given the noise the jets were making. Maybe she'd guessed.

Richard was oblivious, and he also didn't care about having spectators. Pulling Ingrid down to join him under the water, he wrapped his arms around her and started kissing her.

"You are right." Vlad pushed to his feet and offered Wendy a hand up.

When they got inside, they found Leon sitting in an armchair that he'd dragged next to the front window. Other than them, he was the only one in the house, but he was watchful. Even if she had a coat and snowshoes, Wendy doubted she could have snuck past him.

"Do you want hot cocoa?" Vlad asked.

"Sure. There isn't much else left in the cabin. Mey is going to bring supplies, but until then, it's either cocoa, coffee, or tea."

"I could eat," Leon grumbled.

Vlad nodded in agreement. "Me too, but all I can offer you is a hot drink."

"I'll take it."

Leon seemed friendly, and so did Bowen, but getting past those two would be impossible. They were professionals. Wendy's only hope was to go on a hike alone with Vlad and then give him the slip. The question was whether the guards would let him take her out. And even if they did, what was she going to do? Bash him over the head and run?

She was a wolf in sheep's clothing, but she wasn't a mean one. It was semi-okay to trick Vlad, but not to hurt him.

The town wasn't far, and she could convince him to walk all the way there. Then she would suggest a coffee break, go into the ladies' room, and ask someone to use her phone. It would take her only a couple of seconds to tell her uncle where she was, and since she had his private cellphone number, she knew he would answer right away.

Once that was done, she would go out and join Vlad as if nothing had happened.

Easy.

He might never find out that she was responsible for his capture. In fact, she was going to tell her uncle to keep it a secret. No one needed to know how he found them. And once they were in the program, perhaps they could continue their friendship.

Dream on.

This story was not going to have a happy ending, not for Vlad, and not for the others, and perhaps not even for her.

Her heart heavy, Wendy forced a smile when Vlad came back with the hot cocoa. She motioned at his guitar case. "How about you sing Leon and me a song? It will take his mind off the subject of food."

Vlad

After giving Wendy and Leon a singing performance, Vlad picked up the remote and clicked the television on. "Any preferences?"

"Anime, if you can find any," Wendy said.

Leon didn't respond, so Vlad searched through the offerings until he found a show Wendy approved of.

As long as he got to sit cuddled with her on the couch, he didn't care what he was staring at.

An hour passed with Wendy engrossed in the show and him engrossed in her. At some point, Ingrid and Richard came in and went upstairs, supposedly to shower and change. But given the sounds coming from the master bedroom, they were busy doing something else.

He tried not to listen, but it was difficult to ignore. Luckily, Wendy's human hearing spared her the embarrassment.

When Mey's car pulled into the driveway, Vlad sighed. "I should help them carry the stuff in."

"Yeah, me too." Wendy started to rise.

"It's okay. Bowen and I can manage. You can stay and finish watching your show."

She smiled. "Thanks. There are only a few minutes left."

In the garage, Vlad waited for Mey to pop the trunk. It was full to capacity, as was the back seat.

When everything had been brought in, Mey handed him one of the bags. "That's yours."

It had his name written on it with a marker.

"And that's yours, Wendy." She handed her a bag with her name.

"What did you get?" Wendy asked.

He pulled out a puffer coat, a pair of snow boots size fourteen, a hat, a scarf, and a pair of gloves. He left a pack of underwear and a pajama set inside the bag.

"Put them on." Wendy waved a hand. "I want to see how you look in them."

Modeling outfits was girly but saying that would probably make Wendy think that he was a chauvinist, so he'd better not.

"How about you go first?"

"Okay." Wendy pulled out a pair of thick socks. "I love these." She smiled at Mey. "Thank you."

"You are welcome."

When Ingrid and Richard came down the stairs, Mey handed them both their bags.

"Let's see what you've got." Ingrid peeked into hers. "The colors are nice." She pulled out a long scarf.

"The fashion show can wait for after lunch, people." Bowen dug into one of the bags that he'd put on the kitchen counter. "Let's eat first. Mey and I were hungry, and we got hamburgers and fries for everyone."

"Bless your hearts." Leon left his station by the window and walked over to the counter.

Sniffing, he dove into one of the other bags. "I hope you brought enough."

"I second that." Vlad joined him in the shopping bags attack and helped bring it all to the dining table.

Fifteen minutes later, he was done with two hamburgers, his and Wendy's fries, and was still a little hungry.

"That was only to tide us over," Bowen said. "I've got a big, juicy tri-tip roast, and I'm going to put it in the oven. It will be ready in an hour."

"I'm going to check out my new things," Ingrid said.

Once everyone was done going over Mey's purchases, she looked from one person to the next. "Did I forget anything?"

"I got everything I need," Wendy said. "Thank you." She pulled her new hat over her hair and wrapped the scarf around her neck. "I'm ready for a hike."

"Are the shoes okay?" Mey looked at the snow boots she'd gotten Wendy. "Nothing pinches?"

"No, they are great. And the socks are so cozy. Thank you."

Richard got up and turned in a circle. "How do I look?"

Apparently, the guy didn't think it was girly.

"Awesome," Ingrid said.

Wendy got up and repeated Richard's performance. "I want to try this stuff out. Come on." She offered Vlad a hand up. "Let's take a walk."

"Don't go too far," Mey cautioned. "I didn't see any of our neighbors walking outside, but I suggest that you keep that scarf ready. If you see anyone, wrap it around your nose and mouth."

"I will." Wendy's excitement was palpable.

Looping the long scarf around her neck twice, she pulled Vlad behind her and headed for the door.

Given the circumstances, it was surprising that Mey was letting Wendy out of the cabin. The government was searching for the escapees from the paranormal program, the village was under lockdown, and Fates only knew what was going on that had necessitated it. Other than the one-sentence explanation Bowen had given them in the keep, Mey and the Guardians were being tight-lipped about it, probably not because they wanted to keep things from him and Ingrid, but because of Richard and Wendy.

Nevertheless, he was glad that Wendy was getting her wish. After being cooped up in the Keep's underground for days, it was no wonder that she was so eager to get outdoors.

As they started down the road with an easy stroll, all Vlad could think about was Wendy's hand, which she hadn't pulled out of his. They were both wearing gloves, so it wasn't as if he was actually touching her, but he was acutely aware of the delicate bone structure of her small hand, and its warmth that was seeping through the double layers and warming much more than his hand.

Wendy took a deep breath and then let it out slowly. "I love the cold air. It's as if my lungs are getting more oxygen, and I feel more energized."

He smiled. "I think that you are just happy to be outdoors."

"I am, especially in a beautiful place like this, surrounded by nature. Do you want to walk along the road, or do you want to cut through the woods?"

"There might be wild animals in there."

Wendy grimaced. "Yeah, I guess it's called Big Bear for a reason. Are there many bears out here?"

"I don't know if there are a lot of them, but one is enough if it thinks that you smell tasty. Then there are the coyotes, mountain lions, and bobcats. The cats are rare, so I'm not too worried about encountering one of those, but coyotes are plentiful, and they run in packs. They can be just as dangerous."

"Then we should stick to the road." She sounded disappointed.

"If you want, we can venture in a little bit. I doubt the animals would get close to the road in the middle of the day when cars are passing by."

Except, so far they hadn't seen any.

"I would like that."

They stepped off the asphalt, but Vlad kept to a parallel path. The snow cover wasn't deep, and in some places only patches of it remained, but the ground was wet and spongy, which slowed them down.

"Are you okay?" He glanced at Wendy's pink cheeks. "Are you cold?"

"A little, but I don't mind. It's so nice out here."

Was that his cue to put his arm around her? How would she react if he did that?

"I can keep you warm." He tugged on her hand and brought her closer against his body.

When she didn't object, he let go of her hand and wrapped his arm around her. "Better?" His voice quivered only a little.

"Yes. Thank you." She leaned her head against his arm.

Vlad lifted his face heavenward and offered a silent thanks to the Fates.

He was walking with his arm around a pretty girl, and she liked it. That was better than anything he'd dared to hope for.

Except that wasn't entirely true. A kiss was as far as he was daring to dream, but that was probably going too far. He didn't know how to initiate it, or when was the right time to do so, or how was it done.

Bhathian's lesson had covered the consent part, but not the mechanics of the kiss itself. Even if Vlad gathered the courage and initiated it, his lack of experience would be painfully evident and embarrassing as hell. He didn't want Wendy to know that at twenty he had never kissed a girl before.

Kian

"Thank you, Okidu." Kian took the box of cigarillos his butler had delivered and sat at the far end of the war room.

"Whiskey or beer?" Onegus asked.

"Whiskey."

"Coming right up."

Turner smiled. "Getting into character for the call?"

"Yeah, my own." Kian lit a cigarillo and leaned back in the chair. "This is just another business deal with a particularly sharp adversary. Been there, done that."

Kian wasn't a stranger to negotiations, and if he approached this one with the same attitude and confidence that he'd approached a thousand other deals he'd made over the years, he should be fine.

After all, these days Kalugal was a businessman, and his Brotherhood days were long gone. Deal-making was a game he knew how to play and he was familiar with its rules. And since they were both comfortable in that arena, it shouldn't be too difficult to negotiate a deal that would make both sides happy.

The trick was to stay emotionally neutral and not blink first. Appearing nonchalant and making the other side sweat the final offer always resulted in better terms.

"Here you go." Onegus handed him a full tumbler and put the bottle on the table next to him. "Good luck."

"No worries. I got it." Kian placed the call.

He wasn't surprised when Kalugal didn't answer until the fifth ring. His cousin was playing the same game.

"Hello, Kian."

"I spoke with Jin earlier, and she told me that you had my people searched." Putting his adversary in a defensive mode was a good opening strategy.

"Then she must have also told you that it was done respectfully, just as I promised it would be."

Jin hadn't actually witnessed the search. She'd heard Jacki and Arwel talking about it later, but Kalugal didn't need to know that. Kian wanted him to have the impression that Jin was on him every moment of the day.

"She did. Are you convinced now?"

"We found no recording equipment on either of your people. I assume that you and your spy have thought of a solution?"

"I've talked it over with Jin, and there is only one way she can prove the tether's removal. She will have to release and reattach it a couple of times for you to notice the difference."

"What if I don't?"

"Then you'll have to take her word for it."

"You must understand that it's not possible for me to agree to that."

"That's the best offer I can make you. Besides, Jin assures me that you'll feel the difference, and that it will take her no longer than half an hour to convince you."

"I'm not worried about her trying to trick me into believing that she released me while keeping me tethered. If it's at all possible, then I can simply compel her to do that. Her inability to remove the tether is what worries me."

"Jin has tethered and un-tethered many of my people. I know she can do it, and those who paid attention felt the difference. What I worry about is you trying to deny it in order to detain her."

His claim was an exaggeration, but it wasn't a complete lie. Only Edna had felt the difference. The others had taken Jin's word for it.

"Trust me. If the spy upholds her part of the deal, I'll uphold mine."

Kian smiled. "I'm sure you can understand why I can't take your word for it. I've devised an exchange plan that will ensure Jin's release."

"Why do I have a feeling that I'm not going to like it?"

"I don't like bringing her to you either. A workable solution requires compromise on both sides."

"What's your plan?"

"We will meet on your driveway. You will bring out my people together with your second-in-command, who Jin tells me you seem very fond of. I'll hold him hostage until you release Jin. You are not going to take her into your bunker. Instead, she is going to demonstrate the tether's removal and reattachment out in the open on your front lawn. I'll have snipers pointing at you, and you will no doubt have snipers pointing at Jin. Once she is done, you open the gate, she walks out, and your guy walks back in."

For a long moment, Kalugal didn't respond, and Kian imagined him mulling over his offer. He wondered what counter the guy was going to come up with.

Obviously, Kalugal wasn't just going to agree to all of Kian's terms.

"If you want me to risk my own safety and to keep my second-in-command as a hostage, then I want to keep your people until I'm safely back inside. When you return him, I'll release your people."

"No deal."

"Then we are back to the starting point. Your offer is extremely one-sided, and I can't accept it. We can do it the way I suggested it or your way, but without me coming out into the open. Jin will have to do her demonstration in the bunker."

"I can't risk her like that. Her safety is not negotiable."

"I'm not going to harm her. If she can't prove the tether's removal, she will have to stay with me as my honored guest."

Kian chuckled. "The cat hosting the mouse. I don't think the arrangement bodes well for the mouse." He lifted the glass and took a sip of whiskey.

"That's not a good analogy. I prefer to think of it as a king hosting the daughter of a rival monarch. That story could end in an alliance."

As what Kalugal was implying sank in, Kian snorted. "Are you asking for her hand in marriage?"

"Not yet. I haven't had a chance to talk with the lady and see if she is agreeable. But this could be an excellent solution to our problem. Don't you agree?"

This was what Onegus had suggested, but Kian was still convinced that Jin was Arwel's fated mate.

Nevertheless, the fact that Kalugal was thinking along those lines was encouraging. The guy was willing to mate a woman he'd never met to defuse the situation and form an alliance with the clan.

"I appreciate the offer, but I doubt the lady in question would."

Kalugal

Kalugal chuckled. "Let me worry about winning Jin over. I can be quite charming, and the ladies find me very appealing."

He was a good-looking man, but that wasn't why he was confident in his ability to win over every woman he set his sights on.

Kalugal could change his appearance to precisely match the lady's taste in men, and as to his personality, he had enough experience to woo and charm even the most resistant. In fact, he enjoyed himself more when females didn't just drop into his lap.

What was the fun in that?

For the win to be meaningful, it needed to be challenging.

Regrettably, these days most young women had lost their natural instincts and succumbed much too easily. Not only that, many fancied themselves pursuers instead of embracing their traditional role of seductresses.

"I have no doubt. Especially when you compel them to feel that way."

"You insult me, cousin. I never compel women into my bed. I might compel them to reveal information relevant to my business interests, but only if more mundane methods of coaxing it out of them fail, which rarely happens."

In the spy's case, though, he might have to break that rule. If she couldn't prove the tether's removal, and if she was resistant to his charms, he would have no choice but to compel her to mate him. After all, rules were meant to be broken, and pragmatism demanded that he set his moral code aside.

"Let's leave matchmaking out of the deal, Kalugal. You'll have half an hour with her, and it's going to be in full view of my people and yours. Even as skilled as you claim you are in the arts of seduction, I'm sure you can't convince a woman to marry you under those conditions. Not without using underhanded tricks like compulsion or thralling."

Kalugal huffed. "You are one to talk about underhanded tricks. You sent a spy after me, who inserted a mental camera and voice recorder into my brain. How is that better than compelling or thralling someone?"

"It's not the same. You might not be free to do anything in secret, but you still have your free will. The only times

I sanction thralling or compelling is when it's necessary to hide who we are or to save lives, immortal and human."

"I didn't know that you had compellers among your clansmen."

"You don't know many things about us."

"Same here. But if I marry your clanswoman, we can become allies and share information. Maybe even cooperate on some projects."

Kalugal had no intention of getting the clan involved in his dealings, but he would love to know what they were doing. As far as he knew, their goals were to stay alive and to stop Navuh and the Brotherhood from enslaving humanity. For some reason, the clan believed in humanity's ability to govern itself in a democratic and peaceful way, which was an absurd notion. Most of the world was governed by dictatorships of this or that kind, and humans had been at war with each other throughout history. The only way to stop them from destroying themselves and the planet was to make wars impossible.

Under Kalugal's watchful rule, wars and the senseless slaughter of millions would be a thing of the past. Nevertheless, Kian would probably not approve of Kalugal's method of achieving global peace.

"This is the twenty-first century, and political marriages are no longer used to ensure cooperation. After we overcome this impasse, we can sit down and negotiate like two civilized men."

"Agreed. But I still don't like how one-sided your proposal is. I suggest a compromise. I'll release one of your people and keep the other until I'm convinced that the tether is gone. You can have the warrior, whose return you consider vital to your safety. I'll keep the immune."

"Getting Jin is enough. You don't need another hostage."

"But I'm not really getting her. You want her to do the demonstration out in the open while you have snipers aiming at my head. That's not the same as the simple exchange I had in mind. In fact, I assumed that you would trade the spy for your people and withhold communication with my mother until after the spy's release."

"That was my original plan, but I then realized that communicating with your mother might not be as important to you as getting rid of the tether in any way you could. I'm not about to chance Jin's life on your eagerness to talk to your mother. But just so we are clear, if you harm Jin in any way or refuse to return her, I will retaliate by harming your mother. We know where she is each evening, and we can kill her with one well-aimed missile."

Kalugal's blood chilled in his veins. "You wouldn't do that. If any of what you've told me is true, your mother would have your head if you killed her sister."

"My mother is not in charge. I am. I humor her when I can, but I'm not obligated to do so. Don't get me wrong, I'm not looking forward to killing my own aunt, but don't think for a moment that I won't do it if you harm Jin. This is not a warning. This is a promise."

Kalugal chuckled. "I know that you are bluffing, cousin, but you have nothing to worry about. I give you my word that I will not harm the spy. The worst that can happen to her is marriage to me, which in itself is an excellent deal. As my wife, Jin would live like a queen."

Kian let out a breath. "You think that you are so different from your father, but you are not. Navuh keeps your mother in a gilded cage, but at least he loves her. You plan to do the same to Jin, but without the love. That makes you worse than Navuh."

As the truth of Kian's words hit Kalugal, his first instinct was to abandon the plan to marry the spy. But that was a knee-jerk response, and letting Kian's accusation affect him was precisely what Kian wanted.

"You threaten to kill your mother's beloved sister. How does that make you any better than my father? And besides, what makes you think that Navuh loves her? I know that she loves him, but I don't think he is capable of loving anyone."

"If Navuh didn't love Areana, he would have killed her a long time ago. Your father doesn't want anyone to know that Annani is not the only surviving goddess, and that her sister is sequestered in his harem. She could potentially undermine his authority, and so could you and your brother. Provided that your real maternal lineage is discovered, that is. Your blood is purer than his."

"Blood purity is irrelevant in today's world. Navuh is a charismatic leader, and his compulsion ability is incredible. He is in no danger from my gentle mother or from me. Perhaps Lokan poses a threat to him. How is my brother, by the way?"

Kalugal had the feeling that Kian had approached Lokan on behalf of Areana first. Had the spy tethered him as well?

"As far as I know, he is well."

Which meant that Lokan hadn't been tethered. If he were, Kian would have known everything there was to know about him.

Perhaps they hadn't gotten to Lokan yet?

He was curious about his brother and what he was up to, but Kian wasn't going to volunteer any information without getting something in return.

"We need to finalize the terms of the exchange. You get your warrior and my lieutenant, Jin and I meet out in the open, and once the tether is removed, I let her go in exchange for my man. Later, I'll trade the immune for communication privileges with my mother."

Kalugal sighed dramatically. "This is my final offer, Kian. I can't sweeten the deal any more than I've already done. And if she can't convince me of the tether's removal, we will have to negotiate for her to remain with me. I don't have to marry her, but she will have to join my organization and stay by my side. I can't afford to release her and have her report everything I do to you. I'm sure you can understand that. I promise you that other than her freedom, she would lack for nothing."

"How would I know that you won't kill her or keep her locked up in a cell?"

"Simple. She will call you every day, under supervision of course, and report how she's being treated. As you've indicated, you hold my mother's life in your hand. If I break my promise, you have the means to retaliate."

"I don't know how important your mother is to you."

Kalugal rubbed his chest. "Even villains love their mothers, and I'm not a villain. When are we going to do this?"

"Midnight."

Kalugal let out a silent breath.

Without stating it explicitly, Kian had accepted his terms.

"Agreed."

Jin

Jin's heart was beating so fast that she was sure Kri could hear it from across the room.

Kian had actually listened to her plea and arranged for the swap. She was going to save Arwel, Jacki, and everyone in the village, and also prevent a war between the clan and Kalugal.

Except, everything depended on her ability to convince Kalugal that the tether was off.

No pressure.

"You can still change your mind," Kian said. "I can call Kalugal and tell him that the deal is off."

He didn't sound like he meant it, but Jin appreciated him leaving the final choice up to her.

"Not only will I not change my mind, but I am adamant about doing this. And thank you for using my idea to hold Kalugal's second-in-command as a hostage."

"I did much worse than that. I threatened to kill Areana if he harms you."

Jin gasped. "You didn't."

"I had no choice. Your life is on the line, Jin, and I'm not taking it lightly. Kalugal's best option is to kill you. I need a powerful deterrent to ensure that he won't dare do it."

She sighed. "I don't know what's worse. If I can't prove the tether's removal, and the only way to defuse the standoff is for Kalugal to marry me, it would kill Arwel. So maybe it's better for Kalugal to kill me instead."

"Don't talk like that. Do you think Arwel could live without you?"

"Yeah, you are right. I guess I'll just have to convince Kalugal. No one else has doubted it before. Not my teammates in the program and not Edna. It should be okay."

Jin wasn't sure who she was trying to reassure, Kian or herself.

"Let's hope so. Turner is going to arrange your transport back to San Francisco."

"Thank you."

Across the suite's living room, Kri smiled. "I don't know about you, but I'm glad to go home. I miss Michael."

"And I miss Arwel. If everything goes well, I'll have him in my arms tonight."

Just thinking about it made her heart flutter like a happy butterfly. In twelve hours or so, this nightmare was going to be over.

Kian still wouldn't know much about Kalugal, but Jin was sure that during their negotiations, Kian was gaining valuable insight into the guy's character. Maybe when it was over, they could meet somewhere neutral and talk.

Except Kalugal's compulsion ability complicated everything. Kian would have to take Turner with him.

"You didn't tell Kian that you were sick."

Jin waved a dismissive hand. "It's just a stupid cold. I'll load up on fever reducers, and I'll be fine. Do you think that he knows where we are?"

Kri chuckled. "I'm sure of it. Where else could Turner have sent you that is five hours away by plane?"

"Many places. I could be back in New York."

Kri shrugged. "Plausible deniability is good enough. If Kalugal compels Kian to tell him where you are, he can honestly say that he doesn't know."

Jin cradled the cup of tea in her hands. "It's weird to get ready for a flight and not have anything to pack."

Kri nodded. "I'll ask Alena to give you a warm coat to put over the sweater."

Jin was about to decline the offer, but then she thought better of it. She didn't feel well, and a warm coat sounded too good to say no to.

As Kri left the room, it occurred to Jin that the Guardian could have used a phone to communicate with Alena, but she had chosen to do everything in person instead. Was it because she thought it was more respectful to do it this way?

Alena was the goddess's daughter, but so was Amanda, and Kian was her son. Was Kri as polite with them as well?

Thinking back to her conversations with Kian, Jin realized that she could have addressed him more formally, and probably should have. She needed to remember it when dealing with Kalugal. He might not be as forgiving as Kian.

She blamed her Israeli upbringing. Even in the army, her commanders hadn't expected to be treated formally unless it was on official business or a ceremony. On a day-to-day basis, the atmosphere had been informal and friendly.

In that respect, American society was very different, and the hierarchy was still observed in schools and in the workplace. Things were changing, though, and informal camaraderie was slowly replacing the older, more rigid models.

When the door opened, Jin half expected Alena and the goddess to enter, but it was only Kri, and she had a long, wool coat draped over her arm.

It was pink, but Jin didn't mind. It looked cozy.

"Alena says she and Annani will see us off. The Odu is preparing the goddess's jet. And he's going to fly us all the way back to San Francisco. That way, you can sleep comfortably during the flight."

"Awesome. I loved the fully reclining seat."

Pushing to her feet, Jin held on to the couch's armrest, but it didn't mitigate the dizziness that assailed her every time she changed positions.

What a lousy time to get sick.

Kri was next to her in a blink of an eye. "Why didn't you wait for me? Falling down and breaking something would really screw everything up." She wrapped her arm around Jin's middle, propping her up. "Perhaps I should carry you. That would be the safest."

Jin glared at her. "Don't you dare."

"You wouldn't have objected if a male Guardian suggested it."

"Yes, I would. Unless I'm nearly dead, the only one who is allowed to carry me is Arwel, and only under special circumstances."

Kri snorted. "Like when? Over the threshold while you are wearing your wedding gown?"

"I was thinking more along the lines of him carrying me to bed, but I like the threshold idea too. I can't wait for this to be over so we can move into the village and start our lives together. Unfortunately, I need to wait until Wendy, Richard, and Jacki find their mates."

The Guardian slanted her a glance. "I heard rumors about Ingrid calling dibs on the guy."

"She did. But from what Mey is telling me, they are just fooling around. Vlad and Wendy, on the other hand, seem to like each other a lot. The one I'm worried the most about is Jacki. She doesn't seem interested in anyone."

"Is she into girls?"

"It had occurred to me that she might be, so I asked her. Jacki said that she's just waiting for the right guy, and that she's not going to hook up with anyone just for sex. It's either the real deal for her or nothing."

"It might be a convenient excuse for someone who is not ready to come out, so to speak. Not everyone has the guts to do that."

"Maybe." Jin shrugged. "Or she might be telling the truth. Not everyone is into hookups either."

Kri nodded. "I can understand that. Before Michael, I was quite sick of meaningless sex, and I'm a young immortal, so it's not like I had centuries of it. I'm so glad that that part of my life is over, and I feel sorry for those who still have to hunt. Sometimes I feel guilty for getting lucky."

That was an unexpected confession. "Don't you believe in the Fates? From what I understand, immortals credit them with happy matings."

"Not all immortals are believers. I doubt the Doomers even know about the Fates. They worship Navuh's father, the god Mortdh." Kri's lips twisted in a smile that was more of a grimace. "It fits for an evil organization to worship a murderer who singlehandedly ended the gods' era." She pinned Jin with a hard look. "You should remember that when you deal with Kalugal. That's what he carries in his genes, and I bet it's the dominant part."

Arwel

Following a quick rap on the door, Rufsur entered together with another guy carrying a tray, and Arwel immediately picked up on his agitation.

Normally, Rufsur reminded Arwel of Anandur. He was easygoing, positive, and difficult to rattle. Even the club fiasco hadn't affected his pleasant demeanor.

Not that Arwel had any illusions as to how deadly the guy could be. There was a reason that Kalugal had chosen him as his second-in-command, and it wasn't his amiable personality. Like Anandur, the guy probably turned into a killing machine when it came to protecting his boss.

But that wasn't the reason Arwel hadn't tried to overpower him and make a run for it. The place was locked down tightly, and Kalugal's men who had been too far away to get back in time were locked out.

Which led Arwel to believe that there were no escape tunnels.

If there was a secret way into the bunker when it was locked down, Kalugal would have ordered those men to return and not stay away in the city. He didn't have a large force, and every one of his warriors was needed.

"Enjoy your lunch." Rufsur opened the door and let the other guy out.

"What's going on?" Arwel asked, stopping Rufsur with his hand on the handle. "You seem agitated."

The guy turned around. "Our bosses reached an agreement. You and I will be traded for the spy. When she removes the tether, your boss is going to release me, and mine is going to release the spy."

Arwel's gut twisted. "When is that going to happen?"

"Tonight."

Fuck. Was there any way he could prevent the trade from happening?

Maybe he could talk to Kalugal?

Except since the abduction, Areana's son didn't seem interested in them.

"Is your boss going to visit us at all? I find it curious that he hasn't bothered to do so after going to all the trouble of kidnapping Jacki and me."

"Kalugal promised Kian not to interrogate you, so he has no reason to come here. If the spy sees him talking with you or Jacki and reports it to your boss, he might reach the wrong conclusion."

That explained it. Since it seemed like he would get traded without ever talking to Kalugal, Arwel's only chance was to convince Jin not to do that. And the only way to communicate with her was to keep talking to Jacki about it over and over again.

"I'll come again with your dinner." Rufsur looked at Jacki and cracked a lopsided smile. "Which will probably be the last time we see each other." He ran a hand over the back of his neck. "Unless you are willing to go out on a date with me once this is all over."

"I'll give it some thought."

Even without engaging his empathic ability, Arwel knew that she had no such intention. Rufsur was a good-looking fellow, and he had treated them both well, but Jacki wasn't attracted to him.

It was easy to sense the guy's disappointment, but that wasn't the emotion Arwel was interested in. What he wanted to know was the reason for Rufsur's agitation. Since he should have a good idea about Kalugal's plans for Jin, he might be afraid for his life.

Then again, he was probably expecting treatment similar to what he would have gotten at Navuh's camp, and that was reason enough to worry.

Arwel could alleviate his concerns, and if Rufsur was still nervous after that, it wouldn't bode well for Jin's prospects of survival.

"You have nothing to worry about from my people." Arwel pushed to his feet and offered Rufsur his hand. "You've been cordial to Jacki and me, and I'm going to make sure that you're treated just as well by my friends."

It could be that the only reason for Rufsur's exemplary behavior was Jin's tether to Jacki, but Arwel could at least pretend to believe that Rufsur's gentlemanly act hadn't been for Jin and Kian's benefit. "The clan is not like the Brotherhood. No one is going to beat you up or torture you for information."

As Rufsur took Arwel's offered hand, his relief was palpable. "I'd appreciate you putting in a good word for me, but I want you to know that I didn't expect anything in return for treating you right. Even though I was raised in the Brotherhood, I'm not like them. I left with Kalugal for a reason."

"He didn't compel you?"

"He only compelled our silence. We were free to choose."

"How many chose to join him?"

Smiling, Rufsur shook his head. "You sly dog. I was being nice, and you are trying to get strategic information out of me."

"That wasn't my intention. I'm curious about the percentage of Doomers who decided to stay behind. I don't need to know the numbers. Just the ratio."

"Doomers?" Rufsur arched a brow. "Are you referring to Brothers?"

Arwel stifled a smirk. "Doom is the acronym of Navuh's organization. We nicknamed the members, Doomers."

"I see." Rufsur chuckled. "Kalugal will have a good laugh when he hears that."

The fondness in Rufsur's tone helped Arwel relax a little further. The guy liked his boss, and hopefully the feeling was reciprocated. Kalugal wouldn't sacrifice a man who he considered a friend.

"I hope your boss has a good sense of humor."

"He does." Rufsur rubbed the back of his neck. "Kalugal handpicked each of his men. We were not the average Brothers, and when he decided to run, most of us followed him. On our own in the big world, we have become like real brothers. You might think that Kalugal runs a military organization, but that's not how it is. We are a family. But don't think we would be easy to take down. We are all warriors as well, and we've kept up with our training."

"I have no doubt."

In that regard, Kalugal's people were not that different from Arwel's. Annani's clan was a family first and an organization second. The difference was that clan members were related to each other either by blood or by mating, while Kalugal's men were not.

Still, Arwel chose to believe that their bonds of friendship were just as strong as those of blood, and that if Kalugal could help it, he wouldn't let harm come to his second-in-command.

Wendy

Wendy kicked at a patch of snow. "Do you know how far it is to the town center?"

"It's far, and we can't go there. You need to stay hidden."

She huffed out a breath. "No one is looking for me in Big Bear. It's not like my wanted poster is plastered on every utility pole." She leaned on his arm. "Imagine how nice it would be to get a cup of coffee and maybe even a piece of cake."

She didn't have any money, but Vlad did. He wouldn't mind paying for her. "Can you check on your phone? The map application can tell us how far it is on foot."

Reluctantly, Vlad reached into his pocket and pulled out his phone. Wendy had seen him use it before, but she hadn't noticed whether it was one of those new models that were unlocked by scanning his face or a fingerprint.

If she were lucky, it would be a simple phone that required a numerical code, and she could memorize it.

Her prayers were answered when Vlad punched in a series of six numbers that were surprisingly easy to remember.

Why would he use a stupid code like that?

The guy was too naive for his own good. Naturally, she wasn't going to comment on it and let him know that she now knew how to unlock his phone.

"The town center is on the other side of the lake. It would take an hour and a half for us to get there." He showed her their location on the map.

"That's not too bad. We can make it there and back before nightfall."

"I'm not taking you there. If we are gone for more than an hour, Mey is going to send Bowen or Leon after us."

"Bummer." She let her chin drop.

Since the coffee shop plan wasn't going to happen, she needed to come up with a different one.

Could she take Vlad's phone without him noticing it?

She could pretend to need to pee, which wouldn't be a lie, go hide behind some rocks and make the call. Vlad might notice the outgoing call she'd placed to a number he didn't know, but by then, Director Simmons would have sent people for them.

Perhaps she could ask Vlad to give her the phone while she went to take care of business because she needed the flashlight feature?

Peeing in nature was a potentially dangerous endeavor, and he knew how scared she was of spiders and other creepy crawlies that might be lurking between the rocks.

But what if he refused?

This might be her only chance, and she didn't want to risk blowing it. The best thing would be to steal the phone, and to do so, she would have to kiss the boy.

He would be too stunned to pay attention to anything other than her lips on his. And if she used her tongue, he was probably going to faint.

The problem was that Wendy had never kissed a boy, and her knowledge of kissing was based on movies and romance books. Still, it shouldn't be too difficult, especially since she was quite sure Vlad was just as inexperienced as she was. Even if she was a bad kisser, he probably wouldn't know if he had no one to compare her to.

"Vlad?"

He looked down at her. "Yes?"

"Did you ever kiss a girl?"

His cheeks reddened. "Of course."

"I mean a romantic kiss, not a kiss you give your cousin or your aunt."

His cheeks turned crimson. "No," he admitted.

"Neither did I. I mean kiss a boy, not a girl."

"Really?" He smiled shyly. "I was sure that a pretty girl like you must've gotten plenty of kisses."

The guy was just too sweet.

"I've never wanted to kiss anyone before."

Vlad stumbled, but managed to stop himself from falling and turned to her. "And now you do?"

Wendy nodded. "I like you, and I feel safe with you. I haven't felt that way about any other guy."

She wasn't lying. Not about that.

What a pity that after he discovered her betrayal, Vlad was going to hate her guts.

But it was for the best.

Her future had no place for a boyfriend, but Wendy wasn't sure that she was strong enough to push Vlad away. The betrayal would do that for her. She might cry a few tears, but she'd get over it.

Lifting to her toes, she wrapped her arms around his neck and pulled him down. "Let's be each other's firsts."

With a pained sigh, Vlad closed his eyes, but he didn't bring his mouth any closer to hers, probably waiting for her to close the distance. Which was fine by her.

Wendy the seductress was about to be born.

Lowering her hands to his shoulders, she kept going down until she reached his lower back. He'd put his phone in the back pocket of his jeans, which meant that she would have to cup his ass to get it.

That would shock him for sure.

His lips were a mere inch away from hers, but closing that distance took a monumental effort. With butterflies flapping frantic wings in her stomach, partially in excited anticipation of her first kiss and partially in fear, Wendy put her mouth on Vlad's.

As her body got hit by a thousand volts of electricity, it was a miracle that she retained the presence of mind to pull the phone out of his pocket and slip it into the sleeve of her puffer coat.

Once her mission was accomplished, though, her mind did what it had always done in times of extreme stress. It disassociated from the deceit and immersed itself in the incredible experience of her first kiss.

Vlad

As Wendy's lips touched his, Vlad felt like he was getting zapped with a high-voltage current. The overload of sensations short-circuited his brain, and there was a brief moment of blackout, but then his neural system rebooted, reawakening completely rewired.

Suddenly, there was something primal and feral inside him that was utterly new and yet familiar. It felt real, it was still him, but different.

That ferocity that had lain dormant until now burst into existence, and he welcomed it like the first breath of truly fresh air after a lifetime of staleness.

Vlad felt invincible.

His arms, which had been hanging by his sides, shot around Wendy, and he lifted her up, crushing her against his chest and taking over the kiss.

With a husky moan, she melted into him, and as his tongue darted experimentally to lick at the seam of her lips, she opened up for him. At the first taste of her, Vlad got light-headed and nearly lost his footing, but he wasn't going to let her fall no matter what.

Somehow, he knew what to do, and nothing about the kiss felt awkward, but it was sure as hell overwhelming. He wanted to consume Wendy, to become one with her and never let go.

Hell, he wanted to strip them both naked and make love to her right there on the ground.

As frantic as the kissing was, Vlad was aware of how crazy those thoughts were. He couldn't act on them, mainly because Wendy was human, and the ground was too cold and too rough for her, but also because she wasn't ready for that.

Her humanity became painfully obvious when her small hands pushed on his chest, and he realized that she'd run out of breath.

As Vlad let go of her mouth, Wendy sucked in a long gulp of air. "Oh, wow. That was one hell of a kiss. Are you sure it was your first? You are a natural." She touched her lips with two trembling fingers. "Wow."

He couldn't answer because his damn fangs were fully elongated. Instead, he nodded and lowered her gently until her feet touched the ground.

They were out in the daylight, so Vlad could get away with the glow in his eyes, but the fangs were another story. He needed a few moments to beat them into submission.

"I need to pee." Wendy started shifting from foot to foot. "It must be because of all the excitement." She giggled as she glanced around. "I need to find a bush or rock to hide behind."

He just nodded again.

"I'll be right back." She jogged toward an outcropping of rocks.

"Slow down!" he called after her while shielding his mouth with his hand. "You don't want to fall and break something!"

Wendy waved a dismissive hand in his direction, but she did as he asked and switched to a fast walk.

He expected her to stop by the rocks, but she kept on going toward a larger outcropping further away. Was she that concerned about him hearing her pee?

For a human, the first hiding place would have been far enough, and Wendy didn't know about his super-hearing, but perhaps she needed a few more moments to collect herself as well.

He was still panting like a locomotive, his shaft felt like it had grown to the size of a baseball bat, and his fangs were refusing to retreat.

Regrettably, Bhathian's class hadn't covered what happened after the kiss. In Jackson's case, the kiss had usually led to other stuff, which had resulted in biting the girl and then thralling her to forget the bite. But was thralling allowed after only a kiss?

Bhathian had said that it was okay to erase the memory of the bite, and to change what the human female remembered about the immortal male who she'd had sex with, but not the sex itself.

Still, hiding who he was should be the overriding factor, right? If he couldn't retract his fangs, he would have to thrall Wendy to forget what she'd seen.

How did other immortal males deal with that?

Their fangs probably retreated much faster than his, so they didn't need to worry about them showing. Or maybe a mere kiss didn't trigger venom production and their fangs remained dormant.

Vlad was a freak even among his own people, with fangs that were too long even in a resting position and elongated in response to the slightest of triggers.

Not that Wendy's kiss could qualify as such.

It had been earth-shattering, mind-blowing, brain-altering...

He wasn't the same guy he'd been before. From now on, he would think of his life as having two stages. The one before the awakening, and the one after.

Except, what was he supposed to do next?

How would the new Vlad act? What kind of a man was he going to be?

The answer to that was simple. He was going to be Wendy's man. He was going to take care of her, protect her, and make her happy.

Wendy

Wendy's plan had worked without a hitch, but it had also misfired big time.

She had the phone, Vlad was dazed and confused, but so was she. The kiss was supposed to be a diversion for the pickpocketing, but it had turned out to be so much more.

Wendy was still reeling from it.

Instead of Wendy the seductress, she was Wendy the seduced, or Wendy the confused, or Wendy the hot and bothered, or all of the above.

Who would have thought that Vlad was such an amazing kisser? Or that he would take over with such confidence?

Something inside him had snapped, banishing the shy boy and bringing out the man. And it wasn't just the kiss. It was the whole experience. The way he'd effortlessly picked her up and crushed her against his chest, the way his tongue felt and tasted inside her mouth, the way his male scent had intensified, scrambling her senses and making her go limp in his arms.

Wendy had loved every moment of it, and if she were a braver soul, she wouldn't have stopped at the kiss. She would have gone all the way to having sex with Vlad right there and then.

And how crazy was that?

They were both virgins, it was too freaking cold to get naked outside, and she was about to betray Vlad and break his heart.

Maybe she shouldn't?

What if she gave up on her uncle and her cushy future in his organization? What if she married Vlad and had a bunch of babies with him?

Yeah, talk about crazy.

Thinking about a future with a boy because of one hot kiss was even worse than the disassociation she used to employ to escape her crappy life. This was pure la-la land.

Wake up, Wendy! You are not in Kansas, and Vlad is not the wizard.

The only real wizard in her life was Director Simmons. He'd saved her from her abusive father and had given her a fantastic job with even more fantastic pay and a promise of a life she could've never dreamt of.

She wasn't going to let her hormones derail her future.

That was probably what had happened to her mother. When she'd met Wendy's father, she'd probably felt the same way her daughter was feeling now, but unlike Wendy, she hadn't had the wisdom to shake it off.

That one wrong decision had ruined her mother's life, turning her into a drug addict and making her abandon her only child.

Her resolve reinforced, Wendy quickened her step. When she got to the large rock outcropping, she circled to its back and peeked to check on Vlad.

Head hung low, his hands stuffed in his pockets, he was pacing in circles, still looking lost and confused.

Good. She had him exactly where she wanted him.

Crouching behind the rocks, she shook her arm and dropped his phone from her sleeve into her hand.

Quickly entering the six-digit code, she held her breath, and then nearly choked on her own saliva when the screen flashed with access denied. She must have gone too fast and clicked a wrong digit. The second time around, Wendy forced herself to slow down and make sure she hit the right numbers.

Her uncle answered almost immediately. "This is Director Simmons. Please leave a message, and I will call you back as soon as I can. Have a pleasant day."

Damn. He'd probably let the call go to voicemail because he didn't recognize the number.

"Hi, this is Wendy," she whispered into the phone. "I'm in Big Bear, California, with a bunch of people who have paranormal talents. They came to get Jin out of the program, and Jacki and Richard begged them to take them too. I went along so I could tell you where to find them. We are in a cabin on Faulkner Road. The number is 227. I have to go now. Don't return my call. I stole the phone, and I need to give it back."

Disconnecting, she debated what to do with the device. Maybe she should leave it there?

Vlad would think that he lost it.

But what if it had the find-my-phone feature? She should destroy it somehow. Except, if she bashed it with a rock, Vlad would hear it. Would turning the power off do the trick?

Mey

When all the groceries and other supplies were put away, Mey made herself a cup of tea and sat on the couch.

Ingrid and Richard were back outside in the hot tub, Vlad and Wendy were on their hike, and Bowen was sitting next to the front window. He had switched places with Leon, so his buddy could catch a few hours of sleep.

Looking at her, he smiled. "Enjoying a few peaceful moments?"

"I have nothing better to do. You are making a roast, and I already peeled the potatoes and put them in a pot to cook. Ingrid said that she would make the salad."

"You can join Ingrid and Richard in the jacuzzi."

She grimaced. "No, thank you. I think they are very happy to be alone out there. Besides, I need to call my sister."

Mey pulled out her phone and sent a text to Jin. *Can you talk?*

Her phone rang a moment later. "I'm on the plane heading back to San Francisco."

Mey sat up straight. "Why?"

"Kian is trading me for Arwel, but don't worry. We have everything figured out. Kalugal is going to send his second-in-command to be held as hostage until my safe return. That was actually my idea, and I'm so glad that Kian listened to me. Maybe I have what it takes to be an undercover operative after all."

"Thinking outside the box is good for anything that you choose to do. The question is what you will enjoy doing the most. But back to the trade. Having a hostage still doesn't guarantee your safety. Kalugal might decide to sacrifice his guy."

"I didn't finish telling you the whole plan. We are going to do it out on his front yard, with Guardians pointing guns with special bullets at his head. I'm going to show him how it feels without the tether and then with it, and once he is convinced that it's off, I will just walk out of there."

"What about Jacki?"

"Kalugal will trade her for the privilege of talking with his mother. Kian is going to arrange that."

"What if he talks with his mother and then doesn't release Jacki?"

"Then he doesn't get to talk to Areana again. I don't think it will be a problem. Jacki is not important to him. Arwel is the valuable one as far as Kalugal is concerned."

"And you."

"Naturally. Although I want Jacki out of there as well. She is being treated well, and so is Arwel, but that's because they know I'm watching."

"You'll still be watching even after you release Kalugal. No one is demanding that you release Jacki as well."

"That's so true. It didn't occur to me, but you are right. Except, if Kalugal or his men mistreat Jacki, we won't have anything to retaliate with other than withholding contact with Areana."

Mey sighed. "I hope that's enough."

"Kalugal is not a bad guy, but I don't know his men other than the one he talks with the most. That's the guy we demanded as hostage, and he is okay too. If the others are like Kalugal and Rufsur, Jacki will be treated well."

As smart as Jin was, she was still naive. People had many layers, and what they showed on the outside was their best. The ugly usually came out when they thought no one was watching.

"You don't know that. Kalugal might be polite, soft-spoken, but totally emotionless. But then I've never met him, while you've been observing him since yesterday. That's not much to go by, but it's more than any of us have."

"What I saw and heard was mainly his negotiations with Kian, so obviously he was putting on a show. I'm actually basing my impression of him on his interactions with his lieutenant, and on that guy's behavior. Rufsur was never cruel or even unkind to Arwel and Jacki, and that was even before he knew about the tether."

"You told me that he put them in a prison cell."

"Yeah, that's true, but that's because the other rooms inside the bunker don't lock from the outside. I just wonder what Kalugal needs the cell for."

"Maybe he uses it as a brig. You know, for when one of his men does something he shouldn't. Every military organization needs to have disciplinary measures."

Jin sighed. "I guess I'll find out soon."

The knot in Mey's gut twisted tighter. "I'm worried about you."

"I'm worried too," Jin admitted. "But there is no other way. I have to do this."

"When is the exchange going to happen?"

"Tonight. Kian wants to do it after midnight. I want to get some sleep on the plane so I won't be dead when I get there. This freaking cold couldn't have come at a worse time."

Mey switched the phone to her other ear. "Are you certain it's a cold? The symptoms are very similar to transition."

"I'm sure. The doctor checked me, and she said it's a cold. I have low fever, runny nose, and I'm nauseous and dizzy. Those are not transition symptoms."

"The doctor up there has no experience with adult Dormants transitioning. So far, only Kian's part of the clan has found any."

"I've had colds before. It feels exactly the same. By the way, how come you are talking so freely? Are you alone in your bedroom?"

"I'm in the living room, but only Bowen is here. He's one of the two Guardians who have joined us. Richard is out back with Ingrid, playing footsie in the hot tub, and Wendy went on a hike with Vlad."

"Alone?"

"With each other."

"Vlad is not a Guardian in training, is he?"

Mey chuckled. "The kid is so skinny that a strong gust of wind could blow him away. But even if he were as buff as Bowen, Vlad is not Guardian material. He has the gentle soul of an artist. You should hear him sing. And he studies graphic design."

From the corner of her eye, she saw Bowen grinning as he crossed his thick arms over his chest.

Show-off.

"So basically, Wendy is out there with no protection. I don't like it."

"No one is looking for her out here. It's just trees and snow and there is barely any traffic on the street. I think most of the cabins are unoccupied."

"How far is the town? Is it walking distance?"

"Not really. It's on the other side of the lake."

"That's good. It means that they are not likely to encounter many people on their hike."

"My thoughts exactly. Get some sleep, Jin. And call me when you wake up."

"I will."

"Please, don't forget. I want to hear from you before you go into the lion's den."

"I love you too."

When Jin ended the call, Mey put her phone on the coffee table and leaned back. It had been more than an hour since Vlad and Wendy had left.

Maybe she should call Vlad to make sure that they were all right?

"Call him," Bowen said. "For your own peace of mind."

"Do you read minds?"

"It's written all over your face."

Mey lifted the phone. "I would hate to interrupt a romantic moment."

Bowen chuckled. "I doubt it. Those two are so shy that neither would have the courage to initiate anything. Observing them together, I can see the wisdom of old-fashioned matchmaking and arranged marriages. They are perfect for each other, but unless someone gives them a push, nothing is going to happen."

Wendy

Wendy turned the device around, looking for the off button, but it was like no other phone she'd handled before. There were no visible buttons on the sides or on the back. The screen came to life when it was lifted, and a code was needed to unlock it. That was all.

What if it needed a fingerprint or Vlad's face to turn on and off? Or maybe a voice command?

It seemed like she had no choice but to destroy it. The question was how to do that without making a noise. If there was a brook or a pond anywhere near, she could drop the phone into it and hope it wasn't waterproof.

Maybe snow would do it?

Or perhaps she could pee on it? Would that be enough to destroy the blasted thing?

The seconds were ticking away, and she was running out of time. Soon, Vlad would overcome his stupor and come looking for her.

Glancing around, she caught the glint of water several feet away. It was only melted snow, but it was her only option.

Wendy made two steps in its direction when the phone rang, the sound piercing the quiet and making her heart leap out of her chest.

Panic choking her throat, she started running. And when she heard Vlad's boots pounding on the ground behind her, she hurled the device away from her with all the force she could muster.

Hitting a rock with a crunching sound, the phone bounced and landed somewhere she couldn't see.

As Wendy prayed that it was destroyed and wouldn't turn on, Vlad's arms shot around her from behind.

He lifted her up in the air and turned her to face him. His expression a mask of fury mixed with hurt, he held her suspended above the ground and away from him, her legs pedaling in the air. "What have you done?"

"Nothing." Tears started streaming down her cheeks. "I did nothing."

"Why did you steal my phone?"

"I wanted to call my father. I'm sorry. But I missed him, and I wanted to let him know that I was okay. He must be so worried about me."

Vlad's face twisted in a disgusted grimace. "You are lying." He dropped her carelessly and headed toward where the phone had landed.

Crumpling down to the ground, Wendy wept. She was so stupid. What had she thought would happen a moment after she'd succeeded in making the call?

What was Vlad going to do to her?

He picked up the broken device, but since his back was turned to her, she couldn't see what he was doing. Was the thing still functioning?

If she were smart, she would get herself off the ground and start running. Except, Vlad was incredibly fast. How had he managed to get to her so quickly?

He must have crossed a distance of at least two hundred feet in less than ten seconds. Her time perception must have gotten distorted because that wasn't humanly possible. Or perhaps he'd been much closer to her than she'd thought when the phone started ringing, and she hadn't heard him approach.

Except, that wasn't possible either unless he'd hovered above the ground. It was too quiet for her not to hear his boots crunching on the snow and the fallen twigs and leaves under it.

"It's still working." Vlad's words shattered the last of her hopes.

He turned around while returning the call. "Mey, we have a problem. Wendy stole my phone and called someone. She says she called her father, but I think she is lying."

Listening to him talk chilled her to the bone. He sounded so cold, so remote.

She'd expected hurt, anger, accusations, but this was much worse. Vlad had simply shut down. His face was expressionless as he looked down at her. "Mey is on her way to pick us up."

She nodded. "I'm sorry. It was a stupid thing to do."

He arched a brow. "Stupid? I wouldn't call it that. How long have you been planning to betray us, Wendy?"

Vlad

As Wendy looked up at Vlad with a pair of teary eyes, his conviction of her guilt wavered. Perhaps she'd really called her father because she missed him?

That would have been stupid, but not criminal.

Except, he'd clearly smelled the lie on her, and he wasn't even a good sniffer of emotions, which was painfully evident by the ease with which she'd managed to fool him.

Wendy had no feelings for him, and the reality-bending kiss they had shared was nothing more than his pheromones in action. He was so desperately attracted to her that some of it must have rubbed off on her, and that residual had been enough to evoke her passionate response.

And it had been passionate.

Wendy could have faked her feelings, but she couldn't have faked the flaring of her arousal. It had started as just a whiff, and when the kissing had gotten more intense, that scent had bloomed.

"I'm sorry," she whispered. "I had to."

He was about to ask why, and who she'd had to call so desperately, when the sound of a car engine diverted his attention.

They were about two hundred feet downhill from the road, so he couldn't see who it belonged to, but as it slowed down and then stopped, he figured it was Mey. All clan phones were equipped with excellent location trackers.

Vlad heard two doors open, and a moment later saw Mey and Bowen coming down the hill toward them.

Bowen cast Wendy a glare that could chill lava. "Did you find out who she called?"

Vlad shook his head and handed him the phone. "You can check the outgoing calls." The screen and the back cover were broken, but the device still worked.

As a Guardian, Bowen knew the override code to unlock every clan phone and didn't need Vlad's. Finding the outgoing call, he redialed it.

From the corner of his eye, Vlad saw Wendy drop her head between her knees and start shaking all over. Resisting the impulse to crouch next to her and take her into his arms, he looked away.

As Bowen put the call on speakerphone, it rang once, twice, and then it was answered by a recording. "This is Director Simmons. Please leave a message, and I will call you back as soon as I can. Have a pleasant day."

Was there a chance that the voice on the recorded message belonged to Wendy's father?

Given Mey and Bowen's angry expressions, it didn't seem so.

Her hands on her hips, Mey glared at Wendy. "You called the program's director? What possessed you to do that?"

Rocking back and forth, Wendy didn't look up and didn't answer either.

"Isn't it obvious?" Bowen sounded pissed. "She is a spy. We need to get out of here pronto." He handed Vlad his phone back and pulled out his own. "Leon. Put Richard and Ingrid in the car and drive down to Redlands. Wendy is a mole, and she ratted us out. They know our location."

"Aren't we going back to pack?" Mey asked.

"No time." Bowen lifted Wendy off the ground as if she was a sack of potatoes and threw her over his shoulder. "Damn." He shook his head. "I was looking forward to eating that roast." He started up the hill.

The Guardian was going to miss out on a tasty meal, but Vlad was going to miss so much more.

He'd been looking forward to a relationship with a girl that he'd thought liked him. Instead, he was left with an empty cavity where his feelings and hopes for Wendy had been.

Mey put her arm around him. "I'm so sorry, Vlad. She had us all fooled, including Edna."

He shook his head. "That's impossible. Edna is our judge, and everyone knows it's impossible to hide malevolent intentions from her."

With her arm still wrapped around him, Mey urged Vlad to keep going. "Wendy must have an additional talent she was hiding from us. She can mask her true emotions somehow."

"Edna's probe goes deep. I can't believe that she didn't sense anything."

"The best liars are those who believe in their own lies. Maybe that's Wendy's trick. She might have a split personality that she can control."

Vlad hadn't studied psychology, so he couldn't comment on Mey's hypothesis.

Explaining Wendy's actions away as a psychological problem could have eased the terrible sense of betrayal he felt, but it didn't help with the numbness that was spreading from his heart to the rest of his body.

Was that how grief felt?

What did humans do when they lost someone they cared about?

The only thing that came to mind was immersing himself in his art and his music or even baking. Anything that could take his mind off the pain would do.

"Can you tell Leon to grab my guitar? I don't care about the rest of the stuff. But I've had it for years, and I would hate to lose it."

Kian

"You were right about the mole." Onegus walked into the war room with a grim expression on his face. "Wendy stole Vlad's phone and called the program's director. They left the cabin and are heading to Redlands."

Kian shook his head. "How the hell did she manage to fool Edna? I thought that her probe was infallible."

"That's not good," Turner muttered. "That cabin belongs to a friend of mine. I don't want him implicated." He pulled out his phone. "If you'll excuse me, I have damage control to take care of."

As Turner walked to the far corner of the room, Kian got up and started pacing. "Who called you? Was it Mey?"

"It was Bowen. He's asking what to do with Wendy."

"I think it's safe for them to get back to the keep. So far, Kalugal is keeping his promise not to interrogate Arwel, and Jin is verifying that no one else attempts to do so either. Once we trade her for Arwel, the threat to the village and the keep will be gone."

Onegus rubbed a hand over the back of his neck. "Let me check with Bowen first. It's not likely, but she might have given the director the keep's location as well. I'm not sure whether he and Leon bothered to blindfold the two humans when they left the keep."

"Tell Bowen that I authorize thralling her. He needs to know for sure whether the keep is safe." Kian raked his fingers through his hair. "I should have thought of that before. The Guardians should have thralled Richard and Wendy to forget where they've been."

"There was a lot going on."

"There still is." Kian walked over to the cooler and pulled out another bottle of beer.

It was his third that day, and it wasn't going to be the last. He and Turner were still working out the details of the exchange, and he planned on calling Kalugal again and continuing their negotiations.

They had settled the prisoner and hostage exchange, but there was so much more they needed to figure out going forward.

Naturally, now that they knew of each other's existence, things could never go back to the way they'd been. Rules of conduct had to be figured out, and safeguards had to be put in place on both sides.

If only there was a way to counteract Kalugal's compulsion, Kian would have felt much better about dealing with the guy. Kian hated the feeling of vulnerability and the fact that every conversation with his cousin required Turner's presence.

Dalhu had mentioned something about learning to resist Navuh's compulsion. But he'd been able to do that only after he'd been away from the island for a while. Navuh's daily devotions were designed to reinforce his hold over his people, and Dalhu remembered that his thought process had become clearer only after he'd been away for about six weeks.

It seemed that compulsion needed tending to, or its power dissipated over time. Generally speaking that was good news, but it wouldn't help Kian when he was face to face with Kalugal.

Onegus ended the call and walked over to Kian. "Bowen says that Wendy only told the director about the cabin and its location. She didn't even speak with him and only left a message on his voicemail."

"Give the director's number to Roni. Maybe he can do something about that voicemail. If we are lucky, the director hasn't had the chance to listen to his messages yet."

Onegus glanced at his watch. "She called him twenty minutes ago, so that's possible."

"Tell Roni to be careful. We don't want any breadcrumbs trail leading back to us."

"I will."

As the chief talked to Roni, Kian reached into his pocket and pulled out the box of cigarillos. Since Arwel had been taken, he was breaking every rule he'd made about smoking and was excusing his weakness as temporary. What made him feel even worse about it was his relief every time Syssi left the war room. It was the mark of a real addiction when he preferred the ability to light up to the company of his wife.

"Roni is on it," Onegus said. "If the director hasn't heard it yet, he's not going to."

"Tell Bowen to blindfold Wendy on the way back and lock her inside her room."

"What for? She can't go anywhere."

"Punishment. I want her to stew until I can talk to her." Kian lit up his cigarillo and took a puff. "I need to figure out what to do with her next, but I can't dedicate mental bandwidth to her issue while I'm dealing with Kalugal."

"We will need to get rid of her." Turner joined them next to the cooler. "We will give her some pocket change and dump her someplace. She can go back to the program."

Kian nodded. "It will be a shame to lose a potential Dormant, but just like Eleanor, Wendy is a rotten apple, and there is no place for her kind in the clan. Naturally, we will have to thrall away her memory of us, and it is going to be a deep scrub. I hope she doesn't end up with brain damage, but I wouldn't get too worked up over it if she does."

Onegus leaned down and pulled out a bottle of water from the cooler. "There is no rush. We can let her stay in the keep for a little while and have her talk to Vanessa. Maybe the girl has issues that can be fixed. We shouldn't give up on a potential Dormant so quickly."

"Once a rotten apple, always a rotten apple." Turner pulled out a chair and straddled it. "I'm not a great believer in redemption. Then again, we need to investigate Wendy's reasons for doing what she has done. They might have been compelling. It reminds me of Sandoval's nephew. The kid had a legitimate reason for betraying his uncle, and after they ironed out their grievances, the two found a way to work together."

Kian lifted a brow. "So, what is your recommendation? You sound undecided, which is atypical for you."

"I want to hear her out first and then decide. In Eleanor's case, there were no redeeming qualities or extenuating circumstances, but there might be in Wendy's."

Arwel

"You know what pisses me off?" Jacki sat on the couch and crossed her arms over her chest.

Arwel could have made a long list of things, but he wondered which item Jacki was choosing to focus on.

"How come my freaking foretelling didn't warn me about any of this? Before, when I got glimpses of things that were about to happen to other people, I assumed it was because their events were more interesting than mine. But I should have known it wasn't true. I didn't see the program in my future, and I definitely didn't see this." She waved her hand at the room. "It's not fair."

Arwel suspected that Jacki's motive for revealing her paranormal talent was to make herself seem more valuable to her captors. Was she worried about what would happen to her when she was left alone with Kalugal and his men?

He sat close to her on the couch and whispered in her ear, "If we can convince Jin not to do it, you won't be left alone in here."

Jacki wrapped her arm around him and put her head on his shoulder. "We don't know that she wants to do it. Your boss might be pressuring her."

"You know Jin. It's probably her idea, and it's a bad one."

"She loves you."

"And I love her, but she must realize that I can't have her sacrificing herself for me. If anything happens to her, I'm not going to survive it, so her sacrifice will be wasted." Hoping that Jin would hear him, Arwel intended to repeat the same thing over and over again. "Without her, I have no reason to go on."

Jacki sighed. "It's neither here nor there. We can't influence her decision."

"I can. If she tunes in and hears what I have to say, she might reconsider."

Looking up at where they suspected the hidden camera was, Jacki shook her head. "I don't think letting our jailers know how much you care for her is a good idea. You should pretend that she's nothing to you." She smirked. "Maybe we should pretend to be warming up to each other to confuse them."

"At this stage of the negotiations, it doesn't matter if they know that Jin is my mate. Her own freedom depends on her ability to release Kalugal, so it's not like they need to threaten to hurt me to make her do that."

"Yeah, I guess I've seen too many spy movies."

"I just want her to know that she is making a mistake. Once she walks in here, she might never come out." His gut twisted on itself, making him nauseous. "I'm never going to forgive Kian or her for doing this. What the hell are they thinking? Kalugal will not believe that she removed the tether, not even if he feels its absence. His best option is to keep her."

"But then he's not going to get Rufsur back, and he seems to like the guy."

Arwel glared at Jacki even though none of this was her fault. "If you were in his shoes, what would you do?"

"I wouldn't abandon my right-hand man."

Naturally, Jacki wasn't thinking strategically. She was thinking with her heart. Getting to know her better, Arwel realized that her rough exterior was a cover for a soft interior. Jacki was loyal, selfless, and she cared deeply about Jin and even about him.

"Kalugal is a calculating fellow. He will make his choice based on what serves him best, and he will choose Jin because she is a greater asset than Rufsur."

"Would you do that? Would you trade a good friend for a talented paranormal?"

"No, but I'm not Kalugal. The quest for wealth and power is not as important to me as it is to him."

"Let me translate it into terms that are more relevant to you. What if the paranormal was someone who could shield your people from Kalugal's compulsion? Would you trade your friend to gain that protection?"

"I might. But you are only reinforcing my point. Kalugal is going to keep Jin even if it means losing Rufsur. That's why the exchange is such a monumental mistake." He looked into Jacki's eyes, but saw Jin's instead. "Don't do that." And to emphasize, he added, "You think that you are doing this for me, but I don't want to lose you. I'm as good as dead without you. So, if you are hearing this, think again before doing something that I'm never going to forgive you for."

Jacki rolled her eyes. "How many times are you going to repeat the same thing in different words?"

"As many times as it takes. I don't know when she's following the tether to you, so I need to keep saying this like a gif on a loop."

"I should just write it on your T-shirt so she can see it through my eyes. Do you think the guard outside will bring us a pen if we ask for it?"

"I doubt it. He'd probably think that we want to use it as a weapon. Besides, Jin would not be the only one who would see the message." Arwel motioned at the camera. "I don't think Kalugal would allow me to keep the shirt if he saw what was written on it."

"You can turn around and sit on the bed facing the wall and your back to the camera."

Jacki's silly idea was meant to cheer him up, but he was too irate to even smile.

"Perhaps you can write the message on my back."

"Nah, then I won't be able to look at your beautiful eyes. They really are gorgeous. There was a guy in the program that had a similar eye color, but his looked dull compared to yours." She looked him up and down. "And the rest of him also paled in comparison to you. When you dress in clothes that actually fit you, you are one hell of a hunk." She waggled her eyebrows.

Jacki wasn't attracted to him. It was all an act, and not even a very convincing one, but it managed to amuse him despite his bad mood.

"I'm glad you approve."

"Oh, I do." She winked. "I think that you and Jin are perfect for each other."

"Good, for a moment there I thought that you were flirting with me."

"I was." She leaned back. "I need to relearn how to do that. I haven't flirted with anyone in ages."

"Your beauty does the work for you. All you need to do is be there, and guys will flock to you. Magnus had to tell the Guardians to ease up because you seemed bothered by all the attention."

"That was because I wasn't interested in any of them. It's never the guy I actually want to pay attention to me."

He arched a brow. "And who might that be?"

She waved a hand in dismissal. "I haven't met him yet, but if I do, I want to make sure that he notices me."

Jin

As Jin followed the tether to Jacki, Arwel looked straight at her through her friend's eyes, his own blazing with barely suppressed anger. "So, if you are hearing this, think again before doing something that I'm never going to forgive you for."

Gasping, she dropped the connection, and the waterworks started in earnest.

He'd sounded so vehement. What if he really wasn't going to forgive her? What if he dumped her?

It could happen.

Their bond hadn't solidified yet, which meant that they were not mated, and Arwel was free to leave her if he wanted.

Maybe he didn't mean it, and it was only worrying that had made him say that?

Perhaps if she kept on listening, she would hear him say something nice about her, like how much he loved her and appreciated what she was doing for him and his clan.

Instead, she heard Jacki tell him how beautiful his eyes were. Was her so-called friend trying to steal her man?

And what was even worse, Arwel seemed to be responding to Jacki's flirting.

"What's wrong?" Kri leaned over.

"Arwel is angry at me for agreeing to the exchange, and he says that he's never going to forgive me." Jin's chin quivered as more tears spilled out of her eyes. She wiped them off with the sleeve of Alena's sweater. "I don't know why I'm such a cry baby all of a sudden. I'm usually not like that."

"It's the stress." Kri patted her knee. "You are also tired. You should get some sleep."

"I tried. I'm too hyped for that." Jin took a shuddering breath.

She hated to admit her fears, but she needed to talk to someone who had insider information about immortal matings and how they worked from the immortal's point of view.

What was the bond supposed to feel like? How would she know that it was there?

Except, it might be different for a female immortal, and Kri's perspective might not explain what Arwel was or wasn't feeling.

Jin cast her a sidelong glance. The girl, or rather female, acted tough and had the muscles to back her swagger, but despite the breadth of her shoulders, Kri wasn't butch. She wore no makeup, and her clothing was appropriate for her Guardian job, but she softened the look with long hair that was kept in a tight braid, and a light-gray Henley shirt with sparkly buttons that she kept hidden under her leather jacket. Those small touches of femininity made a big difference.

"Arwel and Jacki seem to be getting very close," Jin said in a near whisper. "What if he chooses her over me? He said that our bond didn't solidify yet. Jacki is much prettier than me, and now that they are stuck together, he's definitely noticing her."

Kri shook her head. "Arwel is in love with you. He might like Jacki, he might even show appreciation for her good looks and her misguided heroics, but that's as far as it goes. You have nothing to worry about."

"You don't see them together as I do. They often sit with their arms around each other, and they whisper in each other's ears. I know it's necessary so they are not overheard, but still, they don't need to act so familiarly with one another. I wouldn't put my arm around my cousin and whisper in his ear so intimately, let alone a guy who I know is in a relationship with another woman."

Nodding, Kri twisted the end of her braid around her finger. "I get why you are upset. I would be too. But I'm certain that there is nothing romantic going on between them. I watched Arwel with you. His entire expression changed every time you entered the room."

"Really?" Jin grabbed a tissue and blew her nose.

Kri smiled. "Really. I'm not one to make things up even for a good cause. While all the unmated males were flirting with Jacki, Arwel hardly spared her a glance."

"Things might have changed in captivity. They only have each other, and as you've pointed out, she also tried to save him, which he is surely grateful for. That's enough to spark something that wasn't there before."

The Guardian shook her head. "I've known Arwel for many years, and he is like a brother to me. Most of my Guardian training was with him, and after that, we served together. Since meeting you, he is not the same man that he was before. He's smiling more, and that damn perpetually suffering expression is gone from his face. I haven't seen him get drunk even once, while before he met you the guy was sober only when going out on missions. Do you really think that anything short of falling in love could have made such a change?"

"Mey made a similar comment. She said that Arwel had the tormented artist look."

"You see? Your sister noticed the same thing." Kri let go of her braid and leaned back in the seat. "Feeling better?"

"Much. Thank you."

"Any time. Now try to get some sleep." The Guardian closed her eyes.

Following Kri's example, Jin lowered the back of her seat and closed her eyes, but instead of dozing off, she followed the tether to Jacki once more.

"I'm scared." Arwel looked into Jacki's eyes. "We haven't seen Kalugal even once since he brought us here, and I can't access his emotional grid without him being close. I don't know what his intentions are."

"It's obvious. He wants to get rid of the tether."

"The question is how far is he willing to go to accomplish that. He might decide that killing Jin is the most expedient way to do so, and there is nothing I can do to stop him."

"You can't, but your friends can. You heard what Rufsur said."

Arwel rubbed his temples between two fingers. "As we've seen, the best plans can go to shit. There are no guarantees."

"That's life. As an immortal, you are not as vulnerable, so you don't experience it as acutely as I do as a human, but I know that my life can get snuffed out in an instant. Except, I don't dwell on it because that would be paralyzing. I just do what I can to survive and hope for the best."

"If I lose Jin, I don't want to survive. I can't go on without her."

The sheen of tears in his eyes cut into Jin's heart, and if she could, she would have used Jacki's arms to embrace him and comfort him.

But Jacki didn't need her to animate her arms. Reaching for Arwel, she wrapped them around him. "Have faith. Everything will turn out okay. I promise."

"How can you promise that?" He leaned his forehead against hers. "Did you have a vision?"

"No, but I have a good gut feeling, and I don't get those often. I'm a glass-half-empty kind of girl, and I usually brace for the worst."

Kian

Unease churning in his stomach, Kian paced the length of the war room. Ever since he'd laid out the exchange plan for Kalugal, he had a niggling feeling that they were forgetting something important.

With Turner there, Kian should have felt more confident, but no one was infallible, and they were dealing with an unknown.

Given the circumstances, Kalugal had been a reasonable and agreeable negotiation partner, but that didn't mean that he was a good guy, or that he had nothing sinister and underhanded planned.

After all, Kalugal was Navuh's son, which meant that he was smart, ruthless, and had questionable morals at best, none at worst.

Lokan was Navuh's son as well, and he wasn't all bad, but he wasn't good either. He'd had no qualms about sacrificing Ella and Vivian to achieve his objective, and Kian was certain that Kalugal wouldn't hesitate to sacrifice Jin as well as his lieutenant to achieve his.

They had put in place every safeguard imaginable, but the trade was not as fail-proof as Kian would have liked it to be.

"Do you have any plans to use Lokan?" Syssi asked.

"I'm keeping him as backup. I'd rather not expose his involvement with the clan yet."

Syssi shook her head. "Lokan is playing a dangerous game. He is living with an immortal female. How long does he think he can keep it a secret? We need to bring him and Carol in."

"Not yet." Kian pulled out a chair next to his wife. "When it gets hot for him, and there is no other choice, I'll do that. But in the meantime, he is our ears and eyes on the island. The sense of security it gives me is too precious to give up. If Navuh ever plans something big against the clan, I want to know about it ahead of time. This could make the difference between surviving an attack and not."

"We could pretend to have captured Lokan," Turner said. "Which isn't a lie because we did. You can tell Kalugal that you are holding his brother prisoner. That should be a better deterrent than holding his second-in-command hostage."

"I'm not sure about that." Kian crossed his arms over his chest. "Kalugal's lieutenant has been by his side since the very beginning, and Jin says that he seems fond of him. Lokan might as well be a stranger, and they have never interacted before as brothers or even as members of the Brotherhood. Back then, Kalugal was a young and unimportant commander, while Lokan was already at the top of the Brotherhood's hierarchy."

Turner looked skeptical. "Still, Lokan is his one real brother, son of Kalugal's mother. That carries a lot of weight. I think Lokan would be as important to Kalugal as Rufsur, and having two hostages is better than one."

If Turner thought it was a good idea, Kian wasn't going to argue against it. "Let's see what Lokan thinks about it." He pulled out his phone and placed the call.

"Hello, Kian. I was wondering when you were going to call me with instructions. Carol and I are sitting in the hotel room and biting our nails."

"No, we are not." Carol laughed. "We've been busy doing other things."

Lokan cleared his throat. "Magnus told us that the trade is happening tonight."

"How can we help?" Carol asked.

"That's what I'm calling about. We had an idea to use you as a fake hostage. We can claim that we captured you, and if your brother kills Jin, we will kill you. We won't do that, of course, but Kalugal doesn't know that."

"He won't care. I doubt that he even remembers what I look like."

"You are still his one and only brother, and you are the son of his mother. Part of the deal was to let Kalugal talk with Areana after the trade was made, and even though he tried to hide it, he seemed eager for that. He cares about her, and he wouldn't want to be responsible for the anguish your death would bring her."

"Frankly, I can't predict what Kalugal would do because I don't know him. But I'm willing to put on an act in exchange for another foundation stone for my home in the village."

At his core Lokan was an opportunist, who always looked for his angle in the game, but at least he was upfront about it, and so far he'd helped whenever Kian had asked him to.

"At this rate, you'll have your house ready in no time. But you can't move in until you move out from your island home, and neither of us is interested in that. Not yet."

"I'm playing the long game. But that's not my only motivation. If my mother knows what's going on, which I'm sure she does because Annani keeps her updated, she is probably worried, and she'd appreciate it if I help in any way I can. If you want to offer me in exchange for Arwel, I will gladly do that."

Carol gasped. "No way."

"Relax, darling. Kalugal is not going to harm me. Why would he?"

"Because you are first in line for the throne, so to speak. You are the firstborn son."

"Kalugal claims that he is not interested in the island," Kian said. "He says that it's Lokan's for the taking."

"And you believe him?" Carol asked.

"I do. I have a feeling that Kalugal has bigger plans than the island, and I would love to find out what they are."

"If you trade me for Arwel and Jacki, I can get Kalugal talking."

"I appreciate the offer, but Kalugal's top priority is to get rid of the tether."

"Or the spy who holds it," Lokan said.

"He offered to mate her."

"What?" Carol grabbed the phone from Lokan. "Jin is already mated."

"Kalugal doesn't know that, and I didn't volunteer the information. As long as he believes that it's a possibility, he won't do anything rash. I don't want him to feel cornered."

"But you didn't agree to that, right?"

Kian smiled as he imagined the ferocious expression on Carol's cherubic face. "I told him that it wasn't going to happen and that political marriages are a thing of the past. But he might still think of it as an option, and I prefer to leave it at that."

"It's actually not a bad idea," Lokan said.

"How can you say such a thing?" Carol seethed. "What if Kian offered me as a political bride. Would you be okay with that too?"

"No, but that's different."

"How so?"

"Arwel isn't me, and Jin isn't you. Maybe they are not fated mates."

Kian cleared his throat. "You can keep arguing after we end the call. Just be ready to get picked up."

"Carol is not coming with me." Lokan's tone no longer sounded amused.

"Of course not. She can stay at the hotel."

"Like hell!" Carol exploded. "I'm going with you."

Jin

"Can you turn the heat on?" Jin huddled inside Alena's coat.

Gregor glanced at her in the rearview mirror. "It's boiling in here."

Jin had expected the weather to be more forgiving in San Francisco, but as soon as the pilot had opened the jet's door, she'd been blasted with a cold gust that had taken her breath away. Luckily, crossing the distance to Gregor's car had taken only a couple of minutes, but unluckily, he hadn't turned the heat on, or rather not enough to keep her warm.

"Jin is sick." Kri reached for the control and turned up the heat. "Take your coat off if you're too hot." She shrugged her leather jacket off and tossed it on the back seat.

Jin pulled it over her knees. "Can we stop at a CVS? I need to load up on meds."

Gregor shook his head. "I'd rather not. Turner gave me instructions to drive through the mall, but that's only to make sure we don't have a tail. I don't want to stop."

Kri turned around to face Jin. "Call Vivian and tell her what you need. She can get it for you."

"That's a great idea. I'll text her the list."

Thanks to Kri, Jin hadn't left her purse behind in the club and could pay Vivian back. She hadn't spent any of the pocket money Kian had given her before the mission.

"How are you going to use Turner's maneuver?" Kri asked. "Did you leave another car in the mall?"

"Turner arranged everything. He had a rental car delivered to the mall's parking lot. It has a coded lock, and I have the numbers."

"Cool." Kri leaned back. "Don't you love modern technology? Next thing we know, there will be services delivering driverless cars to us that we can activate from our phones. Like Uber or Lyft, but without the driver."

"I think they already have those in Europe," Jin said. "Personally, though, I don't trust machines that much. Computers malfunction, and I don't want to be stuck inside a driverless car when that happens."

Kri turned around and smiled. "Then you're not going to like living in the village. Our cars take over a few miles before we get home, and the windows automatically turn opaque. It's a safety precaution so if a clan member gets captured he or she can't reveal the village's location."

"So how come Arwel knows it?"

"He is a head Guardian," Gregor said. "And so is Kri. They and the council members are the only ones who know the exact location of the village and the codes to open the underground tunnel. They should have never been allowed anywhere near Kalugal. That was one hell of a costly mistake."

Kri nodded. "He is right."

It was comforting to realize that the mess wasn't entirely her fault, and that Kian and Turner shared in the blame. Then again, nothing could have kept Arwel away from her while she'd tethered Kalugal, so it was back on her. Or was it on Arwel?

Heck, it was everyone's and no one's fault.

"Yamanu is a head Guardian too," Kri said, "but in his case Kian didn't have a choice. We don't have anyone else who can shroud such a large area and thrall so many humans at once."

"Yamanu is careful," Gregor said. "He is staying as far as he can from Kalugal's place while maintaining the shroud, and he has earplugs in."

After changing cars in the mall's parking lot, they continued out of the city for another half an hour or so, and when Gregor parked in front of the motel, it was after seven in the evening.

The place looked like it wasn't ready to receive guests yet, but all Jin cared about was crawling under the blanket and putting her head on a pillow. She was sleep-deprived, sick, and she had a long night in front of her.

Talk about bad timing.

Maybe Kalugal could wait until morning?

Except, even if he did, Kian wanted to make the trade at night. Besides, despite how exhausted she was, Jin doubted that she could sleep.

When Kri opened the back door and offered her a hand up, she reluctantly accepted it. "I feel like an old woman." She didn't object when the Guardian wrapped her arm around her middle and propped her up.

"I don't know how an old woman feels, but the doctor said that you'll be fine in a day or two."

Poor Kri. She was trying to be supportive, and she was incredibly helpful, but she had no idea what it felt like to be so weak and helpless. Immortals never got sick, and Kri was in top physical shape.

"After this is all over, I want to join your self-defense class. I need to get stronger."

Kri grinned. "Awesome."

The door to one of the ground floor rooms opened, and Vivian stepped out. "Welcome to our home away from home." She waved them over.

As soon as they reached her, Vivian lifted her hand and put it on Jin's forehead. "I got you the NyQuil and

DayQuil that you asked for, and I also got you chicken soup."

"Thank you." Jin offered her a placid smile.

Inside, the room was much nicer than the exterior of the motel had suggested. There were two full beds, a table with three chairs, and a door that was opened to the adjacent room.

"Magnus and I are right over there." Vivian pointed. "As soon as I heard that you were coming back, I moved the Guardians who were staying here into another room." She took Jin's hand and led her to the dining table. "Eat your soup before it gets cold."

"Thank you for warming the room up." Jin took her coat off and draped it over the back of the chair. "And for everything else."

Vivian patted her arm. "I haven't been immortal long enough to forget how it feels to have a damn cold."

As Jin sat down, the door opened, and Carol came in. "Miss me?" She walked over and gave Jin a hug and a kiss on the cheek. "I heard that you were sick."

Jin nodded. "I'm so glad to see you, but what are you doing here?"

Carol pulled out a chair and sat down. "Kian, or rather Turner, wanted Lokan to be on standby in case his compulsion ability was needed. We flew overnight and stayed at a nice hotel." She looked around the room. "Much nicer than this place. But anyway, Kian came up with the idea to use Lokan as an additional hostage. Not for real, of course, but just as more leverage on Kalugal."

"Eat your soup." Vivian pointed at the takeout container and then turned to Kri. "There is enough for you too."

"Bleh." Kri took her leather jacket off and dropped it on one of the beds. "I hate the stuff."

Jin wasn't crazy about chicken soup either. Her mother, who also believed in its supposed healing power, had fed it to Jin and Mey not only when they'd gotten sick, but also as a preemptive measure nearly every winter day.

Needless to say, they both grew to hate it.

"I'll have some." Carol reached for the second container. "Does it come with noodles or matzo balls?"

"Noodles," Vivian said.

Jin removed the lid from the container and picked up the plastic spoon that came with the meal.

Fighting nausea, she put a spoonful in her mouth and tried not to gag. It wasn't the soup's fault. The broth was only a little too salty, and the noodles were quite good, but her stomach's churning had little to do with the food.

She was worried, stressed and tired, but she didn't want to repay Vivian's kindness with rudeness. She could force down a few spoonfuls before excusing herself, getting into one of the beds, and crawling under the blanket.

Kalugal

Kalugal brought up the feed from the camera scanning the front yard. "What do you think about the gazebo for my meeting with the spy?"

Rufsur leaned over his shoulder. "Your cranky cousin might object because of the roof. His snipers wouldn't have a clear shot at your head."

Kalugal turned and smiled at his friend. "So, it occurred to you too that he is likely to use drones?"

"They are not going to sit on top of our fence where we can take them out easily, and other than that, there is no conveniently available spot. There are no utility poles or even street lamps to perch on top of. So, unless he brings in a crane or two, drones are his best option."

Kalugal leaned back in his chair and gazed at his front yard, following the surveillance camera as it swiveled around. It was beautifully done, and the landscaping was perfect. There were no tall trees for anyone to hide in, only flowers and bushes that were artfully arranged.

Regrettably, he wasn't set up for offense, and he didn't have drones. His men were stationed on the roof of the house, exposed to Kian's remote-controlled equipment.

He was at a disadvantage, and they both knew that.

His setup was defensive, with state-of-the-art security systems, a bunker that could withstand bombing, and a couple of short escape routes. His men had the best rifles money could buy and an assortment of cold weapons, but that was the extent of it.

Was Kian better equipped?

He could only speculate, but it made sense that the clan would be better armed than he was, even if it was only to defend themselves. Kalugal doubted that his father had eased up on his efforts to eliminate his archnemesis and her progeny.

They needed to be prepared.

Kalugal, on the other hand, had managed to fly under his father's radar. Or so he hoped. Evidently, his mother didn't believe that he had perished during WWII, and she'd probably shared her thoughts with her mate, which made Kalugal wonder why Navuh had never come after him or at least tried to find him.

If Kian had located him, then Navuh could have done so as well.

"What do you want to do with the gazebo?" Rufsur asked.

"I want it to be set up nicely as if it's a romantic date. I'll call Kian to finalize the details of the trade and to let him know that my men are going to venture outside to prepare the gazebo for the meeting. I want the spy to be comfortable and relaxed. I don't know much about her ability, but she will have an easier time if she isn't stressed."

"Got it." Rufsur winked. "A tablecloth for the table, soft cushions for the chairs, candles, wine, a fancy midnight snack. The works."

The bunker was accessible through a tunnel from inside the house, and that was how his men were going to leave the bunker and come back.

The access was set up with a double door system that was controlled from inside the bunker during a lockdown, so getting in without invitation was nearly impossible. The foot-thick reinforced doors could withstand explosives, and the mechanism operating them was just as secure.

With the right equipment, Kian could potentially blow up the first door or the walls around it, but that would be as far as he would get.

The moment the first barrier was breached, all hell would rain down on those trying to cross the distance to the other door. They would be buried alive, and then burned to a crisp. Not even immortals could survive that.

"What about the lights?" Rufsur asked. "We can put on strong ones so the entire front yard is bright and Kian is happy or soft ones that will make the mood more romantic."

"Even if he uses drones, he has no need for strong lights, or any. They are equipped with night vision."

"Just in case, ask him. I don't want a trigger-happy immortal to freak out and activate the drone's guns. Especially since they will be aimed at your head."

Kalugal nodded. "I'll do that." He pulled his phone out and placed the call to Kian.

"Good evening, cousin." As usual, Kian's voice was gruff, but by now Kalugal realized that it didn't mean that he was angry. That was his normal speaking voice.

A charmer, he was not.

"I want to iron out all the small details. Looking at my front yard, I decided that the gazebo would be a nice place to conduct my meeting with Jin. I need to send my men out to set the place up, so don't shoot at them."

"I'll let the field commander know. What else?"

This confirmed Kalugal's suspicion that Kian wasn't in the area and was managing everything from the clan's central location, wherever that might be.

That was not so good, but Kalugal could work with that. The good news was that Kian hadn't objected to the gazebo idea.

"The lighting. Do you want me to turn on the floodlights, or will soft illumination suffice?"

Kian chuckled. "Are you planning a romantic dinner?"

"I want Jin to feel comfortable. If she is stressed, she might not be able to access her talent. We all know that paranormal abilities require a calm mind and concentration. I have heaters in the gazebo, so she'll be warm, and I'll have the table set up for a midnight snack. I'm just being a gracious host."

"I bet. Do whatever you want with the lights. It doesn't make a difference to us."

"I figured that your drones were equipped with night vision."

"Good guess. But what would immortal warriors need with night vision equipment? We can see perfectly well in starlight."

"You've just confirmed my suspicion that you're not in the area. It's cloudy here tonight, and visibility is minimal, even for immortals."

"It will do."

"Of course. Your drones will be equipped with night vision."

Kian

Kian cast a quick glance at Turner, who shrugged and mouthed, "Smart guy."

"What makes you think we will be using drones?"

"It's obvious. Where are you going to hide your snipers? The trees in the neighbors' houses are not tall enough or strong enough to provide support for a grown man or even a slight woman, and sitting on top of my fence would leave your men exposed. If I were you, I would employ drones."

Kian wondered if Kalugal even had them. He didn't engage in offensive or recon operations, so he had no use for such sophisticated equipment. Still, given the guy's penchant for expensive toys, he might have invested in a drone or two just because he had the money to throw around.

"For someone who is engaged mainly in accumulating wealth, you are very well informed about the latest in weaponry. Are you dealing in that as well?"

Kalugal chuckled. "No, cousin. I don't deal in weapons, or drugs, or prostitution, or anything else you might sneer at."

"If you were dealing only in stocks and shares, you wouldn't have needed a bunker."

"Did you forget that I am a fugitive? My father is most likely still looking for me, and I need to protect myself."

"That seems like a waste of resources. I know what it costs to build a bunker that size. What else are you doing in there?"

"That's my business, Kian."

"As long as you don't keep slaves down there or produce meth, I don't really care."

"I can assure you that I don't engage in either of those activities. I'm a collector, and I like to keep my treasures in a controlled environment and safe from theft and vandalism. Does that satisfy your curiosity?"

"Partly. It's good to know that you're not doing anything illegal."

Kalugal chuckled. "I wouldn't go that far. Some of the things I have in here should be in a museum, and the countries they've been collected from don't allow their extraction, but since I paid for their discovery, I think they belong to me."

"That's an interesting hobby."

"You have no idea."

So far, the things Kian was slowly discovering about Kalugal were encouraging.

The guy wanted to make Jin comfortable, which meant that he wasn't planning on killing her. It seemed like he was still entertaining the idea of charming her into mating him.

His cousin was a dishonest businessman, gaining an unfair advantage by getting insider information about mergers and acquisitions before they were publicly announced, but he wasn't a murderer, a drug dealer, or a trafficker. His artifact hobby was of no interest to Kian, and he didn't care which laws Kalugal was breaking to smuggle them out of the countries he'd collected them in.

If that was all the case, and there were no hidden skeletons in the guy's closet, Kian would have no problem forging an alliance with him.

"When we can talk more leisurely, I would love to hear more about your hobby. I bet you have many fascinating stories about the things you've found."

"With pleasure."

Was it Kian's imagination or had Kalugal sounded eager for a meeting that had nothing to do with the crisis they were dealing with?

Time would tell.

For now, they had to discuss the details of the exchange. "We need to decide on the exact sequence of who comes out first and with whom."

Kalugal chuckled. "I'm sure you have it all figured out."

"Obviously. You will send your lieutenant out first, on his own. When we have him in our custody, the field commander will escort Jin to your gate, where you and Arwel will be waiting. Arwel and Jin will exchange places, you escort Jin to your pavilion, and hopefully the whole fiasco will be over in less than an hour."

Kian hadn't mentioned Lokan yet, and he was wondering if he should do that now or right before the exchange took place.

Truth be told, he was reluctant to issue the threat. It had been difficult to pretend that he would hurt Areana if any harm befell Jin, not only because it was a lie, but because so far Kalugal had acted in a very civilized way. Kian didn't want to burn the tenuous bridge they had built between them by also threatening to kill the guy's brother.

Perhaps he should discuss it with Turner and Syssi first. Turner's talent was clarity as to the advantages and disadvantages of such a step, while Syssi's talent was understanding the emotional impact such a threat might have on Kalugal, and how it could affect his decisions.

Kalugal snorted. "This situation reminds me of the riddle about the farmer who has a goat, a cabbage, and a wolf, and needs to cross the river with all three but can only take one at a time. If he takes the cabbage and leaves the wolf and the goat behind, the wolf is going to eat the goat. If the goat and the cabbage are left alone, the goat will eat the cabbage. How does he do it?"

"I know the solution to the riddle, but who is the wolf, the cabbage, and the goat in our story, and how does the analogy fit?"

"If I send out Rufsur together with Arwel, Rufsur might be armed and kill Jin in passing, that's why you want me to send him out first. You don't want him anywhere near her until your men have searched him and made sure that he is unarmed. So, he is the wolf, and Jin is the goat. I guess that makes Arwel the cabbage."

"I don't think he would appreciate the analogy. But you are right about my motive for requesting that your man come out first."

"I'm not going to kill your spy. But we've already covered that, and I don't like repeating myself."

Jin

"Once we get out of the car, put these in." Magnus handed Jin a set of high-quality earplugs. "Keep them in until you pass Arwel."

She nodded. "This is so Kalugal can't compel me to come to him before releasing Arwel."

"Precisely." He put his hand on her shoulder. "How are you holding up?"

Jin had taken four Motrins before leaving the motel, and she was wearing Alena's warm coat over a thick sweater, but she was still shivering.

"I think that the sanctuary's doctor has no experience in treating humans. The last time I ran a high fever that Motrin couldn't take care of, it was a case of strep throat. I might need antibiotics." She huddled inside the coat. "I can't stop shivering."

Magnus cast her a worried glance. "Why didn't you say so before? We need to postpone the trade."

Jin shook her head. "I want this to be over already. Then I'll see a human doctor, get the medication I need, and spend a week in bed. Since this nightmare began, I haven't slept for more than one hour straight. I'm exhausted, but I can't fall asleep."

"The adrenaline is keeping you going." Magnus reached for the pack of bottled water he'd put on the back seat. "Vivian told me to keep you hydrated."

"Thank you."

Sweet Vivian. She'd fussed around Jin, trying to get her to rest and relax. She'd also fed her chicken soup until Jin refused to take another spoonful. Not only had it not done any good, it had made things worse.

She felt as if there was a gallon of soup sloshing around in her stomach, and it was a struggle to keep it down. If she didn't hate barfing as much as she did, she would have excused herself to the bathroom and puked it all out in the toilet.

"Can you take a deep breath, or are you too congested?"

"Too congested." She smiled at him. "Were you going to suggest a relaxation technique?"

"It works." He demonstrated. "Breathe in as deeply as you can, hold it for a couple of seconds, and then release the air through your mouth." He produced a whoosh sound while doing just that.

"I'll give it a try."

They were parked outside the house they'd stayed in before, waiting for the show to begin.

Precisely at midnight, Kalugal was going to send out his right-hand man, and once the guy was in the Guardians' custody, they were going to bring him into the house to search him more thoroughly before taking him to the motel. After that was done, Magnus would drive up to Kalugal's gate and wait for it to open.

When Kalugal showed up with Arwel, Magnus was going to escort Jin to the midpoint, and then walk back together with Arwel.

After that, she would be on her own.

Jin wasn't sure what she dreaded more, seeing the angry look in Arwel's eyes or being left alone with Kalugal and his compulsion power. After experiencing its effects once, she never wanted to be in that helpless and hopeless situation again.

Having someone else take control of her body had been awful, and that was when all she'd suffered through was being stuck in a crouch and unable to move or talk.

If Kalugal was the vindictive type, he could compel her to strip naked in front of his men, and she would do that. Except, right now, what bothered her most about that scenario was not the nudity but the cold.

Just thinking about being naked made her shiver.

"What's wrong?" Magnus looked at her with worried eyes. "Are you feeling worse?"

"No." She sighed. "I'm just having silly thoughts that are not helping me to calm down. Do you know any jokes? I need something to distract me."

He chuckled. "As of late, my arsenal is comprised solely of lame dad jokes."

The funny thing was that Magnus sounded more proud of it than embarrassed.

"Perfect. That's exactly what I need."

"Okay." He grinned. "Tell me something, how does a penguin build its house?"

"Makes a hole in the snow?"

"Igloos it together."

Jin's laughter opened the floodgates to Magnus's store of lame jokes.

"Why is Peter Pan always flying?"

"Because he can?"

"He never lands."

Arwel

Jacki looked at her watch. "It's almost time."

Arwel took her hand and clasped it between his two. "I hate leaving you alone here."

She gave him an unconvincing smile. "I'll be fine for the one hour tops that it will take Jin to convince Kalugal that the tether is gone. He's going to release me right after that."

They both knew that it was the best-case scenario and that not everything was going to work as planned. Hopefully, it would be limited to small bumps in the road, like Jin taking longer than they thought it would, or Kalugal coming up with more demands at the last moment.

Arwel didn't even want to contemplate the worst case scenario.

When the door opened, he was surprised to see Rufsur walk in. "Aren't you supposed to get ready to leave?"

Was Kalugal planning to trick them and send another man? That hadn't occurred to him, but if Kalugal planned on killing Jin, he might have decided to send someone he considered disposable.

"I'm leaving in a few minutes." He rubbed his hand over the back of his neck. "I came to say goodbye to Jacki." He took a step toward her. "After this is over, we are not going to see each other again. Not unless we want to, that is. I was wondering whether you'd had time to consider my proposition to meet me for a dinner or a drink somewhere."

Jacki shook her head. "I'm afraid that won't be possible for reasons that have nothing to do with you."

The smile evaporated from Rufsur's face. "I see. Well, it was worth a try."

Jacki got up and put a hand on his arm. "I'm not giving you an excuse. I'm not from around here, and right now, my life is one big mess. I don't have a job or a place to stay, and until that is taken care of, I can't afford to date. If I could, I would have said yes."

"Then say yes. I can help you solve all of those problems. With me, you wouldn't need to pay for anything. I'm old school."

Jacki smiled sadly. "I like that about you, and I hope that it will help you understand the main reason why I can't date you. You are an immortal, and I am human. If I were the kind of girl who is fine with short-term flings, I would have taken you up on your offer in a heartbeat.

But I'm the type who is only interested in a life-long commitment, and that's impossible for us."

"I understand." Rufsur turned to Arwel. "What are you going to do with Jacki? She knows about immortals, but she can't be thralled or compelled to forget what she knows."

The guy sounded worried for her, which was touching. Maybe after Jacki was free, he would tell the guy that she was a possible Dormant and might turn immortal. But not as long as she was still a captive. Her chances of release would turn to zero.

"We trust her. Jacki has proved herself as a valuable member of our team."

Rufsur lifted a brow. "You didn't tell her what you were."

"No, but she also tried to save me. Don't worry about her." Arwel looked at Jacki. "Your future is secure with the clan."

"Do you have other humans living with you?" Rufsur still sounded doubtful, and rightfully so.

"One, and he was an immune as well."

"Was?"

The guy didn't miss much. No wonder Kalugal had made him his right-hand man.

"He still is. I meant to say that we let him in on the secret even though we knew he was immune. The guy is a strategic genius, and he is very good at keeping secrets. He's been an invaluable addition to the clan."

Turner was also immortal now, but he had known their secret long before approaching Kian and asking to attempt transition.

Rufsur frowned. "Don't tell me that Kian appointed a human as his second-in-command."

Kian must have told Kalugal that Turner was on standby, ready to take over for Kian if Kalugal attempted to compel him.

"Kian doesn't have a second-in-command. The guy I'm talking about is an outside contractor. We've used his services many times in the past, and apparently Kian asked for his help in this. He is definitely capable of taking over for Kian if needed."

Rufsur shook his head. "I can't believe that you let a human reach such a vital position in your organization." He glanced at his watch. "But that's a conversation for another time." He smiled at Arwel. "If your friends are not going to lock me up in a cellar, we can continue our talk while the spy does her thing."

Arwel offered Rufsur his hand. "Gladly."

Kalugal

In a rare display of affection, Kalugal embraced Rufsur and clapped him on the back. "I owe you for this."

Rufsur chuckled. "You bet. I get to choose next month's hunting grounds."

"You've got it."

"It's five minutes to midnight." Phinas punched in the code to open the first door leading to the tunnel.

"Good luck with the spy," Rufsur said as he walked out.

"You too."

Kalugal waited until Phinas closed the door and then headed back to his office. Bringing up the camera feeds, he watched Rufsur make his way into the house, then walk out the side door and stride toward the gate.

"Now?" Phinas asked.

"Open the gate."

Two men were on the roof, and three more were out in the gazebo, preparing the place for his meeting with the spy. The two on the roof had their rifles aimed at the gate, and those in the gazebo carried an assortment of cold and hot weapons.

It was more for show than anything else.

Kian's drones were hovering over the grounds and could take out any of them in an instant.

The truth was that they were outclassed, and the only real advantage they had was the bunker, where they could hole up for months if needed. Except Kian didn't know that, and it was crucial that he remain ignorant as to Kalugal's real military power.

As per their agreement, Kian's men waited for Rufsur across the street, and the first thing they did when he reached them was to frisk him.

That had been expected, and Rufsur had nothing on him aside from a phone, which they examined as well.

One of the men lifted it in the air and then made a show of putting it on the sidewalk.

Careful bastards. But then Kalugal would have done the same. Aside from providing its location, which was damaging enough on its own, all kinds of damage could be done with something as small as a cellphone. Its electronics could be replaced with powerful explosives, which Rufsur could have potentially activated once he reached their headquarters.

A van pulled up to the curb, blocking the view, but when it pulled out, Rufsur and Kian's men were gone.

"Time for stage two." Kalugal swiveled his chair to face Phinas. "Get Arwel and put restraints on him. I'll meet you at the entrance to the tunnel."

"What about the blindfold?"

"Wait for me to get there before you put it on him. I want to talk to him first."

"Won't it be a violation of your agreement with Kian?"

"I just want to say goodbye and apologize for the inconvenience."

Phinas arched a brow. "Regardless of your good intentions, it might be seen as a breach."

Kalugal clapped him on the back. "Don't worry about it."

"Yes, sir."

That was the good thing about Phinas. He knew when to quit arguing and just do as he was told.

Shrugging on his wool jacket, Kalugal took a quick glance at his hazy reflection in the monitor. It had been a very long time since anyone other than his men had seen his real face, and it felt odd to proceed without shrouding himself in one of his guises. It was like going out naked in public, exposed, even vulnerable.

He shook his head.

Habits were stronger than willpower, hijacking a person's brain, or rather circumventing it. Sometimes it was beneficial, like always putting his car keys in the same place so he didn't need to dedicate any cognitive bandwidth to locating them. But the habit of always wearing a shroud made him anxious about being seen, and that was detrimental to his self-perception.

When Kalugal got to the tunnel's door, Phinas had already put handcuffs on Arwel's wrists and was now attaching shackles to his ankles.

Looking at Kalugal, Arwel lifted his hands. "Is this really necessary?"

"I don't want you to run for it the moment we open the gate. But if you are uncomfortable with the restrains, I can compel you to move only when I say so."

Arwel dropped his hands. "I prefer the shackles."

"That's what I thought. I will also need to blindfold you."

"How am I going to walk out like that?"

"I'll lead you, and once we are outside, I'll remove the blindfold. You can walk with the shackles, and once the spy is inside my property, I'll toss the keys to your friends."

Arwel let out a breath. "It's not like I have a choice in the matter." He pinned Kalugal with a hard stare. "A word of warning. If you harm a hair on Jin's head, I will come after you. I don't care how long it takes, or what I have to do, but I'll have my vengeance."

Kalugal had expected a warning regarding the immune who stayed behind, but not regarding the spy, and certainly not the vehemence with which it had been delivered.

Suddenly, the pieces of the puzzle fell into place.

Jacki wasn't Arwel's girlfriend, or even someone he was interested in. The spy was. He had risked exposure and jumped the shooter not to protect Jacki, but to protect Jin, which meant that she wasn't immortal. Otherwise, Arwel would not have been so desperate to protect her because even if she got shot, nothing serious would have happened to her.

Kalugal shook his head. "Loving a human female is a mistake, my friend. You shouldn't have allowed yourself to fall for her. I will not harm her, you have my word, but she will get old and eventually die, leaving you heartbroken."

"I'll treasure every moment I have with her."

The man was a fool, but supposedly love did that to people. Kalugal had never experienced it, so he couldn't judge Arwel.

"Best of luck with that." He clapped the guy on his back. "Before Phinas puts the blindfold on you, I just wanted to offer my apologies for your brief imprisonment. No hard feelings, eh?"

"That depends on whether Jin comes back unharmed. If all I suffer at your hands is a short rest in your bunker, then we are good."

Jin

As Jin waited for the gate to open, the adrenaline in her system kept her legs from turning into jelly, but it also made her heart thud loudly in her chest. If she weren't so young, she would have feared heart failure.

Then again, young people died from heart problems, and she might have an undiagnosed condition.

Stop it.

The last thing she needed was to pile on more stress. She was at the end of her rope, operating on fumes and holding on by a thread.

Finally, the gate started moving, and Jin held her breath, only to release it in a whoosh when it opened all the way. "Why is Arwel shackled?"

Magnus shrugged and pointed to his ear.

How could she have forgotten that both of them were wearing earplugs? No outside sounds filtered through them, but apparently her inner turmoil was enough to fill the void.

As Arwel started walking toward them, Magnus put his hand on her shoulder, gave it a little squeeze, nodded, and pointed at her ear.

His expression combined with that small gesture conveyed everything he wanted to tell her. Good luck, it's time to go, and a reminder to take out her earplugs.

Walking toward Arwel, Jin dreaded what she might see on his face when he got closer. Would he be angry? Indifferent? What was he going to say to her?

With shaking hands, she took out the earplugs and put them in the pocket of Alena's coat.

But she should have known him better.

The first thing she saw clearly were his eyes, which were two glowing turquoise beacons of light, and the next were his lips, which were mouthing, "I love you."

Unable to resist the urge to hold him, she ran up to Arwel and put her arms around him. "I love you so much. Please don't be angry at me for doing this."

He couldn't return the embrace because his hands were shackled, and the handcuffs chained to his ankle restraints. Instead, he leaned his head on her shoulder. "I'm not angry. I'm terrified."

"Please keep moving," Kalugal commanded, but he didn't infuse his voice with compulsion.

"I love you." Jin quickly kissed Arwel's lips and then let go of him. "See you in an hour."

Putting one foot in front of the other, Jin forced herself to keep going. The simple act of ambulating consumed all of her willpower, and there was nothing left to keep her tears at bay. By the time she reached Kalugal, Jin was sobbing quietly.

He looked at her with concern in his eyes and took her elbow. "There is no need for tears." He led her to a gazebo that looked like it was set up for a romantic dinner. "Your boyfriend is fine, and you have nothing to worry about. As soon as the tether is off, and I can verify it, you are free to go."

When he motioned for her to sit, Jin's legs practically folded under her. "I'm sorry. I'm usually not such a cry baby. It's just that I've gotten sick at the worst possible time, and I can barely hold it together."

Kalugal sat right next to her. "Let me pour you some tea."

"Thank you."

He was treating her like delicate china. Every move was slow and calculated as if not to spook her, and his tone was soft and caring.

It was all an act, of course, designed to help her relax so she could do what she was there for, but it was working.

The anxiety was still spinning the contents of her stomach like a bunch of wet clothes in a dryer, but at least it wasn't on the turbo spin cycle.

"Careful. It's hot." He handed her a small porcelain cup with a matching saucer.

"Thank you." She sniffed at the cup he handed her. "What kind of tea is this? It smells woodsy."

He smiled, his perfect lips curving in that signature smirk that Jacki had talked about. "It's not poisoned if that's what you are worried about."

"It didn't even cross my mind. I've just never had tea like it."

The smell wasn't unpleasant, but it wasn't enticing either, and it was still too hot to drink.

"It's a special Chinese tea."

She narrowed her eyes at him. "Is that why you got it? I don't know what a Chinese tea even tastes like."

He chuckled. "How could I have known I would be entertaining an Asian lady when I purchased this tea? I've been drinking it for years. I like it for the unique taste, but it also has many health benefits for humans. Which is most fortunate, don't you think? It might help you feel better."

After taking another sniff, Jin put the cup on the table. "I need it to cool a little." She turned to Kalugal. "May I touch you?"

"Anytime." He flashed her that smirk again.

If she weren't in love with someone else and sick as a dog, she might have found it sexy. The guy had a bad-boy charm that girls went wild for, but it was softened by his good manners and his lighthearted attitude.

Jin had to acknowledge that Kalugal was super sexy, but she was indifferent to his charms. They had no effect on her. It was like admiring a beautiful picture without lusting after it or even wanting to hang it in her living room.

"I need to touch you to remove the tether. And you need to concentrate on feeling its removal."

He offered her his arm. "I'm ready when you are."

Arwel

His mind in a haze, Arwel trudged over to the other side of the street. Twice he stumbled on the chain connecting his ankles, and Magnus caught his elbow before it happened for the third time.

"Let me get you out of these." Magnus crouched and fiddled with the key Kalugal had tossed. "Quit swaying on your feet. You are distracting me."

"I wasn't aware that I was doing that." Arwel stood as still as he could.

Jin had looked haggard as if she hadn't slept for days. There had been dark circles under her eyes, and the spark was gone from them, or maybe they had just been misted with a sheen of tears.

When Magnus was done with the ankle restraints, he straightened up and examined the handcuffs. "Those are weird. They must be custom made." He turned them around until he found the keyhole.

Arwel was about to comment when he noticed the earpiece sticking out from Magnus's ear. Except, it didn't look like the ones William had given them. Was it a new model?

Magnus removed the handcuffs as well.

"New earpiece?"

Ignoring the question, Magnus waved a hand, and a moment later Gregor pulled up next to them. "Let's get out of here."

"Where are we going?"

When neither of the guys responded, Arwel leaned toward Magnus and took a closer look at the device stuck in his ear, and then pulled it out.

"I was wondering why you guys didn't answer me. What's the deal with the plugs?"

Magnus took the other one out. "It was Kri's idea. If we can't hear Kalugal, he can't compel us."

"Did he try?"

"He might have." Gregor chuckled. "We didn't hear him. We wear these when we are within hearing distance of him and use texting to communicate. Our phones are set on vibrate."

"Smart. So where are we going?"

"Get out of your clothes and put these on." Magnus pointed to the paper bag on the seat next to Arwel. "When you are done, put everything in the bag. After we get out, Gregor is going to drive away and drop them in a dumpster at the nearest shopping strip."

It had occurred to Arwel that the *search* Rufsur had done on him and Jacki was not meant to find bugs but to plant them.

"Good idea." He started stripping. "Jin looks terrible. What's wrong with her?"

"She caught a cold," Magnus said. "Poor girl. I don't know much about human illnesses, but I assume that the stress weakened her body and made her vulnerable to viruses."

Arwel's heart skipped a beat. "She might be transitioning."

"She is not. The sanctuary's doctor checked her and said it's just a cold."

"The sanctuary?" He paused with the sweatshirt hovering over his head.

Magnus nodded. "Turner decided that it was the most secure place for her, so he sent her there without telling Kian about it. There was always a chance that Kalugal would compel Kian through the phone and get him to reveal things. That's why he doesn't talk with Kalugal unless Turner is right there beside him. He can take over if needed."

"What a damn clusterfuck. Whose idea was it to trade Jin?"

"Hers. She insisted we do it from the very start. Believe me, Kian tried every possible angle before finally agreeing to the trade. There was no other way. She also came up with the idea of taking Kalugal's second-in-command hostage."

"Jin has a good head on her shoulders. Rufsur and Kalugal are good friends, and Kalugal is not going to forfeit Rufsur's life lightly. Where did you take him?"

"First, we took him to the house, stripped him, and searched him for bugs. After that, we took him to our new location."

"And where is that?"

"One of Turner's many acquaintances has a motel that isn't open for business yet. We've got the entire place to ourselves."

"How has he been behaving?"

"He's complaining about being tied up and claims that you promised he would be treated well."

"I did. But what I meant was that no one was going to beat him up. I didn't promise him a five-star hotel and gourmet meals if that's what he's been expecting. Who is watching him?"

"We have several Guardians there, and Vivian is keeping him company, even though I would have preferred for her to stay away from him."

Arwel wasn't sure how smart that was. Rufsur was an okay fellow, but if he was presented with an opportunity to get free or take Vivian hostage, he'd most likely take it.

"I hope that he is properly restrained and guarded, and that the guys are at least cordial to him." Arwel pulled up the sweatpants and reached into the bag for socks.

Magnus cast him an amused glance. "With Vivian keeping watch they are going to be on their best behavior. Lokan is there as well, but we are keeping him away from Rufsur because Kian is not sure he wants to reveal the connection yet. If needed though, he's going to use Lokan as an additional hostage."

"When did Lokan get here?"

"Yesterday, and naturally Carol couldn't stay away from the action and came with him."

"That's Carol. Even a direct order from Kian wouldn't have kept her away." Arwel pulled the new pair of boots out of the bag and leaned to put them on.

Magnus shrugged. "He's too busy with managing the crisis to care about that."

"I'm ready." Arwel put the clothes he'd taken off into the bag.

"Then let's go." Magnus opened the door and got out.

At the door Arwel was greeted by Kri, who pulled him into a fierce hug. "I'm glad to have you back."

He returned the embrace. "I wish I could say that I'm glad to be back, but I can't while Kalugal has my mate."

"Jin campaigned hard for it. She knew that Kalugal wouldn't agree to anything else and she was right. I know that it's hard for you to accept, but she did the right thing. Now that you are out, the village's location is safe, and Kian has lifted the lockdown. People can go back to work, and those who were caught outside during the lockdown can come back home."

He hung his head. "It's my fault. I should have stopped that shooter before he got into the club. I felt the darkness eating at him, and I knew he was up to no good. But we are not supposed to interfere based on intentions, only actions. Except, it seems that following the rules is not always the right thing to do."

Kri put her hand on his arm. "We can't live our lives agonizing over should've and could've. In hindsight, disarming that man before he reached the club was the right thing to do, but you couldn't have known it. The rules are not infallible, but they keep us from making many more mistakes than what we would have committed in their absence."

"Words of wisdom." Magnus clapped Kri on the back. "I didn't know you were so deep."

Flipping him a finger, Kri smiled and sauntered off.

Jin

Jin let go of Kalugal's arm. "Did you feel it?"

She could've released the tether on her side without touching him, but she wasn't sure he would notice the difference if she did it that way. It was better to remove the hook from his brain than just let go of the tether.

He shook his head. "I'm sorry. I didn't notice any change."

Leaning back, Jin sighed. "I feel like a mental weight lifted off me. Letting go of the tether always feels liberating." She looked at him. "Don't you feel freer? Lighter?"

He smiled. "I didn't feel oppressed or weighed down before."

"When I reattach it, focus inwardly. When you know it's coming, you should be able to feel it. Others did."

"Maybe it's a placebo effect. People expect to feel a difference, so they do."

Jin closed her eyes. "I need a few moments to rest."

"No problem. Take your time. If it were up to me, I would have taken you to a guest room where you could sleep, and we could have continued this the next morning. It was Kian who insisted on doing it so late at night and outside in the yard." He looked her over. "I don't know much about human illnesses, but I don't think you should be out in the cold."

"Thank you for turning up the heaters. I would've been really miserable without them."

"You're welcome." He lifted his teacup and took a small sip. "Tell me something. How come the clan is working with humans? If there is one thing both sides of the divide agree upon, it is that humans shouldn't find out about the existence of immortals."

Crap. Jin didn't know if she was allowed to tell Kalugal about being a Dormant. Mey had said that the Doomers didn't know how to find Dormants in the human population or that paranormal abilities were a good indicator of a person having the immortal gene.

"They are very selective about who they let in on the secret." That wasn't a lie, so it should be okay.

But given the change in Kalugal's expression, it wasn't. In an instant, it turned from easygoing charm to hard determination.

How could someone so handsome suddenly look so terrifying?

"Tell me the truth, Jin." His voice was imbued with compulsion. "I don't appreciate evasive answers any more than I appreciate lies."

"I'm not human," she heard herself say. "Not entirely."

He arched a brow. "How so? Are you the daughter of an immortal mother?"

"I was adopted, so I don't know who my mother was. But she must have been a Dormant, and so am I."

"I see." The smirk was back. "So, you can turn immortal. How come you didn't yet? Has your relationship with Arwel been platonic?"

Embarrassed, Jin reached for her teacup. "Condoms," she muttered under her breath.

"What about them?"

She shook her head. "How come you guys don't know basic stuff like that? To induce a Dormant, it's not enough to have sex with her and bite her. The immortal male's sperm has to actually get inside her and not into a condom."

"Interesting." Kalugal sipped on his tea. "It would appear that my father doesn't know that. He never permitted immortal males to have sex with the Dormants because he wanted to keep them human so they could produce more children. But if condoms are enough to prevent transition, it's not necessary to segregate them."

"He might know about that but doesn't trust the men to use protection."

Kalugal nodded. "That's possible. Navuh is highly paranoid."

"Can I reattach the tether now? I really want to be done with this."

"Not yet. I have many more questions for you."

"That wasn't part of the deal."

He smiled. "But it wasn't explicitly excluded either. I like finding loopholes that I can use to my advantage."

"I bet." Jin grimaced.

"How did they find you? Or did you find them? Are they actively searching for Dormants?"

"They found my sister first, and it was purely by chance. But once she was confirmed as a Dormant, so was I. I don't know how they found the others."

"So, there are more?"

Jin nodded.

"How many?"

"I don't know. I'm new to all this, and I haven't even visited the clan's village yet." She slapped her hand over her mouth. "Crap. I really hate this. But before you ask, I don't know where it is. They kept me in the dark, so to speak."

To buy herself a short reprieve, she took an experimental sip from the tea. "Interesting flavor. What's in it?" She took another sip. It tasted odd, but not unpleasant.

"It's called the Poo Poo Pu-Erh tea, and it was the drink of emperors."

"Poo Poo? That's funny. What does it mean? I know very little Chinese."

"It means exactly what it sounds like. It's made from the droppings of insects that have fed on tea leaves. It's considered a delicacy and costs accordingly."

As Jin's stomach heaved, she only had enough time to turn her head away from Kalugal before everything she'd eaten that day came up geysering out of her throat.

She was dimly aware of Kalugal jumping up and saying something to her, but she couldn't understand what it was. It felt as if she was puking out her brains together with the contents of her stomach, and with every new spasm, her vision blurred further, until she could no longer hold on to consciousness.

Tipping over, Jin's last thought was that falling onto the puddle of puke she'd made was just the perfect ending to the most miserable day of her life.

Kalugal

For the first time in a very long time, Kalugal panicked.

Something was very wrong with the pretty spy, and he didn't know how to help her.

Should he offer her a napkin?

He unfurled one and held it out for her, but she was too busy spilling out the contents of her stomach all over the gazebo's floor to pay any attention to the napkin hanging right in front of her face.

"Tell me what I can do for you."

Oblivious to his presence, she pitched forward, and if not for his quick reflexes, she would have landed right on the pile of vomit.

Catching her by gripping the back of her coat, Kalugal swung her into his arms and started walking. "Bring a doctor!" He yelled loud enough for the warriors outside his gate to hear. "The girl passed out, and I'm taking her inside the house!"

His men gathered around him, forming a wall of bodies to protect him. It wasn't going to help if whoever was controlling the drones decided to shoot, but he hoped Kian's men were aware of Jin's sickness and would not assume that he had done something to her. All it would take to end him was one trigger-happy moron and the right kind of bullet.

"Any of you know how to resuscitate a human?"

The response he got was head shaking all around.

"Bring the immune to the house. She might know what to do."

"Yes, sir."

"I'm taking the girl to my bedroom."

This was no time to think about propriety or what her boyfriend would think.

Taking the stairs two at a time, he held on tight, making sure to clear the banister on one side and the wall on the other. Humans were so damn fragile, and any impact would leave a bruise on the girl that he would have to explain to Kian.

When his phone went off in his pocket, Kalugal cursed under his breath. He had a good idea who was calling him, but he couldn't answer it without dropping Jin.

The damn thing kept ringing all the way to his bedroom and stopped just as he laid the girl on his bed.

"Get me some wet washcloths," he barked at the men who followed him into the bedroom.

"Yes, sir." Shamash rushed into the bathroom.

Kalugal pulled out his phone and clicked return on the last incoming call.

"What's going on?" Kian growled.

"Your spy is sick. She threw up and then passed out. What should I do? I have no experience in taking care of humans."

"I'm getting our clan doctor on the line so she can walk you through it. I'm also sending another doctor to your place, but it will take him about an hour and a half to get there. You might have to take Jin to a hospital."

"That's the best idea you've had so far. I should take her right away."

"Wait. Let the doctor decide if it's necessary."

"If she dies because you made me wait, it's on you."

"She is not going to die. Hold on, I'm connecting you to the doctor. Her name is Bridget."

"Hello, Kalugal." The female sounded calm as if nothing major was happening. "Is Jin breathing?"

"She is."

"Check her pulse. Do you know how to do it?"

Who did she think she was dealing with? An ignoramus?

"Of course. Hang on."

As he took Jin's limp wrist and counted the beats, Shamash returned with the washcloths and started cleaning her up.

"Eighty-six beats per minute."

"That's fine. Since she threw up, you need to lay her on her side. Put a pillow or two under her legs, so they are elevated about twelve inches over her heart."

"Done. What now?"

"Is the room warm?"

"No. But I can turn the heating on."

"Do that, but make sure that she doesn't get overheated. What is she wearing?"

"A coat over a thick sweater and a long skirt that doesn't look too warm. Should I remove the coat? I can cover her with a thick comforter."

"You can do that. Tell me how it happened. Did you give her something to eat or drink that might not have agreed with her stomach?"

"She arrived already sick and said that she had a cold. I gave her tea, which she enjoyed, but when she asked about the tea, and I explained how it was made, she started vomiting. My explanation must have disgusted her."

"What kind of tea was it?"

"It's a Chinese delicacy, which I thought she would appreciate. It's called the Poo Poo Pu-Erh tea, and it's made from the droppings of insects that digest the tea leaves."

"I see." The doctor chuckled. "Poor Jin. She must have been queasy because of the cold, and then you exacerbated the situation with that gross tea."

"It's not gross. It has a unique flavor, is purported to have many health benefits for humans, and it costs over five hundred dollars per pound."

"I'm sure it does, but that's neither here nor there. Stay with Jin and watch her closely. If anything changes, like her pulse accelerates or drops or her breathing becomes labored, give me a call."

"Are you sure that's wise? I'd rather take her to the human hospital. I don't want to be responsible for her demise."

"That's not advisable. She might be transitioning, and they wouldn't know what to do with her. A clan doctor is on his way, and he knows what to do in case she is."

Arwel

Jin threw up and fainted. Kalugal took her inside the house, and Kian is sending Julian over. Bridget thinks she is transitioning.

As Arwel read the text from Magnus for the second time, he wanted to scream in frustration.

Next to him, Kri was reading the same text and cursing quietly. "The damn sanctuary doctor said it was a cold. Maybe she should go back to medical school."

"It still might be just that." Arwel pushed his fingers through his hair. "I need to call Bridget and ask her why she thinks Jin is transitioning."

He placed the call and started walking toward the door.

Kri stopped him with a hand on his shoulder. "Where are you going?"

He cast her an incredulous glance. "Back where I came from. I need to be near my mate when she transitions."

"Don't be an idiot. You are not going anywhere. We just went to all this trouble to get you out."

"Other Guardians are surrounding Kalugal's mansion. I can at least be out there."

"No, you can't. You and I are not allowed anywhere near Kalugal because we are head Guardians, and we know the village's location as well as shitloads of other stuff that the other Guardians don't. If either of us gets captured, it's back to square one."

"I can wear earplugs."

As his call to Bridget went to voicemail, Arwel was ready to throw his phone at the wall. "Why isn't she answering?"

Kri's hand on his shoulder tightened. "You are not going to help Jin by standing outside Kalugal's gate with earplugs in."

"I can't stay here and do nothing either."

"You have no choice. Call Bridget again or call Kian and get an update."

Seething, Arwel redialed Bridget's number.

This time the doctor answered. "I was expecting your call. First of all, don't panic. Jin was under a lot of stress, hasn't slept much, and has gotten sick on top of that. I talked with the sanctuary's doctor, and Rebecca assured me that Jin's symptoms are classic cold and a mild one at that. Then I got a call from Vivian, who told me that she fed Jin lots of chicken soup, which is good for congestion, but it might not have agreed with her stomach."

"So, she is not transitioning?"

Bridget sighed. "She might be, but it's unlikely. From my limited experience with adult Dormants transitioning, they need to be healthy for it to start. Remember Roni? He couldn't transition because his body was weakened after being sick with pneumonia. But just in case she is or in case she's suffering from something more serious, I'm sending Julian over with a bunch of medical equipment."

"If you think she might have a more serious illness, perhaps it's best to take her to a human hospital."

"We can bring in a local doctor, but since Julian will be there in less than an hour and a half, I think it's more prudent to wait for him and have all the possibilities checked out."

"Isn't it dangerous for her to stay unconscious for so long?"

"I was about to call Kian and check whether she still was when your call came in. She might have woken up already."

"When you find out, let me know."

"Of course."

Arwel ended the call and let out a breath. "Jin is probably not transitioning."

"That's what I thought." Kri flipped her braid back. "Come on. You need a drink." She started walking toward the kitchen. "I hope there is some beer left in the fridge."

"A moment ago you were ranting about the sanctuary's doctor not knowing what she was doing, and now you claim to have known that Jin is not transitioning?"

"I thought that Bridget had already spoken with Dr. Rebeca and found fault with her diagnosis. To me, it looked like the flu or a cold. Jin was sneezing and blowing her nose every two minutes, which none of the other Dormants have done while transitioning." Kri opened the fridge and pulled out two beers.

Handing one to Arwel, she leaned against the counter. "If it swims like a duck and quacks like a duck, it's probably not a chicken, even though they look a lot alike." She popped the cap and took a long swig.

"Ducks and chickens look nothing alike, but growing up in the city you wouldn't know that because you've only seen them in the supermarket, cut up and neatly packaged."

Kri waved with her bottle. "Whatever, country boy. You get my meaning."

Kalugal

"Oh my God. What happened?" The immune rushed into Kalugal's bedroom.

For a moment, he was lost for words. If she weren't the only female on his estate, he wouldn't have recognized her.

The mousy brown wig was gone, as well as the makeup that had made her skin look sallow.

Her complexion was a healthy peach color, her hair was a magnificent mane of blond strands that were waist long and lushly wavy, and it flew behind her like a golden halo as she ran through the room.

Bending over Jin, she checked her breathing and then put her hand on her forehead. "She is burning up." Jacki pinned him with a stare so intense that it penetrated the thick layers of rust around his heart. "Do you have any Advil or Tylenol, or do immortals have no need for painkillers?"

He affected a calm expression. "Jin told me that she had a cold and then threw up and fainted. Your boss is sending a doctor."

"If you mean Kian, he is not my boss," Jacki muttered.

"Shamash, check the first aid kit. Maybe it contains some painkillers."

"Yes, sir."

Sitting on the bed next to Jin, Jacki took one of the washcloths that Shamash had left on the nightstand and continued what he had started. "Jin, honey, wake up. I need you to talk to me."

The faint groan Jin uttered in response was music to Kalugal's ears. Why hadn't he thought about coaxing the girl to talk? He could've compelled her to answer him.

But the doctor hadn't said anything about talking. She'd said to watch Jin, which was exactly what he'd been doing. Sitting on a chair next to the bed, he watched the girl's chest rising and falling to make sure that she was still breathing.

"That's a good start, honey." Jacki caressed Jin's cheek. "Can you tell me what's wrong?"

Jin opened her eyes a crack. "Mommy?"

"It's Jacki, sweetheart. Does anything hurt?"

Jin lifted her hand to her throat. "It hurts here."

Jacki turned to Kalugal. "Can you bring her a glass of water?"

"Of course." He pushed to his feet.

"And a bowl with ice water and a couple of fresh washcloths."

"What for?"

She rolled her eyes. "I know that you are an immortal, but living among humans, you should've learned a few basic things about us. I need to reduce her fever, and since I don't have any medication that I can give her, I'll wet the cloths in ice water and put it on her forehead to cool her a bit. It will make her feel better."

"I see."

Kalugal dipped his head before marching to the wet bar in the master suite's sitting room.

Why the hell had he felt the need to do that?

As far as he knew, Jacki was a nobody, but her authoritative tone and lack of fear implied otherwise. She'd also said that Kian was not her boss.

Who was she? And what was her connection to the clan?

Had Kian lied about her not being important? But then he would have asked to trade her first and not the warrior. Except, he might have done it on purpose, so Kalugal wouldn't suspect her real value.

Regrettably, he couldn't compel Jacki to reveal her secrets, and it seemed like she was also immune to his charms, which was no less disconcerting.

Even the spy had looked at him appreciatively, and she was in love with another man.

His curiosity demanded that he find out who Jacki was and what she was hiding, but it was more than that. She knew who he was, knew where he lived, and was immune to thralling. If he let her go, she would walk away with knowledge that no human should ever be privy to.

After scooping cubes from the freezer into an ice bucket, he put some in a tall glass and filled both containers with water.

"Thank you." Jacki took the bucket and put it on the nightstand.

"You're welcome." He handed her the glass. "I'll get the washcloths."

In the bathroom, he took out the whole stack of them from the closet and headed back.

"I need your help." Jacki handed him a pillow. "When I turn Jin on her back and lift her, stuff the pillow behind her. I want her to drink the water."

He put the washcloths on the nightstand. "The doctor said to put her on her side and to keep her legs elevated over her heart."

"Yeah, but that was for when she was unconscious. She is awake now. Sort of."

Bending at the waist, Kalugal put his face a few inches away from Jacki's. "Are you a doctor?"

"I'm not, but everyone other than clueless immortals knows that."

No one talked to Kalugal like that, and he should have felt offended, but instead, he was amused. Hell, he was delighted.

For the first time since he could remember, he was being treated like a regular guy. Even while shrouded, most people sensed his power and trod cautiously around him.

Could Jacki's immunity make her obtuse?

Or was she used to having powerful people around her, and that's why she wasn't impressed by him?

Kalugal was practically salivating with curiosity. Especially since it came with a heavy dose of attraction.

Before this was over and he let Jacki go, he was going to seduce her, and since she was immune to his compulsion as well as to his charms, conquering her would be doubly fun.

"Why are you smirking? It's the truth. For a smart guy, you are incredibly clueless about humans."

"I love it that you do not fear me." He took the pillow from her. "Ready when you are."

She gifted him with a heart-stoppingly gorgeous smile. "I'm glad that you can be reasoned with."

Jin

Jin had the weirdest dream. Her mom was feeding her chicken soup and calling her honey, and her dad was sitting in a chair next to her bed and frowning.

That wasn't like him. Her father was more the brow lifting type, and she'd rarely seen him frown. And when she or Mey got sick, their mom would keep him away from them because he caught every bug and was the worst patient possible. She had also never fed them in bed. Jin couldn't remember ever being too sick to get up to eat.

A cool hand touched her forehead. "I think her fever has gone down a little. She doesn't feel as hot to the touch." That didn't sound like her mother's voice.

"That's a highly unscientific way to measure temperature." The male voice didn't belong to her father either, but it carried the same pompous self-importance that her mom always berated her dad for.

Her mom would tell him, "You're a history professor. That doesn't make you an expert on anything else."

And he would answer, "History encompasses everything. Even science and medicine."

"Outdated science and medicine."

Her father used to say that it was nothing more than his teacher tone, and that he was a humble man. But that was false modesty, and they all knew it but loved him anyway.

"You don't have a freaking thermometer. And until Julian gets here, my hand is all we have. Unless you think that your hand is better at measuring temperature?"

The voice sounded familiar, but it wasn't her mother's for sure. First of all, she would never say freaking, and secondly, she didn't have a southern accent. Hers was New Yorker.

Jin cracked her eyes open. "Jacki?" Her throat felt like it was on fire, and it hurt to talk.

"Oh, thank God. You're awake. Kalugal's guy found some Motrin. Apparently, immortals aren't immune to headaches. They get them when they are hungover. Anyway, you were delirious, and I had to shove it into your mouth and massage your throat for you to swallow it."

Jacki was talking a mile a second, which she'd never done before. She must think that Jin was dying.

As she hovered over Jin, her long hair was hanging like a curtain and blocking the view of a guy sitting on a chair next to the bed. Moving it aside, Jin looked at Kalugal. "Where am I?"

"In my bedroom. You fainted."

And she'd also puked, which explained the horrible smell. It had been that disgusting tea, or rather hearing about how it was made. Just thinking about it made her stomach heave.

"It was that horrible tea. I'm going to puke again." Jin slapped a hand over her mouth.

Jacki shoved an ice bucket under her chin. "In here."

It was full of cold water, with half-melted ice cubes floating around. Reaching inside, Jin pulled out an ice cube, stuffed it into her mouth, and crunched it into small bits.

The chewing helped with the nausea attack, and the icy water felt wonderful on her burning throat. Jin reached for another one.

Jacki grimaced and pulled the bucket away. "That water is not clean. I used it to dunk washcloths in." She turned to Kalugal. "Can you get Jin another glass of water with ice cubes inside?"

"Coming right up." He pushed to his feet and walked out of the room.

Leave it up to Jacki to boss around one of the most powerful immortals on the planet.

"Did I hear you saying that Julian is on his way, or was it part of the dream?"

"He should be here in less than half an hour. Kian sent him with a bunch of equipment, but I don't know what for. All you need are antibiotics."

"The doctor at the sanctuary checked me and said that I had a common cold, but I think she was wrong. This feels like strep throat."

"What sanctuary?"

Damn. Her brain was fuzzy, and she wasn't thinking straight. She needed to think before she opened her big mouth.

"Um, the clan runs a sanctuary for girls and boys that they rescue from traffickers. That's where I was hiding. They have a doctor there, and she examined me."

"I didn't know they were doing that. It's commendable."

"Yeah, I think so too." Jin looked at Kalugal who came in with a tall glass of water.

"Where is that sanctuary you've been telling Jacki about?" He handed her the glass.

She knew there was no point in trying to lie to him. He would just compel her to tell him the truth like he had done before she'd passed out.

"It's in Alaska."

"Alaska? Why so far away?"

Jin took a sip of water, sighing in relief as it cooled her throat. "I don't know. Maybe it's so the traffickers don't find them? Or maybe because houses in Alaska are relatively cheap."

None of what she'd said was an untruth, just not the whole of it.

Thankfully, Kalugal accepted her explanation. "Makes sense. I'm just thinking that those poor kids deserve better than freezing Alaska." He sat on the chair and crossed his legs. "I might consider contributing to the cause in exchange for some privileges."

Jacki glared at him. "You are so freaking rich. You can contribute without asking for anything in return."

He smiled. "That's true, but what I need from my esteemed cousin doesn't carry monetary value, only sentimental."

That piqued Jacki's interest. "What is it?"

"Talking with my mother. I'm holding you hostage until he lets me talk to her, but once is not enough, and I'll probably need to bribe him to let me keep in touch with her."

Jacki frowned. "Is he holding your mother prisoner? Why can't you just call her up?"

"That's a long story, and I'm not sure I want to share it with you. I can't make you forget anything, and you already know too much."

Jacki swallowed nervously. "What are you going to do about it?"

"Nothing. You are safe with me, but I don't know what Kian plans to do with you."

Jin bristled. "Kian is not going to harm Jacki. She's part of the clan."

Jacki lifted a brow. "I am?"

"Sure, you are. Do you think the clan is going to turn its back on you after you risked your life to save Arwel?"

Leaning forward, Kalugal steepled his fingers. "The question is in what capacity. Kian can't let you walk away. You will be a prisoner of the clan for the rest of your life."

Kalugal

"What about Jin?" Jacki asked. "She is human, right? And so is her sister. How do they fit in with a clan of immortals?"

Kalugal glanced at Jin, who seemed uncomfortable, and not because of the illness.

Apparently, Jacki had been left in the dark about all things that had to do with immortality, which was a good decision on Kian's part. The less she knew, the better.

"Rufsur asked Arwel the same question. Apparently, Kian is not as careful in that regard as I am. He's allowed several chosen humans in on the secret."

Jin let out a breath. "Yeah. Being Arwel's girlfriend, I was granted that privilege. Same for my sister. She knows because she and Yamanu are a couple."

"That's not so smart." Jacki looked at her with sad eyes. "How long do you think it's going to last? You will grow older while he doesn't."

"I don't want to talk about it." Jin closed her eyes. "When is Julian getting here? I feel like I'm dying."

"Let me check." Kalugal pulled his phone out and called Kian. "When should we expect the doctor?"

"Has Jin's condition worsened?"

"No, she actually woke up and talked with Jacki and me for a little bit. But that was thanks to the Motrin Jacki forced down her throat, and the effect seems to be temporary. She says that she is dying, which I'm sure is an exaggeration, but she is obviously very sick."

"There was a slight delay. Julian should be there in forty-five minutes to an hour tops. He's coming with a lot of medical equipment, so make sure to prepare a room for him to set it up in."

"Tell him to leave it outside and come examine Jin first. I need to have that equipment checked."

"Relax. Now that I have my man back, I have no reason to blow your place up."

"Nevertheless, I'm still going to conduct a very thorough check."

"As you wish."

"She is sleeping," Jacki said as he ended the call. "There must be something seriously wrong with her. Jin is a healthy and strong woman, she shouldn't be that incapacitated by a freaking cold. Maybe it's one of those deadly flu strains. And if it is, I'm in trouble because they are usually highly contagious. And if it's a strep throat, that's not so bad because it's not life-threatening, but it's contagious as hell too."

Kalugal pushed to his feet. "May I offer you some tea?"

She scrunched her nose. "Not the one that made Jin puke."

"I don't think it was the tea that caused her to vomit. The Poo-Poo Pu-Erh tea is actually supposed to soothe upset stomach, and it also provides many other health benefits. I suggest that you drink it as a preemptive measure."

Crossing her arms over her chest, Jacki shook her head. "I'm not putting anything in my mouth that has Poo Poo as part of its name."

"Your loss. I'll have a simpler tea prepared for you."

"I'd appreciate it." She yawned.

As he walked out of the room, Kalugal thought back to the moments leading up to Jin's fainting spell. She'd looked bad, and he'd noticed her rubbing her middle when she'd thought he wasn't looking. Perhaps she had food poisoning?

It could have been caused by a virus, or by something she'd eaten before coming there, or it could have been an actual poisoning.

Why would Kian poison his own spy, though? That didn't make any sense. Unless it was all a ploy to get the so-called doctor and his equipment in.

A Trojan horse Kalugal couldn't refuse.

If that was indeed the plan, then he had severely underestimated his cousin's deviousness.

Most of his men were still in the bunker, and he was going to leave them there until the doctor and his equipment were gone. The question was whether Kalugal was going to join them there or remain in the house.

The smart thing to do would be to leave one of the men in charge, but that was not how Kalugal ran his house. He wasn't going to hide in the bunker and leave the skeleton crew he had in the house exposed.

Except, he had to admit that logic and strategy had little to do with his reluctance to go down to the bunker.

The truth was that he didn't want to leave Jacki and her crusty and yet surprisingly pleasant company. She was so refreshing, so different from the women he was usually attracted to.

Looks-wise, she was his type. He liked tall blondes with curvy bodies and peachy skin. But her character didn't match the profile of his companion of choice. He had a feeling that despite her intelligence, she had no higher education.

Jacki didn't sound like a hillbilly, but she was rough around the edges and not nearly as sophisticated as the women he usually picked.

Maybe that was precisely why he found her so fascinating.

Arwel

When Arwel's phone rang, he nearly dropped it in his haste to pull it out of his back pocket. He'd been expecting a call from Bridget, but instead it was Kian.

"I have good news for you. Jin is awake, and Kalugal brought Jacki to take care of her. The bad news is that she is still very sick, and Julian is running a little late. He needed to pick up antibiotics and some other stuff that we don't keep on hand in the village. He should be landing shortly, though, and several Guardians are waiting for him on the strip to help him with the equipment."

"Is there a way I can talk to her or Jacki?"

"It's not advisable. In case Kalugal tries to compel me while I talk to him, I have Turner to take over and Onegus to stop me from doing something I'm not supposed to. You have no such protection. He could compel you to tell him what he wants to know, and no one there can stop him."

"What if you make a three-way call? If Kalugal tries his tricks, Turner can disconnect it. It's the same as if I were there with you. I'll have Kri chain me to a pillar, so if Kalugal commands me to come to him, I won't be able to do that, and if he asks me a question I shouldn't answer, Turner can disconnect the call before I reveal anything."

"Hold on a moment. I'll ask Turner what he thinks."

A long moment passed until Kian came back on the line. "Turner says it can work. Call me back when you're chained to that pillar."

"Thank you. This means a lot to me."

"No need to thank me. I get it." Kian ended the call.

Kri lifted a brow. "What do you want me to use for chains?"

"There must be something in the garage we can use."

"I have reinforced handcuffs." Gregor leaned over the second-floor railing.

Arwel looked up. "What can we attach them to that I can't rip off?"

Gregor scratched his stubble. "The railing is wrought-iron. Even if you tear it off the wall, you can't drag it with you through the door. And if you try, I'll knock you out."

"Sounds good to me. Get them."

"It could work. You can sit on the stairs and have one hand cuffed to the railing. That way, you'll still have the other one to hold the phone." Kri walked over to the railing and shook it. "It's sturdy."

When it was done, Arwel placed the call. "I'm ready."

"I hope Kalugal won't object," Kian said.

"If he does, let me talk to him."

Kalugal's parting words implied that he didn't want any hard feelings, and allowing Arwel to talk to Jin wouldn't cost him any advantage.

A short moment later, Kalugal came on the line. "Has the doctor arrived?"

"Not yet," Kian said. "Arwel is on the line, and he asks to speak with Jin if it's possible."

"She is asleep."

"Can I talk to Jacki?"

"Sure. I'm putting you on speakerphone. Go ahead."

That was easier than Arwel had expected. "Hi, Jacki. How is Jin doing?"

"I think she has strep throat."

"What's that?"

"Come on, you too? I thought that only Kalugal was so ignorant because he lives isolated from the world. It's a bacterial infection in the throat, and it can get pretty nasty. It's not life-threatening, though. You can Google it."

"How do you know it's that and not something else? You're not a doctor."

"Jin's throat hurts, she has a high fever that doesn't respond well to fever reducers, and when she talks, she sounds raspy. I've seen so many cases of strep throat that I can diagnose it like a doctor. Foster homes usually stick three to four kids in the same bedroom, and when one gets it, all the others get infected too."

"Can you do me a favor and call Kian when Jin wakes up? I want to talk to her."

"It's not up to me."

"I'll place the call for you," Kalugal said.

"Thanks. I appreciate that."

"No hard feelings, right?"

Arwel shook his head. "That still remains to be seen, but I'm grateful to you for allowing me to talk to Jin."

Kalugal sighed. "I'm a reasonable man, Arwel, and I'm not cruel when I don't have to be. As long as it doesn't endanger my men or me, I have no problem accommodating your or Jin's requests. You and Kian seem to forget that this whole mess was created by you, not me. I'm only defending myself and my men the best I can."

Kalugal

"The doctor is here," Phinas announced from the other side of the door.

"I'll be right out." Kalugal pushed to his feet and looked down at Jacki. "I assume that you want to be here while he examines your friend."

"Naturally. He will want me here as well. When a male doctor examines a woman, a female nurse is usually present. I'm not a nurse, but I meet the first requirement."

He smirked. "You certainly do."

"Are you flirting with me, Kalugal?" Her eyes narrowed, but her lips were curved in a little smile.

"I'm just stating a fact. You are unmistakably female." He left before she had the chance to answer.

Spending time with Jacki was an interesting experience. He enjoyed the constant banter and the fact that she didn't give him an inch. He would probably grow tired of it shortly, like he did with most people, but that was okay. She was leaving soon, and until then, he was going to enjoy her company without analyzing the reasons for it.

Phinas was waiting for him out in the corridor. "A van full of medical equipment is parked outside, but the doctor says he can perform the initial examination just with what he has in his bag. The equipment will be needed only if the lady requires monitoring, whatever that means."

"It's what they do in hospitals. The equipment monitors the patient's vitals, like heartbeat, respiration, pulse, etc."

"How do you know that?"

"Movies. And I've also checked on doctor Google. These days you can find any information you want on the internet. No need to go to the library or attend lectures, it's all there at your fingertips."

Phinas assumed a smile. "At the ready for you to exploit."

"I'm just taking advantage of what's freely available to anyone who cares to investigate. The problem is that much of it is not reliable, and it takes a discriminating mind to know what's factual, what's speculation, and what's straight-up lies and manipulation. Where did you put the esteemed doctor?"

"In the library. Shamash is frisking him and checking his bag."

"Good. I don't want any more surprises tonight. We've had enough excitement to last us a year."

This time Phinas smiled for real. "I can't say that I don't enjoy it. Our lives are pretty boring, and sometimes I miss the old days of going out to fight."

How soon people forgot and romanticized the past.

"You've never believed in the cause, my friend. And you hated killing people for no good reason."

"That is true. What I liked about it was the adrenaline rush and also the camaraderie."

"You still have the second one. And if you need a rush, you can take up skydiving or something similarly dangerous."

Kalugal opened the door to the library and walked in.

"Doctor Julian, I presume?" He offered his hand to the immortal. "I'm Kalugal."

"I know." The guy shook it. "Your portrait hangs in our headquarters. Can you take me to Jin?"

Kalugal turned to Shamash. "Is the doctor clean?"

"Yes, sir."

"Follow me." Kalugal waited for the doctor to pick up his bag. "What is my portrait doing in your headquarters, and how did you get it?"

"That's a long story that I'm sure you'll find fascinating, but it will have to wait for another time. I have a patient to see."

"Of course."

Kalugal opened the suite's door and motioned for Julian to go ahead of him. "Jacki says that you need her present for the examination."

"I don't need her to be there, but I don't mind it either."

As they entered the bedroom, Jacki jumped up, ran up to the doctor, and hugged him. "You have no idea how glad I am to see you."

The rage gripping Kalugal was totally unexpected, and he struggled to stifle the growl rising up in his throat. Why had seeing Jacki embracing the handsome doctor evoked such an intense reaction in him?

What the hell was going on?

He'd never felt jealousy before or any overly intense emotions for that matter. He was a logical man, and not one who was ruled by basal urges. And what's more, he had no right. Jacki didn't belong to him, and if she wanted to wrap her arms around the neck of some guy that was too good-looking to be a doctor, it was her prerogative.

"Same here." Julian pulled her arms off. "Now, let me examine Jin."

"It's strep throat. I'm willing to bet on it."

"She shouldn't have passed out from a simple infection like that."

"She was tired and stressed out, and then Kalugal gave her Poo Poo tea, and it was the last straw."

The doctor shook his head. "I'm not even going to ask." He looked at Kalugal. "Can you please wait in the other room? You can leave the door open."

"Of course."

Kalugal would have liked to stay, but Jacki would probably threaten to scratch his eyes out if he insisted on it.

The doctor sat on the bed next to Jin and put his hand on her shoulder. "Jin, it's Julian."

Kalugal walked out into the sitting room and headed to the wet bar. Pouring himself a drink, he listened to the conversation in the other room.

"Can you open your eyes for me?" the doctor asked.

Jin

"Julian? When did you get here?" Jin whispered because talking hurt too much.

"A few minutes ago. I need to look at your throat."

"It hurts."

"I bet. Can you open your mouth?"

"Am I transitioning?"

"You are ill, Jin. But I'm here to take care of you."

Right. She wasn't supposed to mention transition next to Jacki. Although at this point, it was stupid. Jacki already knew about immortals, so what was the harm in telling her about Dormants?

Except, Jin lacked the energy to argue with Julian.

"She is delirious," Jacki said. "Before I gave her the Motrin, she thought that I was her mother."

Ignoring Jacki's comment, Julian lifted the tongue depressor. "Open and say ah."

As Jin followed the doctor's instructions, producing the ah sound hurt like hell, and it turned into a whimper.

"I'm sorry. I'll be quick." Julian shone his slim flashlight into her throat. "Just as we thought. Your throat is covered with pus. It looks like streptococcus, but it's always best to check. He pulled out a long cotton swab. "Open wide."

That was going to be a bitch, especially since she was starting to think that Julian was putting on a show for Jacki. Maybe she didn't have a throat infection and was transitioning?

Nevertheless, she opened her mouth as wide as she could and almost gagged when Julian swabbed the back of her throat.

"Where is the bathroom?" he asked.

"I'll show you." Jacki got up.

As the two left, Jin reached with a shaky hand for the glass of water on the nightstand. The thing almost fell out of her hand, but she gritted her teeth, tightened her hand around it, and brought it to her mouth.

Mey had said something about transition involving swollen glands, but that was supposed to happen only to the males. But then Mey had grown a pair of tiny fangs, which was an anomaly. None of the other Dormant females had lost or regrown teeth during their transition.

In Mey's case, the fangs had come without venom glands, but maybe Jin was going to get both?

That could be so cool. Talk about being a badass.

On the other hand, it felt like strep throat. The last time she'd suffered from it, Jin was eight, and all she remembered was that her throat had felt on fire and she couldn't even swallow her own saliva. Why would it come back so many years later, though? Strep usually affected kids, and Jin hadn't had contact with any for far too long to get infected.

It didn't make sense.

"It's strep," Julian announced as he came back with Jacki. "The culture tested positive in a matter of minutes."

Was he still putting on a show?

He sat next to her on the bed. "Are you allergic to penicillin?"

"No."

"That's good. I'll give you a Bicillin shot, which is an injectable form of penicillin, and you'll be all better in two to eight hours. It's a one-dose treatment. You won't even have to take pills for ten days."

"Really?"

"The streptococcus bacteria responds very well to antibiotics. The downside is that the shot is painful."

As the daughter of a pediatric nurse, Jin knew all about the shot. Her question wasn't about the speed of recovery or whether it would hurt.

"I know. I had it when I was a kid. But are you sure that I need it?"

"Do you prefer pills? I have those too. But it will take them longer to work."

More and more, it seemed like Julian was serious about it really being a bacterial infection and not the start of her transition. And in that case, Jin would rather heal faster than slower.

She still had a job to do.

"I'll take the shot."

Jacki grimaced. "Is it okay if I wait in the other room? I really hate needles."

Hallelujah.

Finally, she would have a moment alone with Julian.

"Go. I trust Julian."

"Thank you." Jacki scurried out of the room.

Jin put her hand on Julian's forearm. "Do I really have a strep throat, or am I transitioning and this is all for Jacki's sake?"

He chuckled. "If this was a charade, I would have given you sugar pills instead of subjecting you to a penicillin shot. You are not transitioning. In fact, you can't until you heal. We've learned from experience that unless the Dormant's body is healthy and in good physical condition, it's not going to enter transition. The process is incredibly taxing on the body, which is why it can be potentially fatal for older Dormants even if they are healthy."

"So, it's a defensive mechanism. The genes don't activate unless they have the right environment."

"That seems to be the case."

Jin sighed and turned on her side. "Do it quickly."

"Try not to scream. We don't want Kalugal and his men running in here to save you from me."

"I won't."

Just to make sure though, Jin grabbed a pillow and held it in front of her face. "I'm ready."

Kalugal

"I won't be needing the equipment after all." The doctor walked into the sitting room. "It's a simple bacterial infection that responds very well to antibiotics. Jin is going to be fine in a matter of hours."

Kalugal rose to his feet. "Best news I've had today. Thank you." He offered the doctor his hand.

"I'm going to check on Jin." Jacki walked up to Julian. "Thank you for coming, and say hi to everyone else in the gang for me." She leaned and kissed his cheek. "Bye, Julian."

Even though there was nothing going on between the two, Kalugal didn't like her touching the male.

Forcing a smile, he turned to the doctor. "Would you like to stay the night, or are you going back to your people?"

"I doubt Jin will need my services, but I don't mind staying around if it's okay with you."

An unexpected relief washed over Kalugal. "I would very much like for you to stay. I find myself out of my element with an ill human, and I must admit that I didn't enjoy the feeling of not knowing how to help her."

The doctor nodded. "I know how you feel. Sometimes doctors can't help either, and that's incredibly frustrating, even depressing. It was difficult for me to work in a human hospital and be exposed to suffering I couldn't alleviate."

"Are you an empath?"

"Not a strong one. But it would have been hard for any immortal with a sensitive nose. I hate the scent of despair."

Kalugal nodded. "I hear you. There are many emotional scents that I find repugnant. My favorite by far is the smell of female arousal," he added to lighten the mood.

Julian cracked a smile. "Isn't it every male's?"

"You guys are gross." Jacki walked back into the sitting room, the color of her cheeks a deeper peach color than before.

Was she embarrassed?

"My apologies." Kalugal dipped his head while stifling a smile.

When they were waiting for Julian to administer the shot, he'd caught a very slight whiff of that best scent, and now that Jacki had heard his and Julian's exchange, she must've realized that her secret was out.

She waved a dismissive hand. "No need to apologize. All it proves is that all men are the same. Immortal or human, sophisticated or not, educated or not, it doesn't matter. Leave you alone for a few minutes, and you turn into adolescents, spewing locker-room humor."

Julian shrugged. "There's no harm in that. It just proves that we are female aficionados. Imagine a world in which males were indifferent to female charms."

"I could do without your appreciation for certain female-specific scents. But speaking of smells, I helped Jin to get into the shower. Can I borrow some clean clothes for her?"

"Certainly." Kalugal opened the door and motioned for Shamash to come in. "Can you show the doctor to a guest room?"

They'd never had guests before or had planned on having any, so there was no spare room in the house that was dedicated for that purpose. But since most of the men were still in the bunker, Shamash could put the doctor in one of their rooms.

"I don't intend to sleep," Julian said. "Point me to an armchair, and I'll spend what's left of the night reading."

"Then you will enjoy my library."

The doctor's eyes sparkled. "I definitely would. I'm also going to call Kian and give him an update if you don't mind."

"Not at all. It will save me the trouble."

Julian waved a hand at Shamash. "Lead the way."

"Bye, Julian." Jacki waved before turning to Kalugal. "You didn't tell your guy to get clothes for Jin."

"She can have some of mine. Follow me."

"Where?"

"To the closet, of course."

Jacki snorted. "That's the worst pick-up line I've ever heard."

"You have a one-track mind, Jacqueline."

As Kalugal walked back into the bedroom, he expected to be greeted by the smell of vomit. But Jacki had opened the windows, and most of it was gone.

"What do you mean?" She followed him into the closet.

"You keep insinuating that I'm flirting with you, but I am not." He was, but so far, he had been so subtle that it could have easily been interpreted as friendliness.

She rolled her eyes. "My mistake." Her tone dripped with sarcasm.

Naturally, a beauty like Jacki was used to a lot of male attention, and the best way to deal with someone like her was to appear unaffected by it.

He pulled out a set of silk pajamas and handed them to her. "If the pants are too loose, she can use only the top."

"Jin is tall. It might not be long enough to cover the essentials." Looking around his cavernous walk-in closet,

Jacki pointed to a bank of drawers. "Do you have a pair of new boxer shorts by any chance?"

"I sure do." He opened the drawer and handed her a pair that still had the tag attached to it.

She ran the fabric between her fingers. "It's so soft. Is everything you wear next to your skin made from silk?'

Was she thinking about him in the nude, wearing only his boxer shorts or pajama bottoms?

The thought was very arousing.

"I like how it feels." His voice dropped half an octave.

The peach color of Jacki's cheeks deepened. "I bet. Only the best will do for you."

Jin

After showering, Jin already felt significantly better. First of all, the disgusting smell of puke was finally out of her hair, and secondly, much as she hated to admit it, Kalugal's silk pajamas were incredibly soft and luxurious.

Arwel would not have approved of her wearing another man's sleepwear, especially a sexy devil's like Kalugal, but he wasn't there, and she didn't have a choice.

Not much of the vomit had gotten on Alena's sweater and skirt, but they had still smelled horrible. Jacki had washed both in the bathroom sink, and then one of Kalugal's men had taken them to put in the washing machine and then the dryer. By morning, she could change back, and Arwel wouldn't know she had ever worn Kalugal's pajamas.

"I had tea made for you." Kalugal walked into the bedroom with a tray. "The regular kind." He put it on the nightstand.

Talk about ego-boosting. One of the two most powerful immortals on the planet was serving her tea in bed.

Sweet.

She smiled. "Thank you. Where is Jacki?"

"She fell asleep on the couch in the sitting room."

Lifting the chair that Jacki had moved aside, he brought it closer to the bed and sat down. "How are you feeling?" He poured the tea into a porcelain cup.

"A thousand times better. I can't believe how fast that shot worked." She took a sip from the tea. "Earl Grey?"

"Yes. I told Shamash to use the plainest tea we had."

Kalugal was such a snob, but for once she was going to keep her big mouth shut and not voice her opinion. "It's the one I like most."

"I'm glad that I was able to oblige your preference." He eyed her with that signature smirk lifting one corner of his perfect lips. "You must be disappointed."

"About what?"

"You thought that you were transitioning."

She nodded. "I'm glad it didn't happen now. I still need to show you that the tether is off. As much as I appreciate your hospitality, I want to be out of here by morning."

The smirk became more pronounced. "Given the way you were staring at my lips, I thought that you might want to stay a little longer."

Damn. The man was not only a snob but also full of himself. Still, she was going to tread lightly, and treat him as politely as a former Israeli soldier could. Some flattery wouldn't hurt either.

"You have the most beautiful lips I've ever seen on a man, and it's hard not to stare, but my heart belongs to another. Besides, your eyes can't compete with Arwel's."

He chuckled. "Indeed. He has the most uniquely colored eyes. But I'm sure that's not the only reason you gave him your heart."

"It was the first thing I noticed, but I fell in love with the whole package. There isn't a single thing I would change about Arwel." She scrunched her nose. "Except for his wardrobe, but that's a work in progress."

"A wardrobe is easy to fix." He sighed. "I want to wish the two of you the best of luck, but I have to be honest with you. If you can't prove to me that the tether is off, I won't be able to release you."

"I'll prove it." She scooted aside, clearing space on the bed, and patted the mattress. "Come sit next to me, and let's do it."

Gracefully unfolding his limbs from the chair, he shifted over to the bed and offered her his hand.

She took it and held it between her two. "I'm going to reattach the tether now. Close your eyes and turn your sight inward. You should experience a slight mental heaviness."

He nodded and did as she asked. "I'm ready."

Concentrating, she imagined inserting a hook into Kalugal's mind, and then attaching a thick strand of her consciousness to it instead of the wispy one she usually employed. Hopefully, he was going to feel it.

"It's attached. Can you feel it?"

Kalugal opened his eyes. "I think so, but it could be a placebo effect."

"Close your eyes again and focus on that feeling of heaviness. When I remove the tether, you should feel the difference."

"Okay."

"Did you feel it?"

He nodded. "I think so. Do it again."

She ended up tethering and releasing him five more times before he was convinced.

Partially.

"I felt the difference, but you might have been doing something differently to make me feel it. I can never be sure that the tether is really off."

"You can even remove it yourself once you know what to look for. One of the people I tethered was able to do it."

"I can attempt to do so, but that is not going to be conclusive either. I might imagine myself doing that, but

I have no way of verifying that the tether is gone. I'll still need to take your word for it."

"Ask me. Compel me to tell you the truth."

"Is the tether off?"

"Yes, it is."

"Did you ever fail to remove the tether from someone you attached it to?"

"No."

"Have you ever encountered someone who you couldn't tether?"

"No. I could even do it to Jacki, who is immune to every other mind trick."

"How do you explain that?"

Jin sighed and looked down. "It's only speculation, but my sister and I think that we are the descendants of a different god. Someone who was not like the others. No one in the clan has ever heard of abilities like ours."

"What is your sister's talent?"

"She can retrieve echoes imbued in the walls. Not of everyday stuff, only conversations and events that were emotionally charged."

"Fascinating. I could use both your talents."

Jin smiled. "If you play nice with Kian, he might let you borrow us on occasion. But just so you know, I don't plan on a career in espionage. My sister and I are going to launch a fashion line."

His eyes widened. "That would be a terrible waste of two incredible talents. You could make millions by offering your special services."

"Or we could get conscripted into government service. That was what happened to me. If not for the clan, I would still be stuck in there. They saved me."

"Tell me all about it. And start at the beginning, please."

By the time she was done, it was light outside, Kalugal had ordered four more pots of tea to be delivered, and he must have asked her a thousand questions.

God only knew what he was going to do with all that information, but it wasn't as if she'd had a choice.

"One last question."

Jin rolled her eyes. "Go for it."

"Do you really love Arwel?"

"With all my heart and everything that I am. I can't imagine my life without him. We are fated mates." She smiled. "I didn't fully believe that until you captured him, but now I do."

He tilted his head. "You seem like an intelligent woman. I'm surprised that you believe in such romantic nonsense."

"It's real. Arwel says that the Fates reward those who have sacrificed greatly for others by giving them their one and only, a mate to form an unbreakable bond with. I haven't sacrificed much, but Arwel has, enough for both of us. Every day out in the field is torturous for him."

"How so?"

"That's more than one question, but it's not like I can refuse to answer. Arwel is a powerful empath, and he is constantly bombarded by human emotions. He would have been much happier in a job that didn't require interaction with humans, but despite the anguish it brings him, he chooses to be a Guardian and uses his special talent to protect the clan."

Kalugal

Kalugal smiled. "That's admirable, and he deserves his reward." He rose to his feet. "I'll let you catch a little sleep."

"Are you going to let me go?"

Even though he wasn't sure about it yet, he nodded. "That's what I promised." He walked out into the sitting room.

Jacki was still asleep, covered in the throw blanket he'd wrapped around her. Hopefully, she hadn't been infected. The bacteria had wreaked havoc on Jin, and he would hate to see Jacki suffer like that.

Except, this time he knew what to do. He would bring a doctor and have him give her a penicillin shot. The thing worked like a miracle.

Sitting on an armchair across from Jacki, he was fascinated by the many shades of blond interwoven in her long wavy hair. He could have sat there for hours and just looked at her sleeping, but he had some thinking to do, and she was too distracting.

As Kalugal got up and walked out of the room, it occurred to him that it would be better if Jacki left as soon as possible. She was an unhealthy obsession that he had no business having, and she was too much of a distraction. A pleasant one, but still.

Except, he worried about the girl.

What was Kian going to do with her?

Perhaps he should continue his questioning to get a better insight into his cousin's motives and modes of operation. Jin didn't know much, and he doubted he could get anything more out of her. The doctor, on the other hand, would know much more.

Kalugal hadn't promised Kian not to interrogate him, but the fact that Kian hadn't insisted on it meant that the doctor didn't know any strategic secrets. Which was fine. He could still answer many of the questions that had been bugging Kalugal for decades.

When he opened the library doors, Kalugal found Julian flipping through one of his tomes on Sumerian mythology. "I see that you've chosen some light reading to pass the time."

Julian weighed the thick book on his palm. "Not as heavy as what's inside. Fascinating stuff."

Kalugal walked over to the library's bar and poured himself a small glass of whiskey. "Would you care to join me?" He lifted the bottle of twenty-five-year-old Macallan.

"Sure. I'm not a great whiskey connoisseur, but even I know that's a good one."

"What do you usually drink?" Kalugal handed him the glass.

"Beer."

Kalugal sat in the other armchair and crossed his legs. "Beer doesn't do it for me."

"Did you ever try Snake Venom?"

"Is it any good?"

"It's potent, and it's the only beer that can give an immortal a buzz."

"I drink for the taste, not to get drunk. Tell me, Julian, are immortal females blessed with the same advantages as the males?"

The doctor shook his head. "Are you using compulsion on me?"

"I'm not going to ask that you reveal clan secrets. Since I've never encountered an immortal female other than my mother, who I now know is a goddess, I'm curious about them and how different they are from the males. My father didn't share that information with his sons, real or adopted."

Julian struggled for a long moment, but Kalugal knew he wouldn't be able to resist for long and waited patiently.

"They are stronger than human females and have the same enhanced hearing and eyesight as the males. But they are not as strong, and they don't have functional fangs. Their sense of smell is not as developed either."

"What about thralling and shrouding abilities?"

"They have them, but since females don't need to use them, very few are good thrallers or shrouders."

"Is it because they are not soldiers?"

Julian chuckled. "It's because they don't bite their sex partners and don't need to erase the memory of it later."

"I see. Is there any way to distinguish them from human females?"

"Not unless they exhibit their strength."

The doctor was trying to resist by giving partial answers, but it was not going to work.

"Please list all the ways in which immortal females are different from human females and how to identify them."

That should close any loopholes Julian might cling to in an effort to resist giving Kalugal a complete answer.

"The scent of their arousal is different than that of human females. The caveat is that you need to know what to sniff for, and the female needs to be aroused at that moment for you to catch it. They also have the same rapid healing ability as the males. But it's not like you can go around scratching a woman's skin and watching how fast it heals."

"What about Dormants? How do you find them?"

"Usually, they find us."

Kalugal arched a brow. "Please explain."

"We've tried all kinds of methods to identify Dormants, but so far, the only indicator we've found was paranormal ability. It's not a sure sign because some humans with no godly genes have supernatural talents as well, and some Dormants have none. Most were seemingly random encounters or the work of the Fates, as some of us believe."

"Do you?"

Julian nodded. "You may say that I was compelled to. Meeting my mate must have been arranged by the Fates. There is no logical explanation for the bizarre set of circumstances that led to our coming together."

"How did you know she was your mate?"

Julian smiled. "One look at her picture was enough. I couldn't stop thinking about her. Every time I closed my eyes, I saw her looking at me, urging me to find her."

"Interesting. So, it can't be explained by pheromones or some other physical reaction."

"Precisely. When I saw her picture, I didn't know that she was a Dormant. All I knew was that the beautiful girl in the photo was much too young for me. The Fates had a different opinion."

"One more question. Can immunity to mind manipulation be considered a paranormal talent?"

Julian nodded.

"Is Jacki a Dormant?"

"She might be. There is no way to know until she is induced. She either transitions or doesn't."

"Has it been attempted with her?"

"No. She is new, and she doesn't know anything about transition or about being a possible candidate for one. We don't tell the suspected Dormants anything until they find a clan member to bond with, or in human terms to fall in love with. The bond guarantees their loyalty, and without it we can't risk the exposure."

That was excellent news. Jacki was a potential Dormant, and that explained why Kian accepted her into the clan and why he wasn't going to harm her when she came back to him.

Except, she might not.

Kalugal smirked.

Perhaps the Fates the clan believed in had arranged all of this to deliver Jacki to him. If she was indeed a Dormant, he could induce her transition and turn her immortal.

Suddenly his horizon appeared so much brighter.

Jacki could give him immortal children.

There was no guarantee that she possessed godly genes, but on the remote chance that she did, he couldn't let her go until he had seduced her and attempted to induce her transition.

Jin

After Kalugal left, Jin didn't go to sleep. She didn't even try.

Was he going to let her go?

He'd said he would, but he hadn't looked convinced. She could imagine him pacing the hallways of his sprawling mansion and plotting how to keep her without it causing a war with the clan.

Damn.

Now that she was feeling so much better, all kinds of crazy ideas were swirling in her head. The door to the suite was probably unlocked, and the Guardians were just outside the gate. Could she make a run for it?

Kalugal's men were not going to shoot her, so if she was fast enough and could scale that fence, she could get free.

How tall was that fence anyway?

Jin had watched it so many times from the balcony of the rented house, she should have known that, but for some reason, the details were hazy. Was it built from blocks or from bricks?

The master suite Kalugal had put her in faced the back yard, so she couldn't just look out the window and check.

If the fence was six feet tall, she could climb it with ease, she could even manage eight if there were small crevices that she could stick her fingertips into.

Except, she wouldn't make it to the wall before one of Kalugal's men tackled her to the ground.

Maybe Jacki could create a diversion?

Nah, those were all stupid thoughts. Kalugal would have no choice but to trade her back. The small suspicion still lingering in his mind was not enough for him to abandon Rufsur.

The sun was all the way up in the sky when Kalugal walked in with her clothes neatly folded in his arms. "You are awake."

"I couldn't sleep."

"How are you feeling?"

"As good as new."

"Excellent. That means that you can walk out of here on your own two feet, and Julian doesn't need to carry you out." He put the clothes on the chair next to the bed. "Get dressed. I'm letting you go."

Jin flung the blanket off and jumped up. "You don't have to ask me twice." She padded toward the bathroom. "I'll be out in a minute."

"No rush. I called Kian and told him to bring Rufsur back. We agreed to make the exchange at ten-thirty, which is two hours from now."

"Oh, okay."

"After you get dressed, come down and join Julian and me for breakfast."

"What about Jacki?"

"She stays. But you need to remove the tether from her as well."

"Why?"

"Because I don't want a spy in my house."

"Ouch."

"If you don't untether her, I will have to keep her locked up. If you do, she can be an honored guest instead of a prisoner."

Jin shook her head. "What's the difference? Jacki can tell us what she saw later, when you release her. I don't feel safe leaving her here with you without knowing what's going on with her."

"Do you want to go home, Jin? Because I can trade Jacki for Rufsur and keep you. You are a much better prize than your friend."

Damn him for leaving the choice up to her.

Maybe if he hadn't told her already that he was letting her go, she could have done the right thing and chosen to stay so Jacki could go. But with the taste of freedom already in her mouth, Jin couldn't bring herself to do that.

"It's only for a few hours, right?"

"Maybe a little longer. I don't know when Kian can arrange for me to speak with my mother."

That didn't sound too bad. Even if Jacki had to stay another night. After all, Kalugal would want more than one phone call with his mother, and if he did anything to Jacki, Kian would cut him off.

"Shouldn't Jacki join us for breakfast?"

"If you want to wake her up, you are welcome to do so. She is still passed out on the couch in the sitting room."

"I can't go without saying goodbye to her first."

He shrugged. "Then wake her up."

Why did she have the feeling that Kalugal had no intention of letting Jacki go anytime soon?

After Kian let him talk with Areana, it made no sense for him to keep her. Jacki didn't know anything useful, and even if she did, he couldn't compel her to tell him anything unless he planned to torture it out of her, but Jin doubted he would resort to that. Kalugal was a stuck-up snob who thought he was all that, but he wasn't evil.

Besides, Jacki seemed to like him. Maybe something had started between the two while she had been out of it?

That could be an interesting development.

After getting dressed, Jin combed her hair with her fingers because she didn't want to use Kalugal's brush, but she did use some of the hand lotion he had on the vanity to moisten her face. She looked like a damn ghost and there was nothing else she could do to improve her appearance. As they had suspected, it seemed that Kalugal never brought females home because there was nothing in his bathroom to suggest otherwise.

There was no leftover foundation, or eyeliner, or an extra robe. Even though the place was immaculately clean and luxurious, it screamed bachelor.

When she was done, Jin pulled on her shoes and walked into the sitting room.

Asleep on the couch, Jacki had a soft pillow tucked under her cheek, and a thick blanket tucked around her.

Had Kalugal done that? That was nice of him.

The two made a most unlikely pair, but maybe that was part of the attraction. Jacki had never met a guy like Kalugal, and he had probably never met a girl like Jacki, and not only because one was an immortal and the other still a human.

He was a prince, and she was a foster kid without a penny to her name.

Talk about Cinderella. Except, this one came with a sharp tongue and equally sharp claws. Jacki was no damsel in distress in need of a rescuer.

Or maybe she was?

Perhaps that was what Jacki had been looking for in a guy? Someone who would take care of her so she wouldn't have to worry ever again about where her next meal would come from or where she was going to sleep?

Except, if that was true, Jacki would have stayed in the program. She'd had a guaranteed income, including all-expenses-paid accommodations, and she'd given it all up for freedom.

Crouching next to her friend, Jin shook her shoulder. "Jacki, wake up."

"What? Why? Is it morning?"

"It is. Do you want to come down for breakfast?"

Yawning, Jacki stretched and sat up. "You look so much better. How are you feeling?"

"This is better?" Jin pulled on the skin under her eye. "I look like the walking dead."

"Trust me, this is better. Last night you looked like the non-walking dead. This is a big improvement."

Jin snorted. "Thanks for the compliment."

"You can always count on me to tell you the truth." Jacki put her feet down and got up. "I need to use the bathroom."

"I'll wait for you."

When Jacki was done, they took the stairs to the lower floor and followed the appetizing smells toward the dining room.

"I'm surprised that there were no guards posted outside the bedroom." Jacki stopped next to a painting. "Is this an original Picasso?"

"How should I know? It's possible. Kalugal likes expensive stuff."

"Who doesn't?" Jacki moved over to the next painting. "But I don't think those are originals. He wouldn't have hung them in the hallway."

"Probably. By the way, Kalugal is letting me go."

Jacki stopped and turned to look at her. "You managed to convince him?"

"Yes. After you fell asleep, he came back to the bedroom, and I attached and then removed the tether several times until he started noticing the difference."

"Thank God." Jacki pulled her into a crushing embrace. "It's over."

"Not yet. He is keeping you for a little while longer, and he wants me to remove the tether from you."

"I don't mind." Jacki waved her arm in an arc. "It's not every day that I get to stay in a place like this. More like never. This is a palace."

"You are not scared?"

"Of what?"

"You know, improper advances and stuff like that. There are no other women on Kalugal's estate, and without the tether, no one will know what's going on in here." She leaned closer. "Arwel says that all immortals are notoriously horny."

Jacki chuckled. "I hope that you know that from personal experience and not just hearsay."

Jin felt her ears warm up. "I certainly do."

Given the mischievous gleam in Jacki's eyes, she wasn't done teasing her. "Be careful not to set the house on fire." She leaned to whisper in her ear. "I'll be watching out for the smoke."

"Don't be silly." Jin slapped her arm and then leaned to whisper back. "With everyone fussing around us, we won't get the chance, and hopefully, by tonight, you will join us."

Jacki arched a brow. "I don't swing that way."

Jin laughed. "You know what I mean. Anyway, I'm done with my wandering days, and I hope to rekindle our passion in Arwel's home, not in the rented place or a hotel. I want days of doing nothing but making love, taking romantic walks, and having romantic dinners with my guy."

Arwel

"Kalugal is releasing Jin." Magnus walked into the kitchen holding his phone.

Arwel's legs nearly gave out, and he leaned against the counter to steady himself. "When?"

"In two hours. We need to get Rufsur back here. Once he is at the gate, Jin is going to walk out with Julian. The antibiotics shot he gave her was an overnight cure."

"I'm ready to kiss him."

Kri snorted. "Who, Kalugal?"

"Julian. He cured my girl."

"What about Jacki?"

"I'll kiss her too."

"I meant, is he releasing her as well, or does he still want to keep her until he talks with his mother?"

Magnus shrugged. "As far as I know, that's still the plan. Kian told me to put you, Jin, and Kri on the plane and send you home. He wants all three of you out of here. "

Kri frowned. "Why do I need to go?"

"You know why. You are a head Guardian, and you know where the village is."

"I get it. But I could drive back with Michael." She cast Arwel a lopsided grin. "You and Jin probably want to celebrate on the plane. But if Kian insists, I can stay with Charlie in the cockpit and use these amazing earplugs Magnus has gotten us." She pulled them out of her pocket.

Arwel shook his head. "I just want to hold Jin in my arms and never let go."

"Still, I'd rather drive home with Michael."

"There is enough space for all four of you on the jet," Magnus said. "If you want to drive home, you will have to clear it with Kian first."

"Of course." She pulled out her phone and started typing a text.

"This is how I suggest we do it." Magnus leaned on the counter next to Arwel. "I'm going to bring Rufsur to the gate, collect Julian and Jin, and load them into my car. You and Kri will head to the airstrip and wait for us there."

Arwel wanted to argue that he could wait in the car, but he knew it wasn't prudent. Even staying in the rented house had been a risk.

Except so far, Kalugal hadn't tried anything underhanded or unexpected. He was holding up his end of the deal and doing exactly what he had promised to do.

In fact, Arwel had to admit that the clan had acted less honorably than Kalugal by sending Jin after him, and that he'd been very reserved in his response.

Was he reading the situation all wrong?

In the brief moments he'd had with Kalugal, Arwel had tried to read his emotional grid, but it hadn't been easy. Not because Kalugal was so complicated, but because he just wasn't the emotional type.

If they weren't on opposite sides of the fence, Arwel could have enjoyed the guy's company. Calm, collected, and logical were precisely the type of people Arwel liked to hang out with. That was why accountants were his favorites.

But what if Kalugal was just a cold and calculating bastard, and he was lulling them into a false sense of security?

Arwel needed more information about the guy, and he knew where to get it. "I'll come to collect Rufsur with you. I haven't had a chance to chat with him yet. I can continue from there straight to the airstrip."

"You're welcome to come, but don't expect to get any information out of him. The guy only appears easygoing and friendly. He has a sharp mind, and he keeps his guard up. I talked with him for hours last night and got basically nothing."

"I have a slight advantage over you. I can sense his emotional response, and that gives me additional insight. Besides, I promised him a chat, and I didn't make good on it."

"Sorry to disappoint you," Kri said after reading the return text from Kian. "He doesn't want me and Michael to waste time driving. We are coming with you and Jin on the plane. Julian is going to stay another day in case Jacki caught the bug from Jin and needs him, but the medical equipment that he brought with him goes back with us."

"That's okay. I wasn't planning on joining the mile-high club just yet."

He and Jin had eternity together, and there would be plenty of time to try new things. Making love in the sky could wait.

Jin

Excitement swirling in her belly, Jin hugged Jacki. "See you soon."

"I hope so. Give Arwel a kiss for me." Jacki winked. "On the cheek. The other kisses are all yours."

"I can't wait."

"Then go." Her friend pushed her away. "I'll be fine."

Taking a deep breath, Jin nodded and walked over to Julian and Kalugal, who had been waiting patiently for her to say goodbye.

Jin pinned Kalugal with a hard stare. "Be good to her."

"Don't worry. I'll treat her like a visiting dignitary."

He sounded sincere, but Jin still felt like she was abandoning Jacki in a lions' den, and she wasn't sure whether Kalugal was more like Mufasa than Scar, or the other way around.

As the gate opened, Jin expected Arwel would be waiting for her, and her heart squeezed in disappointment when she saw Magnus standing on the other side of the street with Rufsur and not her mate.

With a nod from Kalugal, she and Julian started walking, and so did Rufsur. The guy smiled and winked when he passed them, but he didn't stop and kept walking.

She turned around, wanting to issue another warning about Jacki, but Julian's hand on her elbow propelled her forward.

"Welcome back." Magnus opened the passenger door for her.

Hoping to find Arwel inside the car, she ducked her head, but he wasn't there. "Where is Arwel?"

Magnus shook his head and got behind the wheel.

"He can't hear you. He has earplugs in," Julian explained as he got in the car.

"Oh."

That was smart. If Magnus couldn't hear Kalugal, he couldn't be compelled.

Glancing at the rearview mirror, Magnus drove for about fifteen minutes before pulling his earplugs out. "Arwel is waiting for you at the airstrip, but first, I'm going to drop Julian off at the motel."

Jin's heart sped up. They were finally going home. "Can I borrow your phone to call him?"

"Use mine." Julian handed her the device. "He's listed under Arabella."

Magnus chuckled. "That's clever, but not very imaginative. You should have listed him under Beatrice or some other name that bears no resemblance to his."

Julian shrugged. "That's the first thing that came to my mind."

Ignoring their banter, Jin placed the call.

"Julian," Arwel answered. "Is Jin all right?"

"It's me. I'm calling from Julian's phone."

She heard him release a breath. "Are you okay?"

"I'm great. The antibiotics shot cured me overnight. I can't wait to see you."

"I wanted to be there when you came out, but Kian didn't want Kri and me anywhere near Kalugal. We know too much."

"I get it. Are we going to the village? Or are we going back to the keep?"

He hesitated for a moment. "We are going to the village. I have some upsetting news for you. Wendy is a mole. She contacted the director."

Jin shook her head. "There must be some mistake. Why would she do that?"

"I don't have the details."

"Damn." Jin slumped back in the seat. "I should have tethered her like Kian asked me to do. I could have caught her before she had a chance to call. What did she tell him?"

"Just the location of the cabin they moved into after I was compromised, and the story we told your friends about who we are."

"Are you sure that this is all?"

"One of the Guardians thralled her and confirmed the information. What I'm afraid of, though, is that she might have an ability to shield parts of her consciousness. Otherwise, she wouldn't have been able to fool Edna."

"Do you think the Guardian saw a false memory?"

"It's unlikely with a fresh memory, but not impossible. The clan's psychologist should have a talk with her."

"Perhaps I should talk with Wendy. Where is she?"

"Kian had her locked up in the keep."

"Can we go there instead of the village?"

Magnus shook his head and mouthed *no* while looking at her in the rearview mirror.

Jin frowned. What was that about?

"You need to rest and regain your strength," Arwel said. "Let someone else take care of this for now."

"You don't have to twist my arm too hard. I really want to finally see the village, but I feel responsible for Wendy. How about I go see her tomorrow?"

"First, let's get home and then make plans for the future. Que sera, sera."

"Whatever will be, will be." She smiled and switched the phone to her other ear. "The future is not ours to see. But there is one thing I know for sure."

"What is it?"

"My future is with you."

The Adventure continues
JACKI & KALUGAL'S STORY IS NEXT
The Children of the Gods Book 38
Dark Overlord New Horizon
Turn the page to read the excerpt—>

Join the VIP Club
To find out what's included in your free membership, flip to the last page.

Dark Overlord New Horizon

Jacki has two talents that set her apart from the rest of the human race.
She has unpredictable glimpses of other people's futures, and she is immune to mind manipulation.
Unfortunately, both talents are pretty useless for

finding a job other than the one she had in the government's paranormal division.

It seemed like a sweet deal, until she found out that the director planned on producing super babies by compelling the recruits into pairing up. When an opportunity to escape the program presented itself, she took it, only to find out that humans are not at the top of the food chain. Immortals are real, and at the very top of the hierarchy is Kalugal, the most powerful, arrogant, and sexiest male she has ever met. With one look, he sets her blood on fire, but Jacki is not a fool. A man like him will never think of her as anything more than a tasty snack, while she will never settle for anything less than his heart.

Jacki

As Jacki escorted Jin to Kalugal's front door, she had a sinking feeling that she was never going to see her bestie or her other new friends again. In the short time that she'd spent with the bunch, they'd become like a family to her, and finding out that most of them were immortal hadn't changed the way she felt about them. They were her teammates, and she was going to miss them.

Thankfully, a feeling wasn't a vision, so it might not come true. Jacki's gut had been wrong about things before. Besides, being left alone with Kalugal was reason enough for the churning in her stomach. The rest was just panic induced, and Jacki refused to let it bring her down.

She'd survived worse, and she was going to survive this as well.

"I hope that Arwel isn't still mad at me." Jin took a deep breath before walking out the door.

"He loves you too much to stay mad."

"I know that he loves me. But that doesn't mean that he's not angry."

During their imprisonment in Kalugal's bunker, Arwel and Jacki had become good friends, and at the beginning, they had even pretended to be a couple. The thing was, Jin must have witnessed some of their pretend flirting through the mental link she'd had to Jacki, and she must have also heard Arwel ranting about her decision to surrender herself to Kalugal.

Perhaps that had created doubts in Jin's mind?

Jacki wrapped her arm around her friend's shoulders. "I won't lie to you. When Rufsur told us that you were going to be traded for Arwel, your guy was majorly pissed, but that was because he was terrified of what Kalugal might do to you. Since nothing bad happened, and you are going back to him unharmed, all is good in Arwel's world."

Jin nodded. "I was scared too. Thank God that Kalugal turned out to be a decent guy. But while that might be true for me, I'm not sure about his intentions for you." She eyed Jacki with concern. "I hate leaving you behind. Without the tether, I can't check up on you." Glancing at Kalugal and Julian, who were standing further down the driveway, Jin leaned to whisper in Jacki's ear. "I don't like it that he demanded that I remove the tether from you. It should have been enough that I removed it from him, and it was also what he and Kian had agreed on."

"I think that it makes perfect sense for Kalugal to ask that," Jacki whispered back. "If you'd kept the tether to me, you could've spied on him through my eyes. If I were in his shoes, I would have done the same." She gave Jin a slight push. "Get out of here and go to your boyfriend. Everything is going to be okay."

Jin pulled her into a tight embrace. "See you soon."

"I hope so. Give Arwel a kiss for me. On the cheek, of course." Jacki winked. "The other kind of kisses are all yours."

"I can't wait."

"Then go." She pushed Jin away. "I'll be fine."

Thankfully, empathy wasn't one of Jin's paranormal talents, so she bought the lie and the fake smile that Jacki had plastered on her face.

Watching her friend walk down Kalugal's driveway, Jacki didn't feel fine.

She was scared.

When Jin reached Kalugal, she pointed a finger at him. "Be good to her."

"Don't worry. I'll treat her like a visiting dignitary."

Taking a last glance at her friend, Jacki turned around and walked back in. With a sigh, she sat at the dining room table and reached for a piece of toast. Perhaps chewing on it would relieve the churning in her stomach.

So much for thinking of herself as tough, resourceful, and fearless. Except, there was a limit to how much she could take in such a short time.

Jacki felt as if she was staring down a tunnel, and it seemed that with each step she was tumbling deeper into an alternate reality.

The thing was, she knew precisely what had gotten her to where she was now. She'd been having visions her entire life, but the first tumble down the rabbit hole had started with one particular vision, which in hindsight, she regretted not keeping to herself.

As soon as she'd seen the old clunker that her friend Allison had gotten, the vision had hit Jacki hard. The car was going to break down, and Allison was going to end up in a ditch with multiple fractures and spend the next six months in rehabilitation.

Naturally, Allison had dismissed Jacki's vision as nonsense and had taken the clunker on a road trip to

California. Jacki's prediction had come true, and a week after Allison's accident, she'd been contacted by Marisol, who had offered her a job in the paranormal talents' division.

Apparently, during her phone calls to Allison, Jacki had mentioned the words visions and predictions, and the bots had picked up on the trigger words, flagging her as a potential paranormal talent. When her prediction about Allison's accident had come true, her talent had been confirmed.

Still, all of that had been small potatoes compared to what happened next.

Meeting Jin in the program and foreseeing her rescue was the reason Jacki was sitting in the dining room of the fanciest house she'd ever seen, and until a few minutes ago, staring at the face of the most gorgeous, arrogant, sexy man ever born.

Correction.

Not a man, an immortal.

And not just any immortal, one of the two most powerful immortals on the planet.

Damn.

Up until three days ago, she hadn't known that immortals even existed, or that the people who'd helped her escape from the program weren't human.

Her biggest fear was that the knowledge could mean the end of her.

Humans were not supposed to know that immortals had been living among them since the beginning of civilization. If not for her immunity to mind manipulation, they could've erased the memory from her head like they did with all the other humans who had the misfortune of finding out about them. But there was no way to erase Jacki's memories, and she was stuck with what she'd learned.

Even if Kalugal released her in exchange for what Kian had promised him, she would never be free again. The way Jacki saw it, there were three possible outcomes.

One was being Kalugal's prisoner for the rest of her natural life, the other was the same fate at Kian's hands, and the third one was her death.

Was she being overly dramatic? Fatalistic?

Probably.

Jacki doubted that Kian and her new friends would kill her, but she was quite certain that she would never be allowed to go back to her old life.

There was also a fourth possibility.

Kalugal could fall in love with her, and they could live happily ever after.

Right. Talk about fairytales and fantasies.

A man like him might want her in his bed for a night or two, but no more than that.

Except, Jacki was not going to be his or anyone else's plaything, not even to save her life.

For her, it always had been and always would be all or nothing.

Kalugal

"Welcome back, my friend." Kalugal pulled Rufsur into a one-armed embrace and clapped him on the back. "How was your stay with my cousin's people?"

"For the most part, uneventful." Rufsur dug a key out of his pocket and leaned down to open the lock on his leg restraints.

"They gave you the key?" As Kalugal looked down at the chain connecting Rufsur's ankle cuffs, he wondered whether they were the same ones that Phinas had put on Arwel.

"The only reason they did that was so I couldn't run. If I had stopped to open the lock, that would have achieved the same result. They wanted Jin to reach their side before I reached ours." Rufsur tossed the chain aside and straightened up.

"Come, Jacki is waiting for us in the dining room." Kalugal turned and started walking.

Rufsur followed. "She is still here?"

Kalugal arched a brow. "Where else would she be?"

"I thought that you'd already talked to your mother and released Jacki."

He stopped and turned to his lieutenant. "Didn't they tell you about what happened with Jin?"

"Only that the exchange was delayed because she didn't feel well." Rufsur cast Kalugal a regretful look. "You must have been disappointed to find out that she was not an immortal and therefore not a clanswoman. That ruined your plans to forge an alliance with the clan by marrying the spy."

It had been a contingency Kalugal had come up with in case Jin couldn't remove the damn tether she'd attached to him. If that had been the case, he would have needed to keep her by his side, and the only way he could have done so without starting a war with the clan was a political marriage. The alliance with Kian had been a secondary consideration. Luckily for them both, Jin was able to demonstrate that the tether was gone.

The problem was that he wasn't a hundred percent sure that it was.

"Those plans were irrelevant anyway. Jin is in love with Arwel."

"So I heard. Is she all better now? She looked fine to me when I passed by her and that guy. Who was he?"

"That was one of the clan's doctors. Jin got sick all over the gazebo floor before she could demonstrate the tether's removal, and then she passed out. I couldn't let her go, so they sent the doctor. After he gave her an antibiotic shot, she recovered almost immediately."

"And then she proved to you that the tether was gone?"

Kalugal shrugged and resumed walking. "I'm still not convinced that it is."

"So why did you let her go?" Rufsur followed.

"I didn't have a choice. It was either that or start a war with the clan."

"But you felt something, right?"

Kalugal nodded. "I did. But it might have been a placebo effect. I might have felt it because I expected to feel it. I compelled Jin to tell me the truth, but that's not foolproof either. She might have believed that the tether was gone while some of it still remained, or she might be able to re-establish the connection remotely. I've just realized that I didn't ask her about that."

"Do you mean that you forgot to compel her to answer that truthfully?"

"It didn't occur to me to ask about it at all. I've made a mistake, and it might cost me dearly."

"What are you going to do?"

"I don't know. I guess I'll have to trust her that it's gone."

Rufsur arched a brow. "That's not like you."

His friend knew him well. Kalugal had an idea of how to prove the tether's removal, but he couldn't tell Rufsur about it because it would defeat the purpose.

His plan was to pretend that he believed the tether wasn't there, do something that would provoke Kian, and then wait for his cousin to react.

As they entered the dining room, Jacki smiled at Rufsur. "We meet again after all."

He grinned and walked up to her. "You are a sight for sore eyes, Miss Jacqueline the Fair." He took her hand and kissed the back of it.

"I like it. You make me sound like a fairytale princess."

Kalugal didn't like it at all, barely stifling the impulse to grab his lieutenant by the throat and toss him across the room.

Fortunately, Jacki pulled her hand out of Rufsur's. "Are you hungry? There is plenty left over, but it's cold. I can take it to the kitchen and warm it up for you." She started to rise.

Kalugal put a hand on her shoulder. "Sit down, Jacki. Shamash can do it. You are my guest." He put a slight emphasis on the *my*.

But Rufsur hadn't been paying attention and pulled out a chair next to Jacki. "I don't mind that it's cold. I'm not a finicky eater like my boss."

Taking his seat at the head of the table, Kalugal glared at Rufsur. "Tell me your impressions from the time you spent with Kian's men."

Rufsur lifted the coffee carafe and poured the cold brew into a cup. "There was a female there as well."

"A female warrior?" Kalugal asked.

"I don't think so. Vivian is the commander's wife, and she's a very pleasant woman. She made sure that the warriors treated me well and that I was made as comfortable as possible given the circumstances. They had me chained to a chair."

Kalugal looked at Jacki. "Do you know her?"

"Vivian is Magnus's wife, and she is not a soldier."

"Is she an immortal?"

Jacki shrugged. "Did you forget that I didn't know anything about immortals until you captured Arwel and me and informed me about Arwel being one? They told me that they were a group of paranormally talented people."

"Point taken." Kalugal turned to Rufsur. "Is Vivian an immortal?"

"I didn't think it was polite to ask, but I assume that she is. Otherwise, what's the point of marrying her? It's just asking for heartache when she gets old and dies."

Kalugal turned back to Jacki. "Does the clan have female warriors?"

She shrugged again. "How the hell would I know? They didn't tell me anything."

Rufsur loaded his plate with eggs. "Before taking me to where I met Vivian, they took me someplace else to search me thoroughly. There was a female there, who I'm sure was a warrior." He lifted his hands and spread them wide. "She had shoulders nearly as broad as mine, but she was still fine to look at, and so was Vivian. If all the clan females are that pretty, then we should start negotiating with your cousin for visitation rights." He glanced at Jacki. "Not for me, but for the others." He winked at her.

She shook her head. "The reasons why I can't date you haven't changed since yesterday. And as you have mentioned earlier, getting involved with a human is asking for heartache." She leaned toward him. "After all, I'm going to get old and die."

Rufsur reached for her hand, but she snatched it away. Undeterred, he smiled suggestively. "I'll take whatever time you're willing to give me."

She let out a breath. "When you stop goofing around and give it some serious thought, I'm sure you'll arrive at the same conclusion I did."

Kalugal really needed to have a talk with the guy and make it clear that Jacki was his. Otherwise, the moment Rufsur discovered that Jacki was a possible Dormant, he would redouble his crude flirting efforts and get twice as bold.

The thing was, Jacki seemed to respond to his lieutenant's unsophisticated approach.

Kalugal had a feeling that Jacki simply didn't know any better because she hadn't met any high-caliber men like him before. All she was familiar with were the clumsy flirtation attempts of uneducated young men, who shared her lowly socioeconomic background.

He hadn't missed her comment about growing up in foster homes. She was a poor girl, with no family and no higher education, and the only things she had going for her were her beauty and her immunity to mind manipulation.

Except, that same ability was an indicator of a strong mind. Perhaps Jacki's lack of education was the result of lack of opportunity, and not the lack of intelligence or the drive to acquire knowledge. If that was the case, he could teach her all she needed to know.

It reminded Kalugal of an old musical he had once seen. *My Fair lady* was a story about a stuck-up professor trying to teach a poor girl to talk and act like a lady.

Had the musical prompted Rufsur to address Jacki as Miss Jacqueline the Fair?

Or was it the other way around, and Rufsur's remark had planted the idea in Kalugal's mind?

Since his lieutenant had probably never watched a musical in his entire immortal life, the second assumption was more likely.

Rufsur had just wanted to impress Jacki with his good manners and fancy talk.

Nevertheless, the idea was sound. Jacki wasn't the perfect companion Kalugal would have wished for, but he might turn her into one yet.

The question was whether she would let him.

Once he executed his plan to verify that the tether was gone, Jacki might never forgive him or allow him anywhere near her, and regrettably, he would not be able to erase the nasty memory from her head either.

Director Simmons

Director Simmons opened the door to his office and motioned for his top recruiter to come in. "Good morning, Marisol."

"Good morning, sir." She walked over to his desk, took a seat in one of the leather chairs facing it, and put her hands on her knees.

"You look lovely."

"Thank you, sir."

"Please call me Edgar. You make me feel like an old man when you address me as sir."

"How about Doctor Simmons? Or Director Simmons?"

"We are friends, Marisol, and we are alone here. Save the titles for when we are in front of the recruits."

"Yes, sir. I mean, Edgar."

"That's better." He smiled and patted her bony back.

He wasn't flirting with the woman, but one of the things he had learned early on in his career was that personal touch always made his subordinates work harder for him.

Maybe if she were better looking and was a little more charming, he would have considered it, but Marisol had the sex appeal of a dull knife, and her personality bordered on sociopathic. Still, the new blonde hair softened her harsh features and made her look a little more feminine, which might help her with luring male talents into joining the program.

Sitting on the chair across from his recruiter, Edgar leaned toward her and steepled his fingers. "Wendy left a very interesting message on my voicemail."

Marisol's eyes widened. "She contacted you? Where is she? Are the others with her?"

He lifted a hand. "Slow down. When she left the message, they were in Big Bear, California, but Wendy must have gotten caught making the call because less than an hour later, there was no one at the address she provided. There was a for rent sign outside the cabin, and the guy that I'd sent to investigate found a cleaning crew preparing it for the next renters. They didn't know who stayed in it before."

"That should be easy to find out."

"Not really. Someone infected the rental records with a computer bug and turned everything into a jumbled mess. Not only that, the recording that Wendy left on my voice mail got erased. I tried to listen to it again, but it was no longer there. We are dealing with professionals, Eleanor."

He rarely called the recruiter by her real name, using it only when they were conspiring to do things that were not approved by the higher-ups.

"Did Wendy say anything else?"

"Yes, and it's more important than the location she provided. Apparently, an organization of paranormally talented people is collecting new members. Somehow, they knew about Jin and came for her. Jacki and Richard jumped on the opportunity to escape, and Wendy joined them so she could report to me and tell me where they were taken. She had to steal someone's phone to do so. Evidently, the organization that took them is not allowing them any more freedoms than we had."

Marisol snorted. "Fools. What did they expect? Some shady paranormal organization that is competing with us is not going to give them better terms or treat them better than we do. We need to stop the weekly leave until we figure out who we are dealing with, or at least beef up security."

Despite her abrasive and mistrustful nature, Eleanor was naive. But she wasn't entirely wrong.

Even though not everything was aboveboard, and not everything that the recruits had been told or promised was the truth, no one could compete with the US government's resources. He had no doubt that the program was leagues better than anything they could expect on the outside.

"We can't stop the outings. Not only are they good for morale, but they are also important for keeping up appearances. Trainees in other programs using this facility get to have days off. We can't treat ours differently. I can, however, increase security. We are already driving them to a different town every week, so the outings are not as predictable as they used to be before the escape."

Marisol's fingers drummed a nervous beat on her knees. "I don't remember much of what happened to me during the time I was gone, but I know that they got the information from me. That whole hotel room with drug paraphernalia was a setup. I've never used drugs, and I would have never gone to a hotel room with some guy I'd just met."

"I know, Marisol. We've been over that, and I don't blame you. It could have happened to anyone."

She looked down at her hands. "I don't know how they found out about me."

"You must have said something to Jin, and she told it to someone. She must have been resistant to compulsion."

Marisol shook her head. "She was so convincing. I can't believe that the girl managed to fool me."

Getting played bugged the hell out of Marisol, but what bugged her even more was that she'd had to change her name and her appearance once again. Her new name was Gina Voldachevsky, and she wasn't happy with it.

"I should start calling you Gina."

"It's confusing to the recruits who know me as Marisol." She touched her blonde curls. "This hair was adjustment enough."

"It looks good on you."

She smiled. "You are a bad liar, Edgar."

He laughed.

She couldn't have been more wrong. There were so many things he was keeping from her while pretending that she was his friend and confidant.

Eleanor, aka Marisol, aka Gina, had no idea that Wendy was his niece.

In fact, Wendy was his grandniece, but the distinction was not important. His sister's daughter was gone, most likely dead from a drug overdose, and his sister had passed away decades ago. He and Wendy were the only family members left.

The other thing Eleanor, aka Marisol, didn't know was that no matter where the missing trainees were hiding, he could find them quite easily. The only reason he hadn't done so already was that finding out who had taken them was more important than finding the trainees themselves.

Unlike Marisol, he was a patient man, and he was waiting for the dust to settle and for everyone to get comfortable and complacent. Not having a large force at his disposal, Edgar needed the recruits as well as those helping them to stop looking over their shoulders before he made his move.

Kian

Eleven in the morning was too early for a drink, but Kian felt like celebrating.

The crisis was over.

Jin and Arwel were on their way to the clan's jet, and they were due to arrive back in Los Angeles in a couple of hours. The village and the keep were no longer in danger, and Turner could go back to the rescue missions that he'd had to postpone while helping Kian manage the near catastrophe.

Kalugal was still a danger to the clan, and he still had Jacki, but by tomorrow morning, that would get resolved as well. Kian was going to put his cousin on the line with his mother, and in return, Kalugal would release Jacki.

The question was how to proceed from there.

The best thing would be to meet face to face and start negotiating a long-term coexistence agreement, but first, he needed to figure a way to protect himself from Kalugal's compulsion.

Dragging Turner with him to every meeting was a possibility, but it was unfair to the guy. Turner was a busy man, with his own hostage rescue operation to run. He helped the clan whenever he could, but there was a limit to how much Kian could ask of him.

"Who wants to join me in a toast?" Kian lifted a bottle of a twenty-one-year-old Suntory Hibiki.

Syssi grimaced. "Shouldn't we do it with champagne? I can have a tiny sip of that."

"You are right." Kian put the bottle down. "I'll have Okidu bring it."

Turner got up and walked over to the cart. "It's too early to celebrate, but I'll have some while we wait for your butler to get the champagne." He took the bottle and examined the label. "I've heard it's excellent."

Kian cast Syssi a sidelong glance. "Do you mind if I have some too?"

"Not at all. Perhaps we should save the champagne for later. Isn't it time we got out of the war room? We can go home and celebrate there."

"I'm expecting a phone call from Kalugal. We can leave after that." Kian turned to Onegus. "How about you? Too early for a drink?"

Leaning back in his chair, the chief had his arms crossed over his chest and a frown furrowing his forehead. He didn't look ready to celebrate just yet. "I'm always game for good whiskey."

"You look worried."

Onegus shrugged. "We are not home free yet. Kalugal is a sneaky bastard, and I wonder what his next move will be. This is not over by a long shot."

"What are you going to do about the Guardians posted around his mansion?" Syssi asked. "He will probably demand that you lift the blockade."

"Not until he releases Jacki. After that, I will no longer have an excuse for it. I will, however, keep tabs on him, just more covertly."

When his phone rang, Kian expected to see Kalugal's contact on the screen, but it was Julian's.

After spending part of the night at Kalugal's home, the doctor had probably picked up a few tidbits of information that he wished to share.

"Hello, Julian. How was your stay at Kalugal's?"

Kian put the phone on the conference table and switched the speaker on.

"Interesting, troubling, disconcerting. He compelled me to tell him about immortal females and how similar or different they are from immortal males. He also got me to reveal that Jacki was a possible Dormant."

"Fuck!" Kian emptied the shot down his throat. "I didn't expect him to do that, but I should have. The bastard took advantage of the situation."

"I didn't tell him anything he could use against the clan."

"I know that. You and Jin couldn't reveal things you didn't know, which was why I didn't stipulate what he was allowed or not allowed to compel you to answer."

Kalugal had told him that he was going to compel Jin because he needed to verify that she hadn't been lying about the tether's removal. He'd also said that he was going to compel Julian to verify that the doctor hadn't been sent to do him and his men harm.

It had occurred to Kian that Kalugal might use the loophole to ask things that were unrelated to those two conditions, but it would have been difficult to start making lists of questions he was allowed to ask and those he wasn't. Given that Jin and Julian couldn't reveal any strategic secrets, Kian had figured there was no need for that.

The one thing he hadn't wanted Kalugal to find out was that Jacki was a possible Dormant, but then he couldn't have stipulated that without giving it away.

"He also compelled Jin to answer his questions," Julian said. "They were mostly about how you found her and how many other Dormants the clan has discovered so far. Jin told him that you found her sister by chance, and that was how you got to her. Luckily, she didn't know the answer to his other questions. She did, however, tell him about the government program we freed her from."

Damn. It wasn't a big deal unless Kalugal figured out the connection between paranormal talents and Dormants. If he did, he might go after the remaining females in the program. Maybe the males as well.

"I need to talk to her and find out exactly what she told him about that. What else did he ask you?"

"How to find Dormants, and how I knew that Ella was my fated mate." Julian let out a breath. "You can't blame him for asking that. Every immortal wants answers to those questions."

"That's true. But now that Kalugal knows Jacki is a possible Dormant, he is not likely to trade her for communication privileges with his mother."

"He might," Syssi said. "Isn't that what we were banking on when Alena posed as Areana for those cosmetics ads? You believed that he would get sentimental and look for her."

Kian shook his head. "My mother believed that, and I humored her. Annani is a romantic and thinks that everyone is motivated by the same things that motivate her. I'm more pragmatic than that. Given a choice, most adult males would choose a chance of having an immortal mate over contact with their mothers."

She arched a brow. "Would you?"

"I would have done anything for you. Even that."

"Kalugal is not in love with Jacki," Turner said. "He might choose Areana."

"Or not," Julian said. "When Jacki hugged me, Kalugal got upset, practically growling at me, but he tried to hide it."

"Maybe he's just easily irritated" Syssi smiled at Kian. "Like someone else I know. After all, you are cousins, and you might share similar traits."

"I don't think so," Julian said. "Kalugal seems much mellower than Kian, and he has better control over his emotions."

The unfavorable comparison grated on Kian's nerves. "He is also more devious, and his morals are questionable. Kalugal might try to come up with a way to have both." He poured himself another shot of whiskey. "I need to find something to hold over him in perpetuity."

"You already have that." Turner handed him his empty glass. "He might give up contact with his mother to keep Jacki, but he wouldn't want anything to happen to her. As far as he knows, you still hold her life in your hands."

Order Dark Overlord New Horizon today!

Join the VIP Club
To find out what's included in your free membership, flip to the last page.

The Children of the Gods Series
Reading Order

THE CHILDREN OF THE GODS ORIGINS

1: Goddess's Choice

When gods and immortals still ruled the ancient world, one young goddess risked everything for love.

2: Goddess's Hope

Hungry for power and infatuated with the beautiful Areana, Navuh plots his father's demise. After all, by getting rid of the insane god he would be doing the world a favor. Except, when gods and immortals conspire against each other, humanity pays the price.

But things are not what they seem, and prophecies should not to be trusted...

THE CHILDREN OF THE GODS

Dark Stranger

1: Dark Stranger The Dream

2: Dark Stranger Revealed

3: Dark Stranger Immortal

Dark Enemy

4: Dark Enemy Taken

5: Dark Enemy Captive

6: Dark Enemy Redeemed

Kri & Michael's Story

6.5: My Dark Amazon

Dark Warrior

7: Dark Warrior Mine

8: Dark Warrior's Promise

9: Dark Warrior's Destiny

10: Dark Warrior's Legacy

Dark Guardian

11: Dark Guardian Found

12: Dark Guardian Craved

13: Dark Guardian's Mate

Dark Angel

14: Dark Angel's Obsession

15: Dark Angel's Seduction

16: Dark Angel's Surrender

Dark Operative

17: Dark Operative: A Shadow of Death

18: Dark Operative: A Glimmer of Hope

19: Dark Operative: The Dawn of Love

Dark Survivor

20: Dark Survivor Awakened

21: Dark Survivor Echoes of Love

22: Dark Survivor Reunited

Dark Widow

23: Dark Widow's Secret

24: Dark Widow's Curse

25: Dark Widow's Blessing

Dark Dream

26: Dark Dream's Temptation

27: Dark Dream's Unraveling

28: Dark Dream's Trap

Dark Prince

29: Dark Prince's Enigma

30: Dark Prince's Dilemma

31: Dark Prince's Agenda

Dark Queen

32: Dark Queen's Quest

33: Dark Queen's Knight

34: Dark Queen's Army

Dark Spy

35: Dark Spy Conscripted

36: Dark Spy's Mission

37: Dark Spy's Resolution

Dark Overlord

38: Dark Overlord New Horizon

39: Dark Overlord's Wife

Jacki is still clinging to her all-or-nothing policy, but Kalugal is chipping away at her resistance. Perhaps it's time to ease up on her convictions. A little less than all is still much better than nothing, and a couple of decades with a demigod is probably worth more than a lifetime with a mere mortal.

40: Dark Overlord's Clan

As Jacki and Kalugal prepare to celebrate their union, Kian takes every precaution to safeguard his people. Except, Kalugal and his men are not his only potential adversaries, and compulsion is not the only power he should fear.

Dark Choices

41: Dark Choices The Quandary

When Rufsur and Edna meet, the attraction is as unexpected as it is undeniable. Except, she's the clan's judge and councilwoman, and he's Kalugal's second-in-command. Will loyalty and duty to their people keep them apart?

42: Dark Choices Paradigm Shift

Edna and Rufsur are miserable without each other, and their two-week separation seems like an eternity. Long-distance relationships are difficult, but for immortal couples they are impossible. Unless one of them is willing to leave everything behind for the other, things are just going to get worse. Except, the cost of compromise is far greater than giving up their comfortable lives and hard-earned positions. The future of their people is on the line.

43: Dark Choices The Accord

The winds of change blowing over the village demand hard choices. For better or worse, Kian's decisions will alter the trajectory of the clan's future, and he is not ready to take the plunge. But as Edna and Rufsur's plight gains widespread support, his resistance slowly begins to erode.

DARK SECRETS

44: DARK SECRETS RESURGENCE

On a sabbatical from his Stanford teaching position, Professor David Levinson finally has time to write the sci-fi novel he's been thinking about for years.

The phenomena of past life memories and near-death experiences are too controversial to include in his formal psychiatric research, while fiction is the perfect outlet for his esoteric ideas.

Hoping that a change of pace will provide the inspiration he needs, David accepts a friend's invitation to an old Scottish castle.

45: DARK SECRETS UNVEILED

When Professor David Levinson accepts a friend's invitation to an old Scottish castle, what he finds there is more fantastical than his most outlandish theories. The castle is home to a clan of immortals, their leader is a stunning demigoddess, and even more shockingly, it might be precisely where he belongs.

Except, the clan founder is hiding a secret that might cast a dark shadow on David's relationship with her daughter.

Nevertheless, when offered a chance at immortality, he agrees to undergo the dangerous induction process.

Will David survive his transition into immortality? And if he does, will his relationship with Sari survive the unveiling of her mother's secret?

46: DARK SECRETS ABSOLVED

Absolution.

David had given and received it.

The few short hours since he'd emerged from the coma had felt incredible. He'd finally been free of the guilt and pain, and for the first time since Jonah's death, he had felt truly happy and optimistic about the future.

He'd survived the transition into immortality, had been accepted into the clan, and was about to marry the best woman on the face of the planet, his true love mate, his salvation, his everything.

What could have possibly gone wrong?

Just about everything.

Dark Haven

47: Dark Haven Illusion

48: Dark Haven Unmasked

49: Dark Haven Found

Dark Power

50: Dark Power Untamed

51: Dark Power Unleashed

52: Dark Power Convergence

Dark Memories

53: Dark Memories Submerged

54: Dark Memories Emerge

55: Dark Memories Restored

Dark Hunter

56: Dark Hunter's Query
57: Dark Hunter's Prey
58: <u>Dark Hunter's Boon</u>

Dark God

59: Dark God's Avatar
60: Dark God's Reviviscence
61: Dark God Destinies Converge

Dark Whispers

62: Dark Whispers From The Past
63: Dark Whispers From Afar
64: Dark Whispers From Beyond

Dark Gambit

65: Dark Gambit The Pawn
66: Dark Gambit The Play
67: Dark Gambit Reliance

Dark Alliance

68: Dark Alliance Kindred Souls
69: Dark Alliance Turbulent Waters
70: Dark Alliance Perfect Storm

Dark Healing

71: Dark Healing Blind Justice
72: Dark Healing Blind Trust
73: Dark healing Blind Curve

DARK ENCOUNTERS

74: Dark Encounters of the Close Kind

75: Dark Encounters of the Unexpected Kind

76: Dark Encounters of the Fated Kind

The Children of the Gods Series Sets

Books 1-3: Dark Stranger trilogy—Includes a bonus short story: **The Fates take a Vacation**

<u>Books 4-6: **Dark Enemy Trilogy**</u> —Includes a bonus short story—**The Fates' Post-Wedding Celebration**

Books 7-10: Dark Warrior Tetralogy

Books 11-13: Dark Guardian Trilogy

Books 14-16: Dark Angel Trilogy

Books 17-19: Dark Operative Trilogy

Books 20-22: Dark Survivor Trilogy

Books 23-25: Dark Widow Trilogy

Books 26-28: Dark Dream Trilogy

Books 29-31: Dark Prince Trilogy

Books 32-34: Dark Queen Trilogy

Books 35-37: Dark Spy Trilogy

Books 38-40: Dark Overlord Trilogy

Books 41-43: Dark Choices Trilogy

Books 44-46: Dark Secrets Trilogy

Books 47-49: Dark Haven Trilogy
Books 50-52: Dark Power Trilogy
Books 53-55: Dark Memories Trilogy
Books 56-58: Dark Hunter Trilogy
Books 59-61: Dark God Trilogy
Books 62-64: Dark Whispers Trilogy
Books 65-67: Dark Gambit Trilogy
Books 68-70: Dark Alliance Trilogy
Books 71-73: Dark healing Trilogy

MEGA SETS

INCLUDE CHARACTER LISTS

The Children of the Gods: Books 1-6
The Children of the Gods: Books 6.5-10

TRY THE SERIES ON

AUDIBLE

2 FREE audiobooks with your new Audible subscription!

PERFECT MATCH SERIES

VAMPIRE'S CONSORT

When Gabriel's company is ready to start beta testing, he invites his old crush to inspect its medical safety protocol.

Curious about the revolutionary technology of the *Perfect Match Virtual Fantasy-Fulfillment studios*, Brenna agrees.

Neither expects to end up partnering for its first fully immersive test run.

KING'S CHOSEN

When Lisa's nutty friends get her a gift certificate to *Perfect Match Virtual Fantasy Studios*, she has no intentions of using it. But since the only way to get a refund is if no partner can be found for her, she makes sure to request a fantasy so girly and over the top that no sane guy will pick it up.

Except, someone does.

> **Warning:** This fantasy contains a hot, domineering crown prince, sweet insta-love, steamy love scenes painted with light shades of gray, a wedding, and a HEA in both the virtual and real worlds.
>
> Intended for mature audience.

Captain's Conquest

Working as a Starbucks barista, Alicia fends off flirting all day long, but none of the guys are as charming and sexy as Gregg. His frequent visits are the highlight of her day, but since he's never asked her out, she assumes he's taken. Besides, between a day job and a budding music career, she has no time to start a new relationship.

That is until Gregg makes her an offer she can't refuse—a gift certificate to the virtual fantasy fulfillment service everyone is talking about. As a huge Star Trek fan, Alicia has a perfect match in mind—the captain of the Starship Enterprise.

The Thief Who Loved Me

When Marian splurges on a Perfect Match Virtual adventure as a world infamous jewel thief, she expects high-wire fun with a hot partner who she will never have to see again in real life.

A virtual encounter seems like the perfect answer to Marcus's string of dating disasters. No strings attached, no drama, and definitely no love. As a die-hard James Bond fan, he chooses as his avatar a dashing MI6 operative, and to complement his adventure, a dangerously seductive partner.

Neither expects to find their forever Perfect Match.

My Merman Prince

The beautiful architect working late on the twelfth floor of my building thinks that I'm just the maintenance guy. She's also under the impression that I'm not interested.

Nothing could be further from the truth.

I want her like I've never wanted a woman before, but I don't play where I work.

I don't need the complications.

When she tells me about living out her mermaid fantasy with a stranger in a Perfect Match virtual adventure, I decide to do everything possible to ensure that the stranger is me.

THE DRAGON KING

To save his beloved kingdom from a devastating war, the Crown Prince of Trieste makes a deal with a witch that costs him half of his humanity and dooms him to an eternity of loneliness.

Now king, he's a fearsome cobalt-winged dragon by day and a short-tempered monarch by night. Not many are brave enough to serve in the palace of the brooding and volatile ruler, but Charlotte ignores the rumors and accepts a scribe position in court.

As the young scribe reawakens Bruce's frozen heart, all that stands in the way of their happiness is the witch's bargain. Outsmarting the evil hag will take cunning and courage, and Charlotte is just the right woman for the job.

My Werewolf Romeo

The father of my star student is a big-shot screenwriter and the patron of the drama department who thinks he can dictate what production I should put on. The principal makes it very clear that I need to cooperate with the opinionated asshat or walk away from my dream job at the exclusive private high school.

It doesn't help matters that the guy is single, hot, charming, creative, and seems to like me despite my thinly-veiled hostility.

When he invites me to a custom-tailored Perfect Match virtual adventure to prove that his screenplay is perfect for my production, I accept, intending to have fun while proving that messing with the classics is a foolish idea.

I don't expect to be wowed by his werewolf adaptation of Red Riding Hood mesh-up with Romeo and Juliet, and I certainly don't expect to fall in love with the virtual fantasy's leading man.

The Channeler's Companion

A treat for fans of *The Wheel of Time*.

When Erika hires Rand to assist in her pediatric clinic, she does so despite his good looks and irresistible charm, not because of them.

He's empathic, adores children, and has the patience of a saint.

He's also all she can think about, but he's off limits.

What's a doctor to do to scratch that irresistible itch without risking workplace complications?

A shared adventure in the Perfect Match Virtual Studios seems like the solution, but instead of letting the algorithm choose a partner for her, Erika can try to influence it to select the one she wants. Awarding Rand a gift certificate to the service will get him into their database, but unless Erika can tip the odds in her favor, getting paired with him is a long shot.

Hopefully, a virtual adventure based on her and Rand's favorite series will do the trick.

Note

Dear reader,

I hope my stories have added a little joy to your day. If you have a moment to add some to mine, you can help spread the word about the Children Of The Gods series by telling your friends and penning a review. Your recommendations are the most powerful way to inspire new readers to explore the series.

Thank you,

Isabell

FOR EXCLUSIVE PEEKS AT UPCOMING RELEASES & A FREE COMPANION BOOK

Join my *VIP Club* and gain access to the VIP portal at itlucas.com
To Join, go to:
http://eepurl.com/blMTpD

INCLUDED IN YOUR FREE MEMBERSHIP:

YOUR VIP PORTAL

- Read preview chapters of upcoming releases.
- Listen to Goddess's Choice narration by Charles Lawrence
- Exclusive content offered only to my VIPs.

FREE I.T. LUCAS COMPANION INCLUDES:

- Goddess's Choice Part 1
- Perfect Match: Vampire's Consort (A standalone Novella)
- Interview Q & A
- Character Charts

If you're already a subscriber, and you are not getting my emails, your provider is sending them to your junk folder, and you are missing out on **important updates, side characters' portraits, additional content, and other goodies.** To fix that, add isabell@itlucas.com to your email contacts or your email VIP list.

**Check out the specials at
https://www.itlucas.com/specials**

Printed in Great Britain
by Amazon